LAYING THE GHOST

LAYING THE GHOST

JUDY ASTLEY

LARGE PRINT
Oxford

First published in Great Britain 2007
by
Bantam Press,
an imprint of
Transworld Publishers

Published in Large Print 2007 by ISIS Publishing Ltd.,
7 Centremead, Osney Mead, Oxford OX2 0ES
by arrangement with
Transworld Publishers,
a Random House Group Company

British Library Cataloguing in Publication Data
Astley, Judy
    Laying the ghost. – Large print ed.
    1. Single women – Fiction
    2. Large type books
    I. Title
    823.9'14 [F]

ISBN 978–0–7531–7916–1 (hb)
ISBN 978–0–7531–7917–8 (pb)

Printed and bound in Great Britain by
T. J. International Ltd., Padstow, Cornwall

Acknowledgements

Massive thanks to the following people for top-of-the-range friendship, invaluable research help, gossipy lunches and shared secrets. This book couldn't have happened without you:

Chris Chesney
George (sleuth) Edwards
Linda Evans
Katie Fffffforde
Rebecca Gregson
Michelle (rock chick) Hurst
Nicola Joss
Frané (hacker) Lessac
Rory MacLean
Rowena (Rosie) Milne
David Snelling
Terry Whitworth
Barbara Williams

Laying the Ghost is entirely fiction. Nobody I know or have ever met is in this book; not even you. In fact — especially not you.

My friends, we will not go again or ape an ancient rage,
Or stretch the folly of our youth to be the shame of age,
But walk with clearer eyes and ears this path
   that wandereth,
And see undrugged in evening light the decent inn
   of death;
For there is good news yet to hear and fine things to
   be seen,
Before we go to Paradise by way of Kensal Green.

"The Rolling English Road"
G. K. Chesterton

CHAPTER
ONE

Four Seasons In One Day
(Crowded House)

Comfort food. Nell savoured the words and felt her taste buds sparkle. What a delicious, creamy, heart-warming phrase. Some women (and although Nell wasn't one of them, she could sympathize here) hit the bottle when their life partner leaves them for the kind of glamorous new love interest that they naively imagine will never — even in the far-ahead fullness of time — require them to unblock a drain at midnight or dig deep enough in a frost-hardened garden to bury a run-over cat. But Nell had recently discovered that she was one of the other sort: those who take joyfully to food as their new soulmate. If she were to be photographed now with the current love in her life, she would be snuggled up beside her fridge; possibly almost *inside* her fridge, fondly embraced by its door, and as close as she could get to the chocolate supply she kept beside the butter. She was well aware that either of the drink/food options had the dangerous potential to turn her into the kind of vast, unkempt bloater that much reduced the chances of filling that recent, and still

lividly scarred, love gap in her life, but at least this way
she wouldn't morph into a pissed-up wreck with a shot
liver. Food as solace didn't cost you your driving
licence, did not leave you with a lingering whiff of stale
wine or have you wondering what it was you'd said
(and, oh Lord, where and in what circumstances) that
was making the leery man from no. 13 ask if you'd got
the purple ones on today. She thought of this now as
she contemplated with deep and true affection the food
on her plate: her choice was, given where she was,
possibly the most unlikely item on the menu.

"You're not going to eat *that*?" Great, Nell thought,
loaded fork halfway to her mouth. Along came the
eternal family critic just as she was about to savour a
truly memorable feast.

Mimi glared across the table at her mother's lunch
choice as if she'd never seen anything so completely
crazy presented as foodstuff in her entire life. How does
a fifteen-year-old girl do this, Nell wondered. How
could Mimi twist her face into something that so clearly
expressed incredulity, disdain, disgust — all at the same
time and all without losing her essential clear-eyed
beauty? Anyone over twenty would look demented. This
must have been what Picasso had been going for when
he first painted two eyes on the same side of a woman's
head. That would be it: cubism kicked off with nothing
more mysterious than the great artist capturing the
expression of a teenager in a full-scale adolescent strop.

Mimi's nose was sugar-mouse pink from the fierce
sun and beginning to peel, but in the interests of
enjoying a final peaceful lunch on this too-brief

one-week escape, Nell decided this wasn't the moment to nag her yet again about sunblock. Or to tease her that if she kept that face on, the wind would change and she'd stay with that look for ever. A row would follow. Lunch would be rushed and ruined. Only a few hours from now they would be at the airport, checking in for the homeward trip and smoothing out the creases on snuggly coats in which to greet the freezing early-morning Gatwick air. The chance of another shot of blazing heat would be months away, if not years. This impulse trip to avoid being around to watch Alex moving his possessions out of the family home had wiped out his Air Miles account very satisfyingly but with Alex no longer keeping it topped up for their use, future holidays would have to be within driving possibility and could even (and Nell would prefer not to consider this), if more profitable work wasn't forthcoming, involve *tents*.

"What's wrong with shepherd's pie?" Nell asked. "You like it OK when I make it."

"That's in *winter*, at *home*," Mimi growled.

"It *is* winter," Nell pointed out. "You can't get much deeper winter than February."

Mimi now gave her the sneering *derrr* look, the one that comes free (and so very, very frequently) with every teen girl. "Like *cold* winter? Like, not *here* in this *heat*? You're mad." She instantly cut off and started on her salad.

"Mad." So. The usual verdict then. Not even remotely a surprise. And yes, I probably am mad, Nell thought, tracing her initials (newly single EJW, not her twenty-years-married EJH) across the mashed potato with her fork. Possibly her scorching hot shepherd's pie at the beachfront Lone Star restaurant, Barbados, wouldn't be everyone's automatic selection from a menu that also offered tuna tartare or — Mimi's choice — lobster and prawn salad with papaya salsa and cucumber mint dressing. But when the perfect comfort food was so conveniently available at a moment when you very much needed comfort, nothing else would do.

Nell would need all the help she could get, from every possible source, to survive the moment the next day when she arrived home and opened the front door on to the still, silent space left by her newly absent husband. It was going to be *the* major moment in the start of the rest of her life. There should be a sort of ceremony involved here. On the drive home from the airport she'd phone and run that one past Kate. Wasn't that what your best friends were for? To be ready with the bottle of fizz (or in this case, given the early hour of the day, tea and a bacon sandwich) in times of stress?

Strange, in the last year during Alex's so-frequent business trips ("business", ha! Definitely a loose term in this case. Under "business", see "pleasure") she had barely missed him. Coming home to an empty house had had a certain luxury to it. She and Mimi and Sebastian had crashed around in a state of amiable domestic anarchy. But how different would it now be, not only with Sebastian away at the college in Falmouth but never expecting Alex back at all? Would having lots of wardrobe space and no one to complain about your shoe collection be any compensation for the long lonely evenings and Nell's nagging fear that she could end up as one of those women with seventeen cats and a hallway heaped with old newspapers? No — that wouldn't happen. It was Alex who had left home, not Nell's fully functioning brain cells. But all the same, in the jet-lag pre-dawn hours during this lovely tropical escape, she had sometimes wondered . . .

Nell watched as Mimi picked up a prawn between her perfectly (and expensively) manicured nails and shelled it as neatly and delicately as an otter before biting it cleanly in half with her perfectly (and expensively) straightened teeth. Her perfectly (and expensively) streak-blonded hair wisped in the breeze and Nell wondered how this overindulged daddy's girl would survive without all the princess accoutrements she'd been so used to, now that her father had found another princess to cherish.

"Mum?" Mimi looked anxious, her face losing six years and reverting almost to little-girl again. The perfect nails tore a rocket leaf to shreds and laid them out evenly like petals around the edge of her plate.

"If Dad comes home to see us, will he . . . will he, like, bring *her* with him? Will I have to meet her and be nice?"

Nell thought about this for a moment, picturing them all trying to do the "let's be civilized about this" thing, all doing too much icy smiling in a restaurant where you could see that the sharp-eyed waiters were canny enough to be taking bets on who'd be first at your table to crack and break into an entertaining full-scale tantrum. She promised herself then and there never to get into that scenario.

"There's no 'if' he comes to see us . . . well, to see you and Seb anyway, he's promised he will . . ." Nell wavered, wondering what, exactly, to say next. There'd been a lot of promises over the years, starting with the ones about for richer for poorer, and till death us do part. All the best ones had been broken. Alex wouldn't be back on the British side of the Atlantic for a long time to come; New York was now his home. A fat-mouthed redhead, name of Cherisse, was now the woman he was promising eternal love and loyalty to, unless New York thirty-somethings were content to settle for much less when it came to a man moving in.

"But I don't know . . . I suppose it'll be up to you in the end, whether you want to meet his new . . ." Nell hesitated. Perhaps she should say "*Your* new"? Mimi's new what? Would Cherisse become Mimi's stepmother? Quite possibly, quite likely, one day. Very determined, New York women. Cherisse was thirty-one, and in the photo Nell had unearthed from feverish and furious delving down the back of Al's Haliburton briefcase, possessed broad, Channel-swimmer's shoulders, a terrifying set of all-American cheerleader teeth and that peculiar over-bouncy long hair that made you suspect the daily use of Carmen rollers. Some kind of corporate lawyer (wasn't everyone, over there?), she wasn't going to let the ink dry on the decree absolute before whizzing Alex down to Connecticut to the family clapboard/picket-fence villa for a gilt-chairs and floral-bower wedding ceremony. She would almost certainly get Alex to email Mimi to say that it was all right, she understood how uncool being a bridesmaid could be when you're a teenager and she'd Respect Her Feelings by not asking her, instead surrounding herself with an array of spooky mini-me beauty-pageant infants and a no-competition pair of diet-failure contemporaries in unflattering peach satin.

"Because I, like, *really* don't want to meet her." Mimi stripped another prawn and bit it clean through its middle. "I don't want Dad getting the idea that I'm *ever* going to think it's OK for him to go off and be with someone else. And suppose . . ." She looked at her next prawn as if she'd just noticed something truly bizarre about it. "Suppose . . ." she hesitated again. "Oh God, do you think they might . . .?"

Nell couldn't eat any more, not without choking anyway. What a waste — only half of this delicious food gone. It was now too much to ask even of shepherd's pie to provide comfort here. For this was the big question, wasn't it? Would Alex and Cherisse make beautiful New York babies together? How long would it take Nell to get to the point where that kind of question, any kind of question about Alex, simply didn't matter? They didn't tell you the answer to that one in *After He's Gone*, the Brown-Owl-brisk, faux-jolly guide to post-divorce life that so-efficient, so-helpful Kate had provided as essential holiday reading. On balance, Nell thought she'd have preferred some blood-curdling thriller-chiller.

"You know what, Mimi? I can't even begin to guess what they might do," Nell told her, adopting the book's recommended rise-above-it attitude. "I don't want to think about any of it — not until we get home anyway, and even then I think we should all get going on the moving-on stage. Let's just enjoy these last few hours here, shall we? We don't want to lose sight of what this week was all about. It's been about *us* and about having a good, fun time. But right now it's only about lunch, OK?"

She could feel her voice becoming artificially bright. She'd even been *that* close to saying the tritest thing, that schmaltzy "And whatever's happened between Alex and me, he'll *always be your dad*." There'd been a lot of that brightness lately; a lot of trying on a "make-the-best-of-it" tone so that Mimi wouldn't sink into a depression. Seb didn't agonize — or didn't seem to. He just did that boy thing, that "*Please* don't make me talk about feelings" look of dread whenever such a possibility loomed. His idea of a bad day wasn't his dad leaving to shack up with a floozie on the far side of an ocean, but his mum dragging him and Mimi into the kitchen and saying, "Let's have a group hug." Not that Nell would, she'd known better than that since they'd stopped falling over in the playground and grazing their knees. And besides, *she* didn't fancy the group-hug thing either. It would be one more all-American irritating item to add to the list.

Anyway, Seb was away now, on an art course in Falmouth where he could shut down completely from home concerns and simply get on with becoming whatever he wanted himself to be. His opting out was so absolute that he had completely immersed himself in surf life and spent every spare weekend in the sea. Still teen-selfish, he made it pretty clear on his few home visits that, fond as he was of his home and family, each second spent in south-west London would be better spent in south-west England. Where did "divorce" come on that well-known scale of the most traumatic life events? For the absent Seb it might rate no worse than maybe a flat tyre, but for Nell, well, she'd read that it was rightly considered one down from a family death, but was it above house-moving and giving birth, or maybe between the two? And at what level was it going to be for Mimi?

Mimi had finished her prawns, rejected a little heap of tomatoes and was now digging her fork into the demolished remains of Nell's mashed potato.

"Have I got time for another swim before we go?" she asked. She was already looking out at the ocean, then at herself reflected in the big mirror placed beside the restaurant so diners could always get a sea view; maybe she was watching to see if a turtle might be swimming close to shore so she could go and float lazily beside it. How lucky it was for teenagers that their attention flittered about like a bee on buttercups. Nell had been looking forward to a dreamy couple of hours on a beach lounger, thinking of nothing but what colour to paint the kitchen. She now had a horrible feeling that while considering some fancy contrast tones for the ceiling, she might also be wondering which shade of white (creamy, or bluish, or hint-of-jasmine) would also look OK for the bridal lace of her replacement.

"You can swim if you wait fifteen minutes for your lunch to go down first and so long as you won't complain about spending the night on the plane with cold wet hair."

Mimi sighed, scowled and growled. Nell didn't blame her — she didn't like her own bossy tone either. She'd stopped short of reminding Mimi how much she'd feel the cold in the early Gatwick morning after the blazing heat of this week, but all the same, Nell was fully aware she was going to be the only Bad Cop in the family from now on. How very, very dispiriting.

Nell saw the boy waiting on the pavement as she and Mimi dragged their bags off the Gatwick car-park courtesy bus. From years of living with a football nut, she recognized his top as Manchester United's current away-strip. He was leaning on the side of the bus shelter, chewing his thumbnail and breathing thick drifts of mist into the freezing early air. It was much later when it crossed her mind that not only was the name "Callaghan" beneath the no. 8 on his shirt back in the place where surely "Rooney" should have been, but that with no baggage (not even a coat, and it was freezing), and no in-charge adult, he definitely didn't look as if he was somewhere between parking a car and boarding a plane.

"I'm so *cold*," Mimi wailed as they crossed the road. It was barely light; the rows of tightly parked cars were silvered by frost and all looked the same — line after line of unidentifiable sparkly greyish lumps. Where *was* the bloody Golf, Nell wondered, knowing that if Alex

10

had been with them he would, by now, have been marching firmly in the right direction, having had the exact location logged into his Blackberry. Also, he wouldn't have left the car-park ticket carelessly exposed on the car's dashboard to show a potential TWOC-er that escape from the car park would present no difficulty. And of course, unlike Nell, he'd have prepaid online, triumphantly saving several pounds, via the right website. A long, long time ago he'd found Nell's scattiness amusing. Over the past year he had simply found it annoying, clucking and sighing at every small evidence of inefficiency. "How can you draw so meticulously," he'd said once after she'd left a casserole in the oven for seven flavour-draining hours while she worked on a last-minute alteration to a double spread for *Pond Life* (third in an educational series, sales rivalling Dan Brown's in thirty countries), "and yet be so bloody disorganized?" He was probably right, she now thought as she peered through the blue-grey half-light in the remote hope that her car would get out of its line and come to greet her.

"You are sure you left it in Zone X, aren't you?" Mimi asked her.

"Definitely," Nell told her as she settled her handbag on her shoulder, bumped her case heavily up the pavement edge and wondered if she'd ever be so well travelled that she'd master the art of manoeuvring wheeled luggage. Why was it that some things which were meant to make life easier just created their own difficulties? The bag wobbled and tottered like a drunk companion as she hauled it carefully through many rows of parked cars, trying not to set off alarms or scratch paintwork.

Alex used to deal with the more unwieldy holiday baggage, enjoying any opportunity to pace around looking strong and blokey. Getting the knack of putting together a tiny capsule wardrobe was going to be essential for any future trips Nell might be lucky enough to have. She could possibly never travel again without clothes that would cram into a manageable shoulder bag. That would completely rule out a ski trip, for a start, which actually was not a bad thing, in her opinion. Alex was the sporty one. Not having even to pretend to join in with that was one to put on the list (as recommended for compilation in *After He's Gone*) of post-divorce pluses.

"So *where* then?" Mimi squinted through the shadowy dawn at the cars, as if theirs might have grown a tail to wag at them in welcome.

"Oh come on Mimi, *you* were supposed to be the one who remembered which row," Nell reminded her. "It was the *one thing* I asked you to do. Please don't tell me you've completely forgotten." She wanted to get home. She wanted to listen to early-morning political bickering on Radio 4 and be soothed by *Thought for the Day*. She wanted to sit at her kitchen table and open a stack of terrifying bills while eating toast and thick gooey honey. Then she wanted to decide what to wear to the Mitchells' twentieth-wedding-anniversary party that night, while wondering if going to bed early with a messy three-pack of Cadbury's Flakes and an undemanding novel might be a wiser option than facing the neighbours' collective curiosity and making a defiant, jet-lagged start on this new, single, reality.

"You were the one driving, Mum. Why don't *you* remember where the car is?"

"Oh great — the daughter quits! What a surprise!"

Mimi ignored her and stared up at the sky, dreamily and unconcernedly watching a Virgin 777 approach at what looked like a dangerously slow speed for its size.

"Why don't *I* remember? Because, Mimi, *I* was the one remembering little things like passports and booking references and whether that scrappy bit of computer printout was really going to be enough to get us checked in because I'm old enough to be more comfortable with proper in-your-hand tickets, and then there was whether I'd got the credit card I'd actually used for the reservation, or had I thrown it away because it had expired, oh and the BA club card and all that stuff! And what did you have to remember? It was which zone, which row and to get some factor 25 in duty-free. Nothing else! God!"

Shivering inside creased and inexplicably damp cashmere, Nell pointed her key at the cars in front of her and pressed the remote lock, hoping to see a welcoming flash of orange lights to guide her to the Golf. There was no response.

"Er . . . maybe it was, like row 5 or something?" Mimi pointed vaguely across to the other side of the car park. "I think. I do remember it was a long walk."

"OK — we'll go in that direction and I'll keep pushing the button." Nell felt depressed. There was no one else around now. Everyone who'd been on that bus (all in cosy twosomes, not surprisingly as it was term-time; some of them had been hand-holding honeymoonish — well good luck, was her bitter thought) had claimed their cars and gone. They would be way out on the motorway by now, carloads of post-holiday relaxed pairs, telling each other what a wonderful time they'd had, how they couldn't wait to pick up the dog from the kennels and how brilliant it had felt, escaping from the winter cold, but it was all right, spring would be here soon and the daffodils would be up in the garden. Bloody coupledom. How long would it be, Nell wondered, before she looked at lovers and didn't seethe at Alex's abandonment. Perhaps she shouldn't go to the Mitchells' party. She might end up snarling at any paired-up folk who dared to look even halfway happy together.

There it was, at last. Nell flicked the switch again and along by the fence her Golf responded with a couple of little blinks of light. And that was when the boy swooped. As he wrenched Nell's bag from her hands, time slowed to something that resembled television scenes of dancers caught moving like half-speed angels in strobe lighting. She heard Mimi shriek and swear and felt a rush of warm, cigarette-scented air as the boy shoved against her. Then he raced away. When safely distant but still in full flight, he ripped open the bag, frantically hurling the contents on to the ground. She watched as, just too far away to be worth the chase, he scrabbled among her possessions, grabbing what he wanted and racing off, leaving the rest strewn about like the contents of an upended rubbish bin.

"Shit, Mum! Are you all right?"

Was she? Or was this an almost triumphant final bloody straw that she could blame — one way or another — on Alex?

"Yes. Well I think so, suppose so. That was a nice bag."

It was a mad thing to say; such a frivolous, irrelevant first thought when there was going to be the nightmare of the credit cards to sort. Her driving licence was in there, too, and several store cards. And the bag wasn't at all nice, really. It was hardly a Chloe Paddington, or whatever the current two-thousand-pound must-have was. There was a stain underneath where she'd put it down in a puddle, and the zip was iffy. But you got fond of bags; their shapes became cosy, worn, softened and familiar. She tried not to think: like men.

"Right. OK." Mimi looked, she realized, more nervous of this reaction than of the mugging. Nell leaned against the car, strangely comforted by the feel of its door handle against her hip, the familiar curve of the Golf's door.

"I've still got my passport — it's in my pocket. My phone's locked in the glove compartment, and I've got the car keys." Her mind whirled; having thought of what *hadn't* gone, she tried mentally to list what she'd had in the bag. Not a lot of personal stuff, no irreplaceable photos, thank goodness. She'd stripped the contents down to the minimum for the trip . . . Mimi was stroking the back of her mum's hand and it was going numb.

"We'll go then, shall we, Mum? I'll go and pick up what he's left? We'll tell someone on the way out. Police and stuff?" Mimi opened the car's boot, carefully stashed both bags then opened the driver's door, tenderly pushing Nell into the seat.

Nell sat for a moment trying to remember how to drive, how to breathe. She was shaking but she wasn't going to cry; not here, not yet. She would save that little treat for later when she'd added this one to Reasons for Tears. "Pick up what he's left?" — wasn't that what Mimi had said? There was too much here of what had been left — not just receipts and the paracetamol packet, the lipsticks, pens and spare glasses that were scattered like sad garbage all over the tarmac, but *herself*. Thanks so very much, Alex, you bastard, she thought, finding it easy enough to add this mugging to the list of grievances against him. Just as she turned the key in the ignition, up came that question that had never been quite far enough from her mind — according to Alex's bitter parting words — during the entire twenty years of their marriage. Would it have been like this if, so many years ago, she'd hadn't, after all, left Patrick?

CHAPTER
TWO

Changes
(David Bowie)

"I know how she bloody feels," Alex had muttered on that long-ago day when he and Nell had watched Princess Diana confiding to the biggest TV audience in history that there were three people in her marriage. Nell had laughed, told him to leave it alone, for heaven's sake; it was years ago and he was the one she'd married, wasn't he?

Alex had given her the usual look and she'd gone into the kitchen to pour more wine and have a private moment of wondering what Patrick was doing now. That time she'd pictured him living on a remote island, possibly in the Outer Hebrides, painting lonely landscapes and communing with otters and deer. No women were in this scene, though she'd allowed him an amicable parting of the ways from maybe two or three over the years. No children, though — he'd always been a hundred per cent sure on that one.

When Nell first met Patrick, they were both eighteen, starting their first day as art students. His look had been somewhere between early Sting and the prettiest one from Duran Duran — all floppy blond hair and too much black eyeliner and casually flamboyant clothes that gave him an attractively piratical look. There were so many boys like him at the time. Nell liked the type. It was a softer look than punk, but not yet the trainee-accountant-on-a-weekend image that would define the New Romantics; vain, certainly, but having spent five school years boarding with girls of varying levels of hygiene awareness she knew what she *didn't* want in a potential life partner. Never again, she'd vowed the day she left school, would she share premises with anyone who let their hair become filthy enough to smell of stale cheese, or whose sweaty-hockey-match-to-shower ratio was less than one-to-one.

Nell fancied Patrick the moment she walked into the Oxford Poly (as it then was) Graphics department and saw him slumped on the old sofa in the corner, apparently asleep. It wasn't what you'd expect from a first year — as all the group assembled in this room were. Everyone else was alert, upright, prowling, eyeing each other for cool-rating and the possibility of friendship. To Nell, who was mildly frightened of just about everything and everyone on that first day, Patrick's don't-care detachment gave him a thrilling aura of confidence and superiority. If he was so casually at home on day one in a new college, he could presumably be enviably comfortable anywhere; she wanted to hang out next to him, to see if that blissful self-assurance was catching.

Patrick's long, stretched-out body was wrapped in a multicoloured coat of velvet patchwork and he wore lime green snakeskin boots. Beside him on the sofa was a very battered old black leather cowboy hat. You'd need supreme confidence to wear that too, she'd thought, guessing it would look so wonderful on this slim and elegant boy that by the end of term at least three doting acolytes would have bought cheap and less stylish versions of it.

She was immediately certain she had never seen anyone quite as desirable as him before and wished she'd had more practice at sex so that when she eventually got him into her bed (and she was very, very determined here) she would be skilled enough to ensure he'd want a return visit. That was the trouble with girls'-boarding-school life — it was hardly what anyone would term an all-round education, whatever the fancy prospectus claimed. Lacrosse and Latin were all very well, but they completely failed to give you an edge over sexier, worldly-wise day-school girls.

Nell's experience of sex to date had been just one fumbled summer with another ex-boarding-school pupil — Marcus from the village — who was equally desperate to get the sex qualifications sorted. Both had been using the few months between A levels and college as a crash-course learning opportunity and had spent many stifling hours in the dark in Marcus's attic den, nervously getting the hang of each other's body geography. Their parents were bridge-and-tennis friends and there had been an uncomfortable (but unmentioned — something here to be thankful for) underlying certainty that this was very much an arranged and approved-of coupling, that each set of

parents had considered this match suitable enough to
get the sexual basics out of the way before the two of
them moved on to their next stage of education:
Marcus to Bristol (law) and Nell to Oxford (art and
design). Nell's mother Gillian was a practical sort: she
made sure her daughter left for Oxford equipped with a
full driving licence, a copy of Delia Smith's *One is Fun*
and twelve different-sized sable paintbrushes. It seemed
highly likely that Nell's loss of virginity had also been
orchestrated in the interest of getting another
practicality achieved before the start of term.

"Criminal, those boots. What a fuckin' disgusting
waste of snakes." A girl who smelled of charity-shop
mothballs glared across at the beautiful dozing boy.

"Is it?" Nell immediately challenged. She looked at
the girl and saw, in spite of the glare, a potential rival.
This girl, all pins, rips, lace and Doc Martens, was
taking notice of the lovely boy. She might be finding
fault but she'd clocked him — couldn't take her eyes
off him. This was only one step away from a change of
mind and serious opposition.

"You know what?" Nell took a chance, brazenly
staking her own claim rather than heading safely for the
making-a-friend option. "I can't think of a better use
for snakes."

And so had begun five years of defending Patrick
against many, many a critic.

Ed was early for once. Today he wouldn't be sloping
late into the college with the most laid-back of the

students (the hung-over, the oversleepers, the bus-shelter dope-smokers) and having the principal give him that look that said it was bad enough for the college's image that he dressed like a Kensington Market hippie, circa 1970 — unpunctuality could be the excuse she needed to get him out and smarten the Literature staff up to standards more in keeping with a thriving business. He stashed a heap of marked essays (War poetry — to be dealt with no more than three at a time in order not to feel suicidal), his iPod and a Doors CD to play in the car into his bag, and took a quick glance out of the window at what the weather was doing. The all-enveloping army coat might be needed, or maybe the biker jacket. Next door's Golf, he noted, was back in the shared driveway. Mimi and Nell were just going into their house.

"Oh good. Next door are home," Ed commented to his brother. He backed away from the window; he didn't want to be thought snooping, not by Nell. He'd see her later, at the Mitchells' party, and would ask her how the holiday went. He hoped it had been therapeutic — she deserved some fun after putting up with a bastard husband for so long. And he wasn't nosy, of course not. He was just being neighbourly, and in his opinion there should be plenty more of that. If you insisted on minding your own business and never taking an interest, the whole area would end up anonymous, dead. Of course he knew it was all right for him, he was only around here in south-west London in term-time and on weekdays. He'd got his place down in Dorset to take off to for peace and solitude whenever he felt like it, but you wouldn't want it all day, every day, nobody talking to anyone else.

"We knew they'd be back today. It's written on the calendar, just above the Mitchells' bash. Funny day to have a party, you'd think they'd wait till the weekend." Charles didn't look up from his sudoku. Today was Wednesday so the rating was Fiendish. If he didn't finish it by the time breakfast was over, the day would be spoiled. That ever-present background worry about Alzheimer's setting in would creep up over the hours, and by late afternoon he would be able to picture the exact layout of his future care home, the slurried shades of beige on the thin, murkily floral carpet, the dull pictures on the walls — washed-out landscapes of places that looked too cold to visit — the lumpy ochre paint on the banister rails, the spider plants on top of the bookshelves. The terrible, terrible lack of books. There were people younger than him moving into those places, taking their few final-years possessions through the Doorway to Death. He shivered slightly, feeling the ghost of his future sliding by. "Whatever happened to spider plants?" he asked his brother. "Everyone had them at one time, didn't they? You don't see them any more. I suppose they went the way of peacock chairs and wooden-handled steak knives."

"Spider plant: *Chlorophytum comosum* 'variegatum'," Ed told him instantly. Charles used to know the Latin name of just about any plant, but recently he'd had trouble recalling some of them. He was a good fifteen years older than Ed: was this a sign that his brain was beginning to delete chunks of information? Ed hoped not. He knew the idea of mental decline worried Charles. Well, it worried everyone in time, he supposed. Even he, still only at the beginning of his fifties, went into a slight panic when he forgot what he'd gone into a room for. The worst thing was, being older and more forgetful meant you also forgot that you'd always done this; even children could sometimes be seen hovering, trying to remember what they'd intended to do next. His daughter Tamsin had done this ever since she was small and she seemed, at nearly thirty, still to have the full use of a functioning brain.

"Trust you to know that," Charles grunted. The bottom right-hand square of the puzzle wasn't working out. There seemed nowhere for the eight to go. Please, he asked God fervently, don't let this be a cock-up. Not on a Wednesday, not when the hardest puzzles of the week were yet to come. Was this a sign?

"Did they look tanned?" Charles asked. Perhaps if he had one more cup of coffee his brain might be kick-started back into rhythm.

"What? Nell and Mimi? Hard to say. I only saw them for a second. You'll be able to see for yourself tonight — I know the Mitchells invited Nell to their do." Ed glanced out of the window again, wondering if she would be too tired to go. The Mitchells had invited half the street — which must mean they had some God-awful new consumer durable they wanted admired — but Nell might not be keen to dress up to celebrate a long marriage when hers had just collapsed. No, he thought, she'd probably put in an appearance, to be polite. He'd make sure he talked to her, be

23

cheerful, because if she *did* turn up it would be a defiant and brave act. Neighbours might prefer to keep their private lives private, but the departure of Alex definitely came under Public Knowledge. The Mitchell house would be full of people asking Nell how she was feeling, all agog that she might come up with something more eye-opening and intimate than "jet-lagged". The sad irony of a wedding anniversary wouldn't go unmentioned either, especially by the women. They could be such nasty things.

"She's left the car out on the drive. I don't suppose she'll bother much with the garage now Alex has gone. I hope she fills it up with his leftover possessions. I wonder if she's cut the sleeves off his suits like that woman in the papers a few years back? If that's a book she's taking a leaf out of, we could be in line for his wine collection. We should keep an eye on the front doorstep."

"Unlikely." Charles folded *The Times* carefully and turned to the main section. There was still the crossword to be tackled — one final chance for his intellect to redeem itself. Ed could do a lot worse than to start doing those himself. It was all very well playing Led Zeppelin at full volume and reminding yourself of long-ago dope-addled days, but it wouldn't keep the brain cells ticking over. In fact, Ed was lucky he *had* brain cells. He'd been quite a wild worry in his time. "If she's got any sense she'll drink her way through his cellar in no time — if you can call it anything so grand, that cupboard under their stairs. Alex was no connoisseur; there'll be nothing worth hanging on to.

Christmas before last, at that party they had, I'm sure I saw a *wine box* on the kitchen table."

"I expect it would have been one that a guest brought."

"Don't be ridiculous. Whoever would take wine in a box to a party? Surely a decent bottle of claret would be the very least. Or champagne."

"Well, students would, kids," Ed decreed. "It was probably some friend of Sebastian." He hoped this didn't add up to defending the appalling Alex. Too smooth by three-quarters, that one, and certain to have had an entire string of extramarital women on the go, not just the one he went off to live with. Men like that, sleek and always rushing, forever gabbling into their phones as if every word they uttered was monumentally important, it was a mystery how they found time for complicated sex lives. Businesswise they were the type described as "thrusting", as if that was a good thing to be. Not so good when it crossed over into their private life, was it? Too ironically apt a description.

The new woman wouldn't last, in his considered opinion. Alex would tire. He would either move on to a different one or come to regret opting out of what must have been a pretty comfortable nest. A man preferred the familiar as life moved towards its later stages. Alex would come to realize this in a year or two, when the new one was making noises about starting a family and he was wondering why he was losing touch with the one he'd already got. He would see the whole thing coming round and going round again, and he'd feel dismal and despairing and full of regret. If Nell wanted her miserable excuse for a husband back she only had to wait it out, but Ed sincerely hoped she wouldn't bother. He, so conveniently next door, could be useful to her, now she was living alone. He would make sure she knew he was always there to take in oversize mail and parcels, to feed her cat when she was away, mend the fence after a gale and such. She might even fancy going out for a drink or meal sometime, just casual, nothing intense. He'd like to be useful and there weren't so many opportunities for that, these days, not since Tamsin had grown up.

Well, it wasn't the trauma it might have been, coming home to this Alex-free house. Maybe the mugging had reduced the impact, which made it a strange small mercy to be grateful for. Nell phoned and cancelled the one credit card the boy had made off with (like many shops, it seemed he didn't take American Express — and he had scorned the John Lewis store card too, making off with only the Topshop one). She then wandered from hallway (calmly blue) to sitting room (dark wood floor, Designers Guild turquoise, pink and lilac-vibrant — her insistence, Alex's surrender) to kitchen (trippily patterned burr oak, honed black granite) and through to the conservatory in a jet-lagged daze, clutching a bundle of mail that seemed to be mostly junk, bills and catalogues, and half-expecting (and half-dreading) to find evidence that Alex hadn't packed up and gone after all.

She wouldn't have been completely surprised to find him sitting at the big old kitchen table with a mug of coffee, going through emails on his laptop, saying, "Oh you're back," without looking up, the way he so often and so annoyingly would do. She wondered how she'd have felt if he had still been there, and decided she'd have been furious, actually (as of course, contrarily, she was also furious that he'd gone). That week away had been to avoid the worst of him going, a chance for him to slink out of the house with his possessions — spotted-hankie-tied-on-a-stick style — while she was bravely having fun somewhere else, getting herself ready, mentally, to face this house he'd abandoned. She would have felt completely cheated if, after all that, he'd been there large as life, having casually changed his mind. It *was* a good thing he'd gone. No question about it. She could almost believe the mean temperature of the house was up by a good few degrees. And that had nothing to do with thermostat settings.

"Mum? I'm going to do some emails and then get some sleep. Cup of tea would be nice." Mimi yawned and slunk away towards the stairs, not — no surprise here — showing any sign of wanting to drag her bag up with her to unpack.

"This lot won't be lying in the hallway for the next six weeks, will it?" Nell called up after her. There was no reply. And nothing was *that* different, so far. No Alex around, obviously, but the seagrass stair carpet still had the fluffed-wire effect on the bottom two steps where Pablo the cat had clawed it. There was still a chunk of gouged-out paint on the wall halfway up where Seb had been carrying a chest of drawers with a mildly drunk friend and without enough care. An irrational corner of Nell's brain had half-expected these domestic blemishes to have fixed themselves, for the entire place to have given itself a celebratory makeover.

The new start shouldn't just apply to her. The house — all her own territory now, so long as she could cope with the bills — should be shaping up and joining in too. The paint she had been planning for the kitchen should have somehow got itself bought and applied, and every room should be full of flowers and Welcome to Your New Life cards. Monty Don should be wiring in a fountain as a finishing touch on the back terrace. Flags should be fluttering from every window, like a flamboyant cruise ship boasting its way into port, and sirens should blast all down the street. Instead, silence. Then out of this silence came a full-volume blast of Kaiser Chiefs from Mimi's room.

"That'll be Mimi reclaiming *her* territory," Nell muttered to herself as she went to fill the kettle. She didn't feel inclined to go and ask her to turn it down because the going-upstairs bit would be where the difference would really show, and where a twinge of pain might kick in. There would be no John Grishams heaped on Alex's bedside table. His comfort stack of Nurofen packets (Regular, Plus, Caffeine-free and Gel) would be gone. He would no longer leave shoes in dangerous tripping-over positions in every doorway and at the top of the stairs, as he had each day since she'd met him (to the point where, lately, she'd wondered if he had murder on his mind. From his point of view it would have solved a lot). There would be empty

28

drawers containing nothing but crinkled lining paper with drifts of dust, lost buttons and flecks of wool and cotton. Possibly a few shirts that he no longer wanted would be hanging in his wardrobe, waiting to be bagged up for the charity shop. It wouldn't have occurred to him to take them there himself. A man who had never made himself familiar with the workings of the washing machine wouldn't have given any thought to the disposal of old clothes.

She would, she decided, repaint the bedroom as well as the kitchen. Farrow & Ball's Cooking Apple Green would be good — she'd had it in mind for a while for somewhere in the house. Alex hated green. When she'd run the idea past him a couple of years ago, he had said it would make the room feel cold, and besides, it reminded him of ponds and wasn't magnolia a safer bet? Well, of course it was. And so bland. How typical of Alex, though, whose extramural sex life didn't lack imagination, to have tried to go for the dull and predictable inside the house and expected her to live with it. An old memory whizzed back to Nell: Patrick's room in the Oxford flat had been green — the wall behind the bed a vivid lime and the rest painted deepest velvety emerald — and it hadn't been cold at all. Far from it.

The phone rang while she was shoving bread into the toaster.

"Eleanor, daaarrrling!" Only her mother could spin the word out to a five-syllable descending note. "So. Has Alex really gone?"

Nell heard the accusation "Oh you useless failure of a wife/daughter" in the sentence. Not for the first time. Gillian Wilkinson had perfected a fine line in disappointment over her entire adult life. It had started, Nell was sure, with the arrival of three daughters but no sons. Nell, as the last of these girls, was by definition the biggest disappointment, for after that there were to be no more. "Boys stay so wonderfully *devoted*," Gillian always claimed, with much ill-concealed regret, whenever she was out with Eleanor and caught sight of some elderly dowager being helped into a restaurant chair by what she took to be a loving grown-up son. A generation on, she quite brazenly favoured Sebastian over Mimi, breezily claiming that was "natural"; that all indulgent grandmothers spoiled the first-born, whichever sex they were, but this didn't fool anyone. It would have been just the same if Mimi had been the older one; it would still have been Sebastian who was treated to extra outings, to the bigger presents. Nell had had to come up with a lot of crafty gift additions around birthdays and Christmases when the children were little, to make sure Mimi didn't feel slighted.

"Yes, he's really gone," Nell now confirmed. "And yes, Mimi and I had a lovely week away in the sun, escaping Alex's escape, thanks for asking." She wasn't going to mention the mugging. Somehow this would add to her mother's tally of Nell's failures. She could do without a lecture on how to hold on to a handbag.

"And Alex was such a reliable sort." Nell's mother sighed the deep, sad sigh of the reluctant betrayee. It had to be someone's fault. Guess whose? Nell pulled a knife out of the drawer in preparation for spreading deep swirls of honey on her toast, and wished that phones still had curly cables. How satisfying it would be, right now, to saw right through one.

"But Alex was *not* so reliable, as it turned out."

"Oh but he *was*, darling, for very nearly twenty years; dull of course, but . . ."

"There is absolutely no 'but'." Nell cut her mother off before she could get into full regret flow. "Alex has gone and I don't want to talk about him. Let me tell you about the hotel . . . you'd love it there; it was quite a small place, right on the sea, perfect pool, fantastic seafood, spa . . ."

"Yes, yes, but daaarliiing . . ." There it was again . . . that drawn-out note, the "but". "What on earth are you going to do *now*?"

"I shall come down to Guildford, Mother dearest, and move in with you, of course." Nell crossed her fingers suddenly, in case what was spoken in jest was misinterpreted by the spiteful gods as something she'd truly wished for. You had to be careful with that. Losing a husband to a girl who was just a toddler when Pink Floyd played *The Wall* at Earls Court was bad enough, but being sent by the teasing immortals to live with your mother in the Surrey gin and Jag belt would be a humiliation too far.

"What? Oh don't be silly, Eleanor. I meant . . ."

"I know what you meant. I'm going to have some toast, tea and then a couple of hours' sleep. Catch up on emails, see if any work has come in. Order some paint supplies. I've got a whole series on vegetables with diseases to illustrate for *Home Grown* magazine, so I need the right colours for potato blight."

"But . . . if you tried, you know . . . even now, I'm sure . . . You see, men at a certain age, they do silly things. They don't mean them. And you know, Eleanor, it isn't entirely ungracious to *forgive*. And of course then you would *have the upper hand.*" This was said in almost whispered intimacy that suggested a mutually understood code. Nell didn't, quite, understand but guessed it might involve the acquisition of valuable guilt presents. That could explain why her mother had such a collection of sparkly jewellery. She really didn't want to know about any wanderings of her late father, and hoped fervently that Gillian wasn't planning an intimate lunch at which she would decide it was time to tell all in the interests of trying to spare her daughter a lonely old age. Five years after his death (car crash on the A3, alongside a woman in scarlet dungarees who, it turned out, delivered more than bouquets from the local florist), she really didn't think such details would add anything helpful to her memories of her father.

"Mum, are you trying to say that Alex really didn't *intend* to move three thousand miles to live with another woman? That he didn't *mean* to have had at least four full-on affairs before the great big catastrophically destructive final one? Which silly thing that 'they don't mean' would apply, in this particular case, to Alex?"

Gillian Wilkinson sighed again. "Well if you're going to be like that, Eleanor . . . But one thing I will say: in spite of everything and the way it's turned out, I still think you did the right thing, marrying *him* and not . . ."

"Now don't even *start* on that!" Nell warned, feeling her voice rise and wishing she was a more controlled type. Press the right keys and her mother would still always play the same tune, so many years on. "Just don't say *anything* more. Not a word!"

"You know what I mean, Eleanor. After . . ."

"OK that's it. Goodbye Mum, I'm going to get some sleep now. I've got a party to go to tonight. I want to be awake enough to enjoy it." Nell clicked the phone off and wished she hadn't said that last bit. It smacked of So There defiance, of Look at Me, I Do Have a Life, You Know. Gillian would sense desperation. She had a nose for it. Too late now and so what anyway; Nell opened the fridge. Oh, God bless Andréa — a big bottle of milk. And a massive, massive multipack of Cadbury's Flakes. Nell's eyes filled with tears. She wiped them away quickly with the nearest useful item (a damp J-cloth, smelling strongly of Astonish. Never mind, it was probably good exfoliation), took out one of the Flakes and snapped off half of it, sending shards of chocolate to the floor. She wasn't going to feel sorry for herself. No. Not at all. She would be positive and abide by Chapter Three in *After He's Gone*: "Treat yourself daily to one item that always makes you feel good". Just now, to kick things off, she reckoned it would take four to do the trick: toast, honey, chocolate and tea. The well-muscled boy who'd stacked the beach chairs at the hotel would have been a good addition to this list, but hey, you couldn't have everything.

★ ★ ★

I am now the Responsible Adult in Charge in this house. Thanks for that, Dad. Mimi thought this as she wriggled her way down beneath her duvet and tried to blot out the shaft of weak sunlight that was searing in through the gap at the bottom of the wooden blind. Neither Adult nor Responsible were terms she was comfortable with. She was way too young. For one thing, if she had to be responsible for keeping her mother's spirits up, where did that leave her own needs? How was she going to carry on doing Being Fifteen and all the glorious self-centredness that went with it, if she had to think about being careful not to add to her abandoned mother's woes? She'd had a quick skim through the *After He's Gone* divorce book over in Barbados, but the author had carelessly left out a chapter aimed at teenage daughters who were going to have to deal with the fallout from . . . well, the fallout. There were girls younger than her — she'd seen *The Jeremy Kyle Show* — who were looking after entire dysfunctional families almost single-handed. Kids with no money, having to juggle the lone mum's benefits and drug habits and casual loser boyfriends. Obviously she hadn't got it *that* hard. But that was the trouble with it not being *that* hard by regular standards. There just wasn't any kind of manual for it. And what a number her dad had laid on her: "Take care of your mum. Keep an eye on her." Final fucking last words before the one-way to New York. Great, so helpful. Lay it all on me, why don't you?

Mimi closed her eyes and thought of lying in the sea again, weightless and carefree. Her hair still had a slight sandy residue and smelled of sea life and she pulled a thick strand of it across her mouth, tasting salt. This time yesterday . . . the boy who strolled up the beach in the mornings selling shell necklaces, palm-frond hats and ready-rolled spliffs; the tiny silver-striped fish that nibbled her ankles as she paddled out to the waves. The sun blonding her hair, the heat making her body tender and lazy. All of it was stuff that made you feel good. Not like this huddly cold, not like this late-winter loneliness. What a long, long time it was going to be till summer.

CHAPTER
THREE

No Surrender
(Bruce Springsteen)

"Nell! *Lovely* to see you!" Evie Mitchell kissed the air alongside each of Nell's ears as she let her into her pink-lit hallway. From further into the house Nell could hear distant-motorway waves of conversation and party laughter and suddenly wished she'd stayed home, in bed with the chocolate, the cat and some well-worn comedy repeats on the telly. Evie was an excited blonde flurry of cream lace and spray tan and looked like a cappuccino. "I'm so sorry about it being a school night," she giggled. "It's just that . . . I know it seems odd but Don and I always think it's *really* important to celebrate our wedding anniversary *on the actual day*, don't you agree?"

Evie's eyes then widened and she clapped her hand (café-au-lait nail extensions) over her mouth. "Oh I'm *so* sorry, Nell! How tactless of me! And you were *so* sweet to come tonight!" She lowered her voice as her daughter Polly sidled up and, with a sullen lack of grace, due to being under strict orders to be helpful, grabbed Nell's coat out of her hands and stamped up the stairs with it. There was an airport duty-free Dior lipstick in the left pocket — would it still be there when she went home? Mimi had said Polly was on a warning at school for thieving cash from the Year Sevens.

Evie took hold of Nell's wrist and gave it a waggle. "We'd have *completely understood* if you'd decided to give us a miss, you know. We'd have been sorry if you had, of course, but we'd have understood. Drink?" She handed Nell a glass of champagne and then steered her towards a relatively uncrowded corner of the sitting room, a space that Nell rightly guessed to be unpopular because of the icy blast coming from the open French doors, beyond which she could see Don Mitchell out on the terrace. He was waving a big knife, tending skewers of something on his gas-powered all-dancing barbecue and being effusive to whoever would listen about the upside to global warming, under a pair of blazing patio heaters and an array of multicoloured fairy lights. Why would anyone want to have a barbecue in February? Wouldn't a vat of warming goulash or comforting cassoulet have been more the thing?

Inside the house, huddled close to the log fire, women who'd anticipated Evie's usual stifling heating shivered in strappy silk. Nell started to shift towards a warmer spot. "No, no, I wasn't going to miss your party. It's good to be out," she tried to reassure her hostess. "And happy anniversary. It is china isn't it, twenty years? I got you this . . ." She handed her prettily wrapped package to Evie. Of course she knew it was china. Hadn't her mother said it was such a shame she and Alex hadn't quite made it to the actual day, she'd been so looking forward to handing on the Wilkinson family Crown Derby soup tureen? Alex had said that was almost a good enough reason in itself for separating, which had made her laugh for the first time in a while till she remembered that she wasn't supposed to find Alex the slightest bit amusing any more, for that way lay the possibility she'd have to admit she might miss him.

"It *is* china," Evie agreed, ripping the paper off a piece of traditional Bajan blue decorated pottery, bought last-minute at the Bridgetown airport shop. "Well, *traditionally* it is." She smiled and fingered a sparkly earring. "But in the more modern lists it's down as *platinum* . . . Ooh Nell, this is *lovely*. Very . . . arty," she said, kissing Nell's ear vicinity again. "I'll just go and find somewhere to . . . er . . . put it. Do mingle, sweetie. You know lots of them, obviously."

"The platinum'll be Don's Amex, poor bastard," Ed whispered to Nell as Evie wafted away to offload her present and deal with guests who had less potential for being emotionally volatile. Nell giggled and took a long deep gulp of champagne, hoping it would speed to her head. It would be good to get cheerful. A few hours' light sleeping in the daytime had left her with a feeling of other-worldness. That, combined with the jet lag, was making her certain her brain was made of soft cheese. She liked Ed, liked his velvety old-hippie, fashion-oblivious, long-haired and mildly dishevelled style, and was glad he seemed to be turning into a permanent fixture with his new job at the college, rather than just the visitor he'd been before the death of his mother. Maybe it was due to all those years living in a village community down in Dorset, but he was the rare kind of neighbour who wouldn't think twice about challenging an unfamiliar bloke up a ladder claiming to be your new window-cleaner. She hoped he'd never come off worse for being that sort — she'd hate to find him bleeding in the road, stabbed by some lowlife he was telling off for trying car doors. He'd been the one who'd babysat Seb the time Nell had gone off in the ambulance blue-lighting three-year-old Mimi to the hospital with febrile convulsions. Where, exactly, had Alex been selling global networks that week? Munich or Maine? Who knew? She remembered she couldn't get hold of him at the time and had cursed the miracle that was the so-called communications business.

"I don't think Evie was keen on the china aspect of the anniversary and I'm ninety per cent sure that platinum-wise," Nell said, "we were meant to clock the earrings. In a straight choice between Ming or bling, for her it's no contest."

"Why are they having a barbecue, for heaven's sake?" Ed asked. "It's freezing! They're mad, aren't they?"

"Being able to afford your fuel bills, it's the new swanking. In-your-face eco defiance. The same way her Range Rover is absolutely essential for the children's safety, as if any parent who drives a nice economical Prius is deliberately putting their kids at risk. Did Charles come with you?"

"He's in the kitchen trying to get Evie to open something that doesn't take the enamel off your teeth. He hates champagne — says it causes fights."

"Hmm. He might have a point." She and Alex had had some of their worst rows after champagne. The first time he'd packed and left had been five years ago after her own birthday dinner when she'd thrown a lemon tart at him because he'd left the table three times to take phone calls and she'd found him sitting on the stairs, smiling and murmuring silly tendernesses at some unknown down-the-line slapper. "There's a demon in every bubble", that was what Patrick used to say. Not that they drank much of it in their student days. Who did, back then? It was a big-occasion treat, not something you picked up in the supermarket for any old Friday night, like now. But she remembered being at his sister's wedding, on one of those rare, hot midsummer nights at his family's farm in Hampshire. Late in the evening, she and Patrick had drifted to opposite ends of the marquee. She was on the dance floor, mildly drunk and unused to endless supplies of Pol Roget, propped up in a crush of people against the warm, solid body of Patrick's oldest friend Simon. The place was steamy hot and smelled of damp vegetation from the crushed grass underfoot and the swags of overripe flowers that were now dropping their exhausted petals.

The Eagles' "Desperado" was playing — the slow, sensuous music doing its seductive tricks so that she didn't pull away when Simon's hand edged under her top and slid across the bare, clammy skin of her back, but instead relaxed closer against him and let the heat and the moment get to her. Even now, she remembered how his breath against her neck had made her tingle.

She remembered wishing he'd bite her, just gently. Then the spell had abruptly shattered as Patrick pulled her away, viciously kicking at Simon with casual, warning spite. There was drink spilling, someone shouting, "Oy, watch it, pisshead." Her arm hurt — Patrick was hauling her out of the marquee, not saying a word, and he didn't let go till they'd crossed the garden and reached the orchard, far from the range of lights. Without a word he'd pushed her to the grass and pinned her down, gripping her wrists above her head as he kissed her, too hard.

The things that stay with you, she thought now while she pretended to be interested in Isabelle from no. 14's battle with the council over cardboard recycling. She remembered the sound of the hens fussing and shuffling in their night-time lock-up, the uneven, tussocky grass pressing into her back, the syrup scent of the stickily ripening plums on the tree above her as Patrick fucked her till she screamed. She'd cried after that, overwhelmed by excess pleasure, not from misery. That was something else champagne did. Made you all emotional, all unnecessary. Now she looked at the inch of bubbly drink left in the glass and decided that tonight, from here on, she'd stick to water. It wasn't really the ideal day to indulge in champagne memory games. All the same . . . she wondered if Patrick ever thought of that night. If she ever found out where he was, and if she spoke to him, mentioned the word "orchard", would he look at her blankly and wonder why she was talking free-range fruit, or would he smile

41

and remember the tender circlet of bruises on her wrist?

"You were mugged by a ginger boy called Callaghan? How do you know? Did he swop his schoolbag for your Mulberry one? Was his name all over his homework? How amateur!" Kate's voice sounded too bright and shrill for Nell, who braced her muzzy head in her hands as she sat over steaming coffee at her kitchen table. How obviously rude would it be to cover her ears, just lightly? She felt very much as if she was hearing all this with an echoed delay, like watching a TV film with badly synchronized sound. Jet lag. She and Mimi had only been away for a week — hardly any time at all. Because it was such a short break, and so Mimi could get back easily into early-morning school time, they had deliberately not tried hard to adjust to the Caribbean time zone, and yet after only twenty-four hours at home she felt as if it would take days and days of constant sleep to sort her woolly brain out.

"'Callaghan' was on his Manchester United shirt. The police knew exactly who he was — seems he's the only red-haired ASBO kid stupid enough to wear his name in big print when he's out robbing. He only took my Visa card, Topshop card and my cash in the end, too. No more than about thirty quid. He even left my purse — just emptied it out, scooped the money and fled. Obviously my driving licence and Amex were way beyond his fencing skills."

"So far . . . By the time he's had a year or two in a Young Offenders' gaff he'll be well qualified in profitably off-loading the full contents of any wallet or bag. Your gym membership will be up for grabs on eBay and the points on your Nectar card will be getting a family of five into the theme park of their choice for free." Kate, reaching for a fifth chocolate digestive, shifted in the pink Lloyd Loom chair which creaked and protested under her considerable weight.

One day Kate would surely get firmly wedged in that chair and Nell would have to find the wire-cutters to slice through the woven strands and loosen her out of it. That would be a sad day (not least for the ever-dieting Kate: this week her faith was in a Porridge and Parsnip regime, though clearly not when she was in other people's kitchens) — for this was the last of six non-matched Lloyd Looms that she and Alex had collected over their early years together. The others had taken their turns at disintegrating, having all eventually fallen to bits from being carelessly left outside on too many bad-weather nights, till they'd rotted enough for it not to be worth bringing them back in.

As soon as the spring sun started to warm the terrace, she would consign this chair to the garden for good. Before Kate's torso expanded to chair-destruction point, the last one deserved a final brave outdoor summer. Each evening at six, she would take a glass of chilled white outside, water the agapanthus pots on the terrace, then sit in this rickety chair and think over the day. She would let it absorb every summer thunderstorm, every ray of blistering sun, alternately soaking then stiffening till its shards of woven raffia unravelled and broke, and the seat inevitably gave way and split from the sides. It would be like setting a caged pet free. And for the kitchen she would tempt bankruptcy by buying eight Philippe Starck Ghost chairs, regardless of how out of place they would look with her ancient pitch-pine table. She loved them; Alex hated them: when she'd suggested the chairs a year or two back he had gone all sniffy and said the transparent Perspex would remind him of his mad mother's Tupperware collection and he wasn't having them in the house, thank you. What, he'd asked, was wrong with solid traditional wooden ladder-backs? "Where do you want me to to start?" she'd snapped. How could she ever have thought it would work, an artist setting up home with a man who'd thought Ron Arad was a footballer and Terence Conran an Olympic ice skater?

"So — what did you think of *After He's Gone?* Helpful? Tina said it was her absolute bible when Micky left her for that dancer in Hartlepool."

Nell laughed. "Well, it was very . . . um, practical. If I followed it to the letter I wouldn't have a single second to think about missing Alex. I'd be out every night at car maintenance classes or speed-dating."

"Well, *do* you think about him?" Kate was never one to skirt the issue.

"I missed him in bed last night."

"Ahh . . . well now, sex . . ."

"No, *not* sex! It was a bit cold, that's all. I needed someone to put my feet on. For the first time ever I could see the point of those cashmere bedsocks that I've always thought were a bit disgusting. Still do, actually. It can't be right, can it, being in bed in socks? It's like going to bed with all your make-up on."

Kate grinned. "But I do that sometimes, don't you? I thought everyone did, or is that the sign of a hopeless slattern? What about when you've come home from a party a bit pissed and you can't be arsed? Or you're both in that mood where you've just got to have sex *right now*. Sorry, sorry! Should have remembered your new celibate state. Mustn't mention the 's' word."

"So I'm going to buy an electric blanket." It sounded so dreary, Nell thought; the defeatist decision of a sighing woman who has given up. Well, that was true enough, for now.

"You can't give up sex, not at your age. You need another man." Kate had a sly, scheming look on her face. Nell hoped she wouldn't find she was already signed up to a dating agency "as a present".

"Kate, no, I really *don't* need a man. When you've just had Pest Control round, you don't rush out and buy a pet rat. What I need is more coffee." Nell got up and switched the kettle on again.

"No, really, you do need a man," Kate insisted. "A nice new shiny one to do lovely sex with so that you don't turn into a desiccated old stick. And you need to join things, make yourself a life. No giving up, no surrender, babe."

"It said that in *After He's Gone*. I've already *got* a life. I've got a job." OK, working alone, from home, she conceded privately. "And friends and a social life and a family." (Well, Mimi still, anyway; she wasn't out half the time. Yet.) "And I don't want to join things; and

45

please not a reading group. I can't think of anything worse than sitting around on other people's uncomfortable sofas drinking nasty wine and talking about books I'd never have chosen to read. Nor do I want to go to the theatre on a weekly basis to see plays I've no interest in, or trail round galleries in a group pretending to be fascinated about paintings I wouldn't even hang in the garden shed. Sorry . . . got a bit carried away there. I didn't mean to sound so vehemently negative."

"No, you were just being contrary. At the risk of you clouting me, I'd say you already sound a tad old-maidish."

Nell couldn't argue with that. She reminded herself of Mimi as a small child, having a foot-stamping "I'm *bored*" moment.

"Well why not? Who *are* these people who do all this 'joining', anyway? When are these abandoned-but-putting-a-brave-face-on-it women supposed to earn a living? There isn't a moment in the day for that little consideration, apparently, not once you've got all those activity things out of the way. According to the book, you get up early and pimp your body down at the gym, then it's hair, manicure, a gossipy lunch with someone, then an afternoon doing something worthily cultural. The implication is that that's *every single day*! How exhausting, expensive and totally self-indulgent is that?"

"Well, one thing you're definitely signing up for is the Stay Safe course they're doing down at the gym. While you were away a notice went up on the board. It's a mixture of self-defence and tips on personal safety measures that any fool should already know but of course we don't. I can't go, the classes are on my Pilates night and God knows, I can't skip those, but you should do it. Go and learn the stuff for both of us so that next time some little mugger twerp grabs your bag you can deck him and give him a fright."

"You know, that's not such a bad idea," Nell told her. "If I'm going to be living on my own permanently I could use a few self-defence tips. Even when Alex was working away, I sort of felt — stupidly, I know — that I was safe once the chain was on the door, but I know it's not enough. As for the other stuff, well — I guess I'll just carry on as normal. Alex and I had pretty much separate lives for the last couple of years anyway, so nothing much has changed. And OK, you're right in a way, I suppose sex would be good, maybe a long time ahead. Not yet though. Don't relationships deserve a decent period of mourning?"

In this case, it crossed Nell's mind, possibly she could do with a few months and an uncomfortable check-up to be sure Alex hadn't left her with some unpleasant little health issues. What a sod he'd been, this last year or so.

"Ah! You see? I was right!" Kate looked triumphant, beaming at Nell in a way that made Nell think she'd already got a plan, ready hatched. She sincerely hoped not. Kate was good at plans — for other people. Not so good at her own, though. After her two sons hit the teenage stage she'd planned on a full-time post-grad course, but suddenly found she was the mother of a third boy, accidental Alvin.

"Well, OK, it was the climate in Barbados," Nell admitted, laughing. "I always was a bit solar-powered in that department. Now that I'm back in freezing February England with layers and layers of clothes, sex seems very much less desirable. And out there in the steamy heat, it's easy to blame the cocktails."

"Well, a drink or two on a sultry night and we all feel a bit rampant. It's natural. It's how we ended up with Alvin." Kate slid her fingers slowly up and down the edge of her mug, clearly thinking along the lines of Faye Dunaway giving the come-on to Steve McQueen in the *Thomas Crown Affair* chess game.

"There was this cocktail list at one bar we went to that got to me," Nell told her. "All the drinks had provocative, raunchy names like Sex on the Beach, Between the Sheets, Slow Comfortable Screw, all the sort of smirk-inducing stuff that you felt a complete idiot asking the barman for. You couldn't help thinking about sex. And then I started wondering, and I had this bit of panic: a kind of, suppose I never, ever do it again? Now that Alex has gone, suppose that's it, for evermore? Shop shut, without even a closing-down sale. A Screaming Orgasm could end up as no more than a choice on a tacky cocktail menu, not a real-life option with a real-life man."

"Well you could always . . ."

"No! Don't even go there, Kate. I know what you're thinking and I don't want a Rabbit! Mimi has to live here too, remember. I don't want anything in the house that I'd be embarrassed for her to find. Not to mention the buzzing. And besides, it's not the same." Nell had actually considered this DIY option, back when Alex had given away his guilt by using bed-avoidance tactics. She'd concluded that sex with a bright pink, glittery plastic item would be too much like playing with toys meant for Barbie. On a bigger scale, of course.

"You wouldn't want your cleaner to find anything like that, either. I knew a woman who had a lovely big shiny black vibrator that she kept in her knicker drawer and one day the cleaner got it out, polished it up and put it right in the middle of the bedroom window ledge where all the neighbours could look at it."

Nell giggled. "Wow, what was the cleaner doing searching through her underwear anyway? Andréa never would. That would be one employee you wouldn't want to undertip at Christmas!"

"Too right. And me, I'd have fired her. Now as for . . ."

"I told you . . ."

"Yes but I was just going to suggest . . ."

"No, Kate. Give me a break."

"No, not a new *live-with* man. What you need is a *comfort* man! Haven't you got some nice safe old boyfriend from way back tucked away somewhere that you could dig out and play with for a bit? Just to get you back into the market in a sort of safe, easy way? You should always hang on to a spare from the past, you know . . . it says so in . . ."

"In *After He's Gone*. Yes I know." Nell had read that section with yet another feeling of failure. No, she hadn't got a backup sex supply, ready and available like a roadside rescue service. Who had?

"What about that man next door?"

"What? *Charles?* Are you mad? He bats for the other side, I think."

"But you don't know?"

"He lived with his mother all his life. She only died a few months ago."

"There are often good reasons for that."

"Well, she was pushing ninety . . ."

"No, I meant reasons for living with their mothers."

"Are you kidding? Name one, Kate. Today's challenge. Oh and he's a sudoku obsessive."

"OK. You win on that one. But then his brother is there in the week, mostly, isn't he? Don't tell me he's gay as well. Is it statistically likely?"

"Ah now, Ed. Used to come and stay a lot but now he's got a job at the sixth-form college and is here for every term-time week. He's lovely, but only in a friends way. He's the sort you ask to help when the fence blows down in a gale or your battery's flat. The car one, I mean," she giggled. "Not the one on your Rabbit!"

"Friends is a good enough way to start. Was he there at Evie's party last night?"

"He was, and he is very sweet, but . . ."

"OK, we'll keep him on hold for later. What about ex-lovers? Don't you have an address book somewhere with the old shag list?"

"I didn't have a shag list," Nell admitted. "There was only really . . ."

Kate recoiled. "Oh God, Nell, don't tell me there was only Alex! You surely weren't a virgin bride?"

Fleetingly, Nell wondered if there was any such thing any more. It was almost tempting to tease Kate by saying yes, she had been, and see how long it took for Kate to email such a rare fact to all her Internet mates.

"No . . . There was Marcus, who doesn't really count, then Patrick for nearly five years. And then a string of non-serious boyfriends who didn't much matter before Alex. But really, I don't want . . ."

"What . . . to see him again? I bet you've thought about it! Good grief, five years . . ."

"No — I don't even want to talk about him, actually. There's no point. I haven't seen him since we split up."

She'd reread his old letters, though. No emails back then, just proper, personal handwritten items you could hold and smell and remember. What would Mimi and Seb's generation have to remind them of the poignant times? Printed-out emails? Memories of two-word texts that were no more than CUL8R or LUVU? She wasn't going to tell Kate that these letters were only feet away from her, in the dresser drawer.

"Acrimonious split?"

Nell laughed. It sounded like a bitter echo. "Oh yes! I'd say that was definitely the word at the time. I met Alex fairly soon after that."

"Ah. Rebound marriage. No wonder it all fell apart. So will you tell me about it? And why haven't you before?"

"It wasn't a rebound marriage," Nell protested. "If it had been, it would have fallen to bits much sooner, wouldn't it? It was . . . oh I don't know, a safe option, a comfort zone."

"And Patrick wasn't?"

"God no! Patrick was never about comfort. He would have been a heart choice. But he'd broken mine, so I went for the head option instead. Someone who made sense." Nell reached across the table and took a handful of tissues from the box. Where were tears coming from, all of a sudden?

Kate took her hand. "Always better to make love than make sense, you know, darling."

"Is it?" Nell giggled through her tears. "Where does it say that in *After He's Gone*?"

"I expect it'll be in the next edition. So what are you going to do about him?"

"Who?" As if she didn't know what was coming. Nell held her breath, waiting for Kate to say his name.

"Patrick. The one you cheated on Alex with."

"I didn't cheat! Not once — I haven't seen him since . . ."

"You know I didn't mean literally. I mean in your head. I bet you thought about him loads over the years. Poor Alex. I'm reluctant to waste my sympathy but, well, you're lucky your marriage lasted twenty days, let alone twenty years. Did he know he played second fiddle to a ghost?"

"That's not how it was," Nell insisted. "There was no chance, no chance at all of Patrick and me getting together ever again. I gave Alex my absolute best shot, honestly."

"Honestly?"

"Honestly. As far as I could."

"Exactly. 'As far as I could.' And on that damning phrase — which, incidentally, reminds me of the thing Prince Charles said, 'whatever love is' — I'll give you just one piece of advice, one word: Google. Find Patrick and tidy up the past. Get whatever it is that still makes you cry so ridiculously easily out of your system, once and for all."

CHAPTER
FOUR

Heroes And Villains
(The Beach Boys)

"Come on, Mimi. Wake up! We're getting off here!" The bus lurched round the corner and Tess bashed Mimi hard on her arm.

"Hey, you, I'll have a bruise there now!" Mimi squealed. An elderly lady wearing a pumpkin-orange crocheted hat tutted loudly from across the aisle. Mimi scowled at her. Old bat. You should have waited till after the school rush, she thought. Shrieky kids are what you get, before nine.

"It won't show on your tan, will it?" Tess grabbed her arm and hauled Mimi out of her seat. Mimi reached back for her schoolbag. There was no arguing with Tess.

"It's not even our stop," Mimi grumbled. It was freezing. No way did she want to walk that extra quarter of a mile to school. It had been bad enough plodding up the road from home to the bus stop with the wind gusting under her hair and down her neck. She was sure it did it on purpose to punish her for that lovely week in the sun.

"We'll be late in now, you do realize that, don't you?" she said as Tess bundled her on to the pavement. It was no good. What Tess wanted, Tess got — was that useful in a best friend? Mimi wasn't sure. It depended on whether the best friend wanted the same as you did. If she did, it could make you lazy — you'd just have to hover around in her orbit and all you wanted (boys, parties, lifts to places) would come your way. But if you didn't, if you wanted different things, you could have a life of battling to be yourself. It was heading that way at the moment. Tess kept having little goes at her: "Your hair would look good with pink highlights," "Not the New Look skirt, it's like, *soo* not."

Tess hadn't always been like this, or had she? When they were seven and in ballet class, hadn't Tess always got the best spot in the front row? Hadn't she always wangled it so she'd been the one on the right when they were paired up for the ballet exams, which was where everyone wanted to be because you got to wear the pink ribbon and not the blue one and you got to go second with the set dance, which meant you also could see how rubbish your partner had been before you had your own go at it and could remind yourself where not to do it wrong? They'd moved on from the days of ballet class, though; it wasn't about crowing over who was better at skipping sweetly through the birdcage dance and who passed the exam with Honours and who only got a Commended, not any more. This was about Boys. It was a big, all-important battlefield. It was the hottest competition. Tess, Mimi realized, was all ready for it today — full-scale make-up and her favourite boots, the high ones she'd been told at school *not* to wear.

"I blame our parents," Tess was saying as they leaned into the bitter wind. "I mean, what were they doing, sending us to an all-girls' school? Like they didn't want us to know what fifty per cent of the population was about? Isn't learning to live with men an education in itself?"

"It is. It's what Seb calls the Reality School," Mimi agreed, feeling slightly more spirited as she caught sight of a promising knot of St Edmund's boys kicking a can around outside Tesco Metro. Joel might be among them. She liked Joel. Tess didn't know this, but even if she did, it didn't matter for once. Tess had already dismissed him as a nerdy boff. He was very quiet and very clever and not full of it like most of the others. Mimi was also inclined to be quiet and clever. She made an effort to be as full of rubbishy chat as everyone else, though, purely as a means of survival. It could be lonely being sidelined. A girl from the year above them had got the sideline treatment a year before and had left. Silent bullying, that had been the lecture they'd all been treated to after she'd taken the overdose. But no one had *actually* bullied her, not really. They just didn't know her. It had been a simple, sad matter of no communication lines on either side, nothing spiteful. It had worked both ways.

"Our mums must have forgotten what it was like, being young and needy," Mimi went on, at the same time scanning the boys for Joel. "Mine went to a boarding school and she said it was like being banged up in prison. They were only allowed out on Saturday afternoons, and not till they were over sixteen. Severe sexual deprivation, that was. Against human rights, gotta be."

"God! Horrendous!" Tess gasped. "Mine went to a mixed comp and said there was a place behind some old air-raid shelter where everyone went for sex. You had to book a time — someone kept a list of half-hour slots for lunchtimes. She probably just meant a bit of snogging, though. God, I hope so."

Mimi shuddered. "How horrible. Everyone'd know what you were doing and who with. They might even come and watch. Gross."

"I asked her about that — she said nobody watched. They just wouldn't. Only she said all that in front of my dad and he got a bit antsy and started going, 'Oh, nice to know there was a fine sense of honour back in the old days.' Sarky sod. But then he is a lot older than her. Sorry Mims, I shouldn't talk about dads, really, should I?"

Mimi shrugged. "No matter. It's not like I haven't still got one, is it? He was always away somewhere working anyway, so it's not much different for me. Only for Mum. Poor old Ma. What must it be like, starting again at her age? I mean, she looks all right, you know. She dresses pretty cool, in a Jigsaw and Joseph way, and she's got an edgy haircut and stuff but she's not a, like, twenty-something babe. When she and her mates go out, they don't exactly go out on the pull, do they? It's all nice cosy suppers and stuff where they've all known each other for about *ever*. And they all wear cashmere because it's *warm*. If 'warm' is top of the list for something to wear, she'll never get anyone new."

Tess said nothing, her attention now fixed on her quarry outside Tesco. Mimi thought some more about her mother, thought about whether she'd be all right on her own and if she'd *be* on her own for ever and ever; would Mimi end up scared to leave home, feeling she'd got to hang about and take care of her, like someone out of Jane Austen? But then if she *did* get someone else, how vile would it be if he moved in and they all had to get used to bathroom-sharing with this new bloke, who might eye up Mimi's body in a non-parental way? Nobody had so far, not that she'd noticed, not unless you counted old pervs on the bus or on the beach.

Mimi had decided Joel might be a good safe one to lose her virginity with one day, but even he had barely spoken to her so far. All she knew was that he might (or might not) be in the group of boys up ahead outside Tesco, and that he might, or might not, be hugely surprised at the fantasy plans she had for him. She also knew that Tess should have given her a bit more notice before dragging her off the bus. How much would a text have hurt before they'd left their homes? If she'd known, she'd have slicked on plenty of lipgloss and brushed her hair. It was a gift from the heavens to have the long blonde stuff, but it wasn't looking its best, straight from bed and tatted. She fluffed it out, running her fingers through it and getting them caught on the tangles. She hoped he'd just think it was attractively wind-blown.

"Y'all right?" Tess had drawn level with the boys, who had stopped can-kicking for a moment to give the girls a lookover. Mimi, hanging back behind Tess, saw Joel coming out of the shop with cigarettes. He quickly unwrapped the pack, throwing the cellophane into the bin outside the store. That was something, she thought, at least he was litter-aware, even if the smoking was a disappointment. But hey, you couldn't have everything. That was something her dad had said last time he and her mum had been rowing. The house was full of shouting, all echoes and anger. "You want it all, Nell, that's always been your trouble," he'd said. And then he'd said the really weird thing: "I was never going to be that 'all' for you, was I? *You* always knew that. *I* always knew that." And then he'd stormed off somewhere in his car and her mum had run upstairs and cried and Mimi had found her later, asleep on the bed with the photo album she'd kept from her college days beside her.

"'Lo," Joel suddenly said to Mimi (not to Tess, she noticed, not to Tess) as he lit a cigarette. He looked uncertain, as if he had no ideas for words that should follow on from this.

"Hi Joel," Mimi said. Did he actually even know her name, she wondered? She'd run into him several times, just sort of around, and at a couple of parties. He knew Tess's brother — they played in the same St Edmund's rugby team.

Mimi sat on the bench outside the shop and watched as Tess revved herself up to full-scale hyper-giggle with the Stuart twins. It wasn't that she wanted to be *like*

Tess exactly, but Mimi did very much envy her easy way with the boys. Apart from all the hair-flicking and pouting and posing, she did have a talent for casual, endless chat. It might be about nothing at all but they found her fun to be with. Mimi, on the edge of the group, waited silently in the cold with her bag on her lap and wondered how snobby it would look if she simply got up and carried on walking to school. Joel was also looking a bit out of place. He leaned against the shop door frame smoking his cigarette, but then stubbed it out halfway through and binned it.

"That's it. I quit," he told her.

"I'm supposed to be impressed?" Oh, that came out wrong, challenging and a bit snide. He looked surprised.

"Sorry — I mean, why now? You just bought those."

"Yeah, but it's a rubbish habit. I just do it at this time in the morning. I don't like habits — they can rule your life. If you want to change you have to do it when you think of it. If I waited till I'd got through the pack it might be too late." He came and sat close beside Mimi on the bench, his leg against hers. "And if you get habits, you get stuck. You need your brain free for thinking new stuff."

"What about when your life changes and you've got no choice about it? Aren't things like comfort habits useful then? Like chocolate or, I dunno, your favourite misery music?" If he asked, she'd tell him about her parents separating. But he wouldn't ask, not yet. He didn't know enough about her, probably actually nothing at all.

Joel was silent for a moment, looking closely into Mimi's face. She smiled, so did he. Nice teeth, she thought. Gentle, blue eyes. His hair was the kind of mid-colour that would be blond by July. It curled at the ends like Johnny Borrell's and had a shaggy, soft look. She had to stop herself reaching across and touching it, to see if it felt soft like a dandelion clock.

"What do you want to do?" he asked her.

"What, now? Um . . . well, I've got double geography in twenty minutes."

Joel laughed. "No, long-term. University, life, all that . . ."

"Ah, *big* questions." Mimi looked across at Tess, who was now having a go at keepy-uppy with a football belonging to one of the Stuart twins. She was hopeless but didn't care. Her short school kilt was flipping up and down and the boys were laughing, urging her to have another go, probably because they liked looking at so much leg.

Mimi thought about how to answer Joel. She didn't know, really, what she wanted to do, but she also didn't want him to think she was some no-brain, clueless loser who didn't care.

"Oh, you know . . . make a difference in the world, ideally. I mean, who wouldn't?" she said. Ugh, that was about as big-time as you could get, she thought. Way too much — it sounded cringingly slimy. "I meant, you know, like kind of build bridges or something."

Joel's eyes widened. "What, *really*? Engineering! You and me both!" He looked at her with shiny admiration.

"Isambard Kingdom Brunel. He's *the* man. Now there's someone to aspire to. *Big* hero."

"Um, yeah. Right." Mimi looked at the pavement, confused. She'd heard of Brunel, but the bridges she'd had in mind had been more of the world-peace variety and even that sounded pompous and silly. Too late. The enthusiasm on his face wasn't something she'd want to wipe out.

"Yeah. Um, engineering's a possibility." She smiled at him. "You're not one of those boys who thinks it's not for girls, are you?"

"No! God, no," Joel said. "We could, maybe . . ." He looked hesitant, shy, suddenly.

Mimi felt her insides tighten. He was going to ask her out, oh sweet joy . . . She looked at him, waiting.

"Um. Only if you'd want to, I mean. Not everyone would but if you're interested . . ."

"Oh I am." Aagh! Too keen! Mimi bit her thumbnail and willed herself to keep quiet.

"Science Museum? Or when it's warmer, go out and look at Brunel's bridges, like Marlow or Maidenhead or something? And Paddington station."

"Joel . . . are you . . .?" What *was* he talking about? Did he have a secret life as a trainspotter?

"OK, sorry . . . no, you're right." He looked crushed. "It's just, Brunel is *such* a hero. Amazing dude. A minority interest, I'll admit, though. So . . . no, probably a bad idea."

"No! Really, whatever you like. I'll tag along. Truly — I'd like to." No way was she going to sit on the end of a platform waving a tape recorder to catch the sounds of engines, but he was very sweet and hey, what was wrong with stations? They all had coffee shops, didn't they? Mimi picked up her bag and stood up. "Text me, call me," she said, digging out a scrap of paper and writing her mobile number down for him. "Any time; whenever. I'll come and look at bridges and stuff with you."

"So what was all that about then?" Tess asked as they hurried towards school. "Don't think I didn't clock you getting cosy with the boffin. Don't tell me you were discussing the combustion point of magnesium with him."

"Bridges," Mimi told her, smiling to herself. "We talked about Brunel and bridges, OK?"

"Yeah yeah. That'll be the jet lag. Get over it, babe, before you start enjoying maths and stuff."

Mimi kept quiet. She actually *did* enjoy maths. Physics, too, but Tess didn't need to know that.

The Body and Soul studio smelled of smoky lavender from Advanced Yoga's candles. The sickly scent seeped out to the corridor from under the nearest of the two glass doors. Inside, the class had reached the end-stage of lying still under blankets, meditating in the dark and the silence. Nell, waiting outside on a padded bench for her own class to start, could see the dark shapes of the bodies lined up, motionless and calm in tidy rows. Shockingly, they reminded her of scenes of makeshift mortuaries after disasters. She tried to delete this horrific image from her head and turned instead to the noticeboard on the wall outside the club's spa, where current special offers were listed. A non-surgical facelift rather appealed, she decided, wondering if it would be more or less effective than the painful-sounding chemical peel or laser dermabrasion.

"If you have that, you can never, not ever again, get your face in the sun." A long, angular woman appeared beside her, pointing at the peel information with a hand that seemed to be no more than bones and paper-thin skin.

For a moment Nell wondered what she meant: why would she want to get her face in the *Sun*? It wasn't her newspaper of choice.

"Oh — right, I see what you mean. Sunshine. Why is that?"

"Epidermis welded to your dermis. Sure as your knee bone's connected to your thigh bone. Your skin goes all thin and sensitive." The woman's voice had a touch of Irish about it. She laughed and looked at Nell, possibly calculating how careless Nell had already been, sun-wise, daring to get a tan on her holiday. Not that it was much of a tan now. Most of it seemed to have flaked off on the plane home. Then several days of grim, late-February weather, combined with keeping extravagantly fierce but comforting heating on in the house, had left her looking blotched and patchily freckled. It wasn't so much a laser peel she could do with, more a deep chiselling with a wallpaper scraper followed by an all-over skim of fresh new plaster.

"Are you here for the Stay Safe class?" Nell asked.

"I am. A lone parent, that's me. You can't be too careful. It only takes one sick loon and you're dead meat. I'd carry a knife but that way you can end up doing time in Holloway and with the kids in care. If I want to be some chick's bitch I'll go and hang out in the Candy Bar."

"And by the time you've found the knife . . ."

The woman laughed. "Yeah, down the bottom of your bag among all the lipsticks and your phone and the old tissues and Tesco's receipts and stuff. I'm Abi, by the way."

"Hi — I'm Nell. And I do hope we're not the only ones coming . . ."

They weren't. As Advanced Yoga trooped out, looking wide-eyed and spacy like baby birds, Nell and Abi were joined by several other potential classmates. There was a tubby, grey-bearded Hell's Angel (or so his T-shirt proclaimed), a large, fierce-looking mother with a reedy, frail-looking teenage son who kept his eyes fixed on the floor, several middle-aged women looking wary on their own, an assortment of chatty twenty-something girls all with their hair pulled back into ponytails, and a couple of reluctant-looking middle-aged men. Nell, remembering Kate's last-minute phoned instructions, quickly scanned these latter for potential date material as they filed into the studio to wait for Steve, their instructor, and found them generally unappealing. It was a relief. She honestly didn't want to start fancying anyone just yet. If ever, in fact. But Kate would demand a full report.

"He's a t'ai chi grand master," the Hell's Angel was telling one of the ponytails, "or was it t'ai kwando?"

"Or tie-dye," Abi hissed at Nell, giggling. And then, as they looked up, there he was. Already on the room's platform in front of the big studio mirrors, setting up a flip chart and waiting for them to notice him. At a guess, he was a couple of years older than Nell was, about half the bulk of the Hell's Angel, and neatly built — more sprinter than shot-putter, with a defiantly youthful athletic bounce to him.

"Hi. I'm Steve. I'll get to know each of you by the end of class one," he said by way of a curt greeting.

Hmm, confident to the point of cockiness, Nell decided, wondering what knack he had perfected that made him think he'd be able to put twenty new names to new faces in one hour.

"First of all, before we do the boring form-filling and so on, I'm going to ask you which of the two doors I came in through. Those who think I came in through the left one, go to the left-side wall, those who think I came in the other door go to the right. Got it?"

Nell looked at Abi and shrugged. She hadn't a clue, but there was a fifty-fifty chance of getting it right, so she chose the left wall with the gawky teenager and his mother, a yummy mummy wearing a bright slick of sparkly scarlet lipstick, and a giggling selection of the ponytails. Abi waved at her from the far end of the room.

"Now you," Steve bounced down from the platform and addressed Nell's group, "you, you got it wrong. Everyone in this room is an antelope and you lot have your heads down, grazing. But you," he sprinted down the studio, "you are aware. You watch, you see, you notice, see what's where. In other words, you get to survive. Out there . . ." He pointed beyond the doors in vaguely the direction of the club's restaurant, reception area and main doors. "Out there is the jungle and it's full of lions waiting to pick you off. Life is divided like this: the antelope graze, keep their heads down and are vulnerable to the lions who prey on them. The antelopes that don't learn to keep an ear and an eye open for the lions, they, folks, become lunch."

Steve waved an arm towards Abi's group. His gestures were exaggerated, like a dancer's, Nell thought. He was whirling, pointing, gesticulating, making sure they got his message. He leapt back on to the platform, landing beside the flip chart, on which were pinned newspaper photos of various teen boys. Their faces were almost entirely hidden by hoods, shoulders huddled, the pictures obviously selected for the maximum brooding menace. It was funny about the hood thing, she'd always thought. Surely a fleecy-lined, hooded top was a sensible item for a young boy to wear? What mother wouldn't want her son to keep his head and his ears warm on a chilly day? And yet such garments were considered something close to the clothing of Satan.

"A *Daily Mail* reader, then," Abi muttered to Nell. Nell looked at the photos. They were ordinary enough young lads, every one — no different from Sebastian who could look as yobby as anyone when in a strop. What was this Steve on about? Maybe yoga would have been better. When the next robber attacked, she could slow him down with a calm invitation to chill and make peace with his chakras. She realized she'd lost concentration already, become a grazing piece of lion's prey. She looked down the room and caught the eye of the Hell's Angel, who smiled. Another dozy antelope then, not quite tuned in to Steve's words of wisdom.

"And these are some of your lions, your enemies," Steve told them, indicating the boy photos, his voice dropping towards an appropriately dramatic growl. "Keep your wits about you and your chances of being someone's prey will be reduced to the absolute minimum. Right, before we go any further, can you all just take a minute or two to fill in these forms?"

He bounded down from the platform and handed round registration documents. "Sorry about this," he said. "The club insists. There's a box to tick for no junk mail."

Nell entered her name where required, and under "reasons for joining this class" wrote "divorce", which just about summed it up, but she hesitated after that and left the spaces for address, email details and phone number blank. She added her form to the pile on the edge of the platform and rejoined the group.

"OK." Steve was pacing the floor now. "The next bit is why are you all here? Have any of you been victims of crime?"

A few hands went up, Nell's included, though warily in case Steve planned a full-scale reconstruction of whatever assaults had taken place.

Wilma, mother of the teen boy, was prodding him encouragingly, but he sullenly folded his arms, blushing.

"Jason had his phone nicked," she announced.

"God, Mum," Jason seethed. "So 'barrassin'."

"What were you doing at the time?" Steve asked him.

"Um. Well, I was tex'in'. Jus' walking down the street, tex'in'."

"Walking down the street?" Steve smiled. "Show me."

"Eh?"

"Show me. Walk towards me with your phone, pretend you're texting, just like you were that day."

Jason blushed but shuffled forward, hand out, pretending to peck at his phone. Head down. And then, so swiftly that no one could swear they'd seen him move, Steve swooped on the boy, slipped the phone out of his hand and whirled past him. "See? Well no, you didn't see, did you? This is the point."

Jason grunted crossly, rubbing his hand. "No I didn't bloody see," he muttered.

"You see . . . a grazing antelope, folks. Wandering around with your head down and something valuable in your hand, you're like horses with blinkers. You make it easy for the thieves. Too many do, just by not taking any notice of what's around. You see it all the time, headphones on, phone in hand, bag held loosely — you might as well hand your valuables out to the first-comer. OK — next. What happened to you?" Steve pointed to Nell.

"Oh, um . . . my bag was stolen in the Gatwick long-term car park."

"Some kid, was it?"

"Well . . . yes. *Not* in a hoodie, though." Nell looked at the photos on Steve's board. None of them remotely resembled the hopeless Callaghan.

"And what were you doing?"

"Trying to find my car in the half-dark, arguing with my teenage daughter, the usual." Nell shrugged. There was a ripple of sympathy from the older women.

"You didn't know where your car was?" Steve looked puzzled, as if he didn't quite understand.

"Well, I'd been away. I hadn't seen it for a week. And don't tell me I should have written down the row number and the exact space. I know all that."

"Oh good. Then I won't have much to teach you, will I? Right . . . next thing. Invasion of personal space . . ."

"Here we go," Abi murmured to Nell. "Time to start beating the crap out of each other."

"I do hope so. I wouldn't mind starting with Steve," Nell replied, though she didn't fancy her chances with him on a dark night. Or on any night. He could swagger you into submission, she thought. Arrogant bugger — yet there hadn't been a single thing he'd said that she could really disagree with. Some people, she thought, simply got your back up, day one. Oh well.

She'd done it again. Where had she parked? After the class, Nell said goodbye to Abi and the Angel (Mike) at the club door and went out to the car park. Now, where was the bloody thing? She flipped the button on her key and looked around. But this time, instead of wandering into the dark and ambling about hoping to stumble across the vehicle, she waited under the lights of the doorway and thought for a moment. She remembered driving in, turning left . . . or was that the last time she'd been . . .? No, definitely left. She stepped out of the light and towards the fence. There it was. She flipped the switch again and the lights winked back at her. Then, just as she was approaching the car, a man appeared beside it and opened the driver's door.

"What the hell are you . . .? Oh Steve, Jeez, what are you doing? You frightened me!"

"You were too far away from it, you see. You should never unlock the car door till you're right beside it. It was unlocked the whole time you were walking across the car park. Another time it could be some low-life between you and safe, lockable space."

So what was this, Nell wondered, personal tuition?

"Yeah, OK, sorry. Put it down to an antelope moment," she agreed, smiling at him. Why was she apologizing? Shouldn't he?

"Can I give you a lift somewhere?" she offered, wishing she wasn't so habitually polite. Telling him to naff off and not go round putting the frighteners on lone females might be more appropriate.

"No — you're all right, thanks. I just wanted a word, actually." Steve took a piece of paper out of his pocket and handed it to her. "You didn't fill in any contact details on the registration form. I don't have your address or any means of getting hold of you. Suppose I have to cancel the class for some reason? You wouldn't want to waste your time coming all the way here."

This was true. Nell wrote her mobile number on the form and handed it back. "There you go. Sorry."

Steve smiled at her. "Is that it? No address? No home number?"

Nell climbed into the car, shut and locked the door, then whizzed the window down a grudging inch and grinned at him.

"Well, no, Steve, I don't think so. Because so far you're still a stranger to me, aren't you? I shouldn't go casually handing out personal details to just anyone, should I? You can't be too careful."

"Touché!" he admitted. "See you next week. Goodnight."

Nell drove out of the car park. Now who's a grazing bloody antelope? she thought. Rooooaaaar.

CHAPTER
FIVE

Time Is Running Out (Muse)

There seemed to be an awful lot that could go wrong with a cabbage. Nell found it hard to believe that a food crop could survive, reach the exacting standards that supermarkets demanded and be perfectly edible, with so much against it. From now on, she would regard the contents of the brassica section in Waitrose as a triumph of nurture over nature, organic or otherwise. If it wasn't an onslaught of cabbage-white caterpillars that were going to do for your crop, according to the pages of guidelines and photographs that Sheila, editor of *Home Grown*, had sent, it would be whitefly, rootfly, wire stem or clubroot. There was also an entire minor league of more obscure ailments that were waiting to scupper your lunch, if it survived any invasion by rabbits, squirrels and pigeons, wasn't dug up by dogs and foxes and if you weren't also stupid enough to keep a pet tortoise roaming free in the vegetable patch. Being individually fitted with cardboard collars and swaddled beneath fine mesh seemed the only way these vegetables could be (almost) guaranteed to achieve harvest point.

In her clapboard studio (which she loved — it reminded her of a village cricket pavilion) beneath the birch trees across the garden, Nell laid out her choice of watercolours in the shades she planned to use, opened the first of her selection of reference books and propped up a fat, healthy cabbage on the shelf in front of her. *Home Grown*'s brief was to paint twenty different vegetables. Each one had to be the entire plant, from tiniest roots to topmost leaf tip, incorporating all the diseases most likely to affect the crops of the keen amateur grower, all on one plant. A cabbage seemed like a good enough place to start. The cool, firm leaves and rich, deep greens suited her current rather uncertain mood, being somehow more soothing to work with than, say, the searing scarlets of tomatoes with their tight, tense skins. She would have to paint a bloody big one, she decided, committing a few pencil lines to a layout pad as a trial guide to the kind of shape she was going for. If it fell victim to even one of the troubles she had to inflict on it, it wouldn't get even halfway to the size she was going to have to make it. Nor would it have any of the plump, veiny, full-size leaves she was going to have to give it, to show these optimistic amateurs what a perfect specimen should look like.

Nell was comfortably settled at her desk and had just sketched out the basic shape she intended to use for her fantasy cabbage when she caught sight of movement up by the house. The side gate was opening, very slowly. Whoever was behind it wasn't yet showing their face. She tensed, nervous suddenly, wary of how vulnerable she really was. The studio door was open to let in the weak March sunshine (the cat was sprawled across the doormat, basking in a sunbeam), the house's back door was unlocked and the keys for the car were lying on the kitchen table, along with her bag which contained credit cards, cheque book, a ninety pounds credit note from Joseph and two silver Tiffany bangles. She'd also left her computer on the worktop, after emailing Seb down in Falmouth to tell him that yes, it was all right, Alex was going to pay for another year of his car insurance.

It was, as Steve would have put it, a grazing-antelope moment. So, not as ready as she'd have liked to be to tackle a vicious burglar (the hands-on techniques came later in the Stay Safe course), she went outside and bravely, briskly, strode across the grass to confront the intruder, just as Steve himself suddenly emerged through the gate.

"God, you scared me — again! What are you doing here?" she demanded furiously, too outraged to care how rude she sounded. How rude was it, after all, to come creeping through people's side gates when there was a perfectly good front doorbell he could have rung? It also rang in the studio — there was no way she could have missed hearing it.

"Sorry, Nell — I didn't mean to frighten you. I did press the bell but I couldn't hear it ring in the house so I guessed it wasn't working. Is it a battery one? It might need a replacement."

"It isn't, actually. I'll check it out and get it fixed. And I hope you're not going to lecture me: I know I should keep that side gate locked. Anyway, come on in, I'll make us some coffee."

Steve followed Nell in through the back door. "Thanks, that would be great. You looked so fierce, I didn't dare mention the lock! I'm going to cover home security in lesson two."

"So — what brings you here? And how did you find me? I didn't give you my address." Had he followed her home after the class? she wondered. It seemed unlikely — after all, why would he? If he'd wanted to spend more time with her he could have accepted her offer of a lift.

Nell then wondered, as she made the coffee, if Steve supplemented his teaching with a spot of burgling. He'd know all the tricks: best method of house entry, whether a metal drainpipe had enough fixing points that hadn't rusted through so that he could get safely up to a window that was open a mere careless centimetre. Perhaps that was why he was here now; he was casing the joint. Well, he wouldn't find a lot; no more than the usual domestic haul of electrical gadgets and non-heirloom jewellery. She was not — unlike her mother — a collector of trophy gems. All the same, Nell, after putting two mugs of coffee on the table, moved her bag out of his way and shoved it to the back of the worktop, beside the bread bin.

"Smash your side window and the bag would still be in reach," Steve commented, watching her.

"Only by an orang-utan," Nell snapped. "It's miles from the window."

"But that jar full of spoons and stuff by the sink isn't. Any burgling scumbag could use those spaghetti-scoop things and grab the handle, no problem."

"Ah yes, but they'd have had to break the window first, and that would have Ed from next door round here in seconds," Nell argued.

"Brave sort, is he, this Ed next door? You should bring him along to the classes. It might save his life. If you go in all confrontational and back someone into a corner it can too easily turn dangerous, and the next thing you know there's blood everywhere. Probably not the scumbag's, either."

Nell looked hard at him. What was he up to? Why was everything down to the worst-case scenario? And wasn't it a good thing that Kate hadn't chosen this moment to call round — she'd be bouncing with unconcealed delight, grinning and winking and making unsubtle enquiries about whether he lived alone and so on. Steve was quite an attractive sort, if you fancied the wiry, athletic type. And he had all his (presumably own) hair, eyes as blue as Steve McQueen's and, in spite of the subject matter, a smile that could charm dragons.

"So, you haven't told me yet . . . what made you come calling on me?" she asked again.

"Ah . . . yes. It's not a big deal, just that Tuesday's class will start half an hour later, that's all. I just wanted to make sure you knew, to save you rushing there and having to hang about. Advanced Yoga are doing a special meditation session with a guest mystic that's going on a bit so they can achieve maximum cosmic depth or whatever they do."

"But I gave you my mobile number. *Not* my address. Don't tell me you're doing house calls round the whole class?"

Steve looked, for once, mildly uncomfortable. "No — I emailed or phoned the others. But . . . I think you missed out a digit when you wrote your number down. Don't know whether you were doing it on purpose — on grounds of security, maybe?" he teased. "But either way, I couldn't get through. So . . . er . . . I looked you up and found where you lived."

"You *what*? Looked me up *where*?" The astounding nerve of it!

"Sorry — and your number was ex-directory, so . . ."

"Yes! Exactly! Ex-directory for a reason!"

"I'm sorry." He put his cup down and pushed the chair backwards. "I'll go, shall I? I am sorry, truly, I honestly didn't intend to . . ."

"No . . . no, it doesn't matter." It did, a bit, but not that much, she supposed, not really. What had she got to be so privacy-crazy about? Too far down that road and she'd end up living in the kind of gated community where even your own children were screened for entry, and the residents were convinced the world just beyond the railings held an eternal threat of terrorism, drive-by shootings and a loitering army of hooded teen thugs.

She softened a bit, saying, "Actually, to be honest I can't recall why we ever *were* ex-directory. It was probably something to do with Alex being in the communications business and not particularly wanting anyone to communicate with him!" Her laugh sounded more than slightly bitter.

"He's your ex, is he? Alex?"

"Yep. That's him. The ex." It sounded odd, applied to Alex. The term "ex" had only figured in her head with regard to Patrick before now. Not a massive total in her life (so far) was it? Only two major exes and a mostly forgotten selection of very short-term minor ones. Some people with far more adventurous lives must have a whole extra address book full of them. She wondered if having so many meant that it became less painful after a certain number, if each addition diluted the angst.

"How did you know he was an 'ex'?" Nell suddenly asked. "I hadn't said anything about that, either."

Steve leaned closer and smiled in the manner of a doctor assuring a patient that it really *was*, for once, more than just a cold. "You didn't need to. Though you did put down 'divorce' as a reason for coming to the classes — that was a bit of a giveaway. My classes tend to attract three sorts of women: the ones who've been on the wrong end of crime, the ones who come with their mates from work for a social giggle and those who are suddenly living on their own and realize they feel newly vulnerable."

"But I also told you I was a crime victim. Surely that puts me in category one?"

"You'd just come back from a holiday with your daughter, in term-time, and you didn't mention a partner who might have been some use seeing off a mugger." He shrugged. "I just figured. And I could have been wrong."

"Are you sure you're not a detective on the side?" Nell laughed.

"Well actually, I was once. I got on the wrong side of a sawn-off and when I was lying there in the hospital, all full of holes, I decided never again."

At least he wasn't offering to show her the scars, Nell thought. A few embryonic cells of an idea were occurring to her, though.

"Um . . . so how *did* you find me? I don't have a website. I probably should, for work, but I have an agent for that. What did you do? Googling Eleanor Hollis isn't likely to find me."

"Oh, it was easy. If you know more or less the area someone lives in, you just go to this fantastic search site on the Internet. I'll show you, if you like. Obviously with anyone you want to find, if you don't quite know where they are, the first stop is Google or Friends Reunited."

"Yeah, yeah, I know that, but if you can't find them that way . . ." Nell murmured vaguely. She took her computer from the worktop and put it on the table between the two of them, moving aside a small pile of Patrick's old letters. She'd been reading through a few of them after Mimi left for school to remind herself of the personal spark that was contained in them, and to see if she'd find a reason *not* to look for him. Mostly, she'd only found a young, confused man who despaired that the world was out of sync with his thinking and who was forever impatient and halfway to furious. Had he mellowed or was he now the ultimate Grumpy Old Bastard? She wanted to know.

"Thank goodness for broadband," Steve said as he tapped the address into the bar. A menu came up instantly, offering the choice of searching for a business or an individual or a map. Steve pressed "individual" and looked at Nell.

"OK — who do you want?" he asked.

Nell held her breath. This was definitely going to be one she'd prefer to try when she was safely on her own. But for now . . . "Let's try my friend Kate. Type in Catherine Perry."

"And the area she lives in?"

"Ah — you definitely need that?" That was a disappointment. For some ridiculous reason Nell had assumed the computer would immediately know exactly which "Catherine Perry" she would mean. Of course it wouldn't — and in turn it wasn't going to know which "Patrick Sanders" she meant, either. There must be thousands of them. And without having a clue where he was living it was going to be next to impossible to find him. And she *definitely* wanted to. She had a sudden painful thought that she might already be too late. Suppose he was dead? Or (and ridiculously it seemed worse) in the process of dying? Time could be running out, fast. For the more than twenty years since they'd split, she'd assumed he was still there, living a parallel life somewhere. Possibly he wasn't, or wouldn't be for much longer. When he vanished into the eternal dark they would never, ever speak to each other again. Why had this never crossed her mind before? It should have.

"Oh — Kate's only a couple of miles away. Try London SW13," Nell told Steve. She wanted him gone, then she could think about how to play with search sites.

All the same, when, in a few moments, he had found not only Kate, her address and phone number but also the names of all her neighbours along the avenue, Nell was both horrified and impressed.

"Is nothing sacred any more?" she said. "Shouldn't we be more able to press a key to opt in rather than have to register to opt out?"

"Depends on how you look at it," Steve pointed out. "It depends on whether you're the one doing the searching or the one doing the hiding. And it's all based on the electoral register, which is public anyway."

"Hiding's nothing to do with it. It's all an unacceptable gatecrashing of privacy, surely."

"Only if you're looking where you shouldn't be," Steve said. "Or if you've got something you'd prefer not to be known."

"I'm not so sure," Nell said, closing down the computer. "It's all a bit identity-card discussion for me. I think I find it all too Big Brother — and not in the television sense, I mean."

"You're probably right," Steve agreed. "But anyway, thanks for the coffee and apologies again for invading your territory like this. I hope I'm forgiven?"

"I suppose so!" Well of course he was forgiven. Hadn't he just taught her a possible way of tracking down Patrick?

Nell went with him to the front door. In her mind was the possibility that if she didn't actually see him go, she might later find him upstairs in a cupboard, from where he'd unapologetically point out her mistake in not watching him leave the premises.

"And don't forget . . ." Steve turned back at the gate.

"I know — half an hour later on Tuesday," she called.

"No . . . I meant get that doorbell fixed!" He waved, unlocked a mud-splattered blue Audi and drove away.

Ed backed the Fiesta into the minuscule slot that the local Waitrose car-park designers had grudgingly allocated for the undeserving sub-species of ordinary folk who didn't qualify for either disabled parking or a generous parent-and-child space. There was, he noted as he switched off T. Rex's "Metal Guru" and opened the car door, barely room to squeeze his normal-size body out between the concrete pillar and the car alongside his. To escape from the tiny gap, he bent the wing mirror inwards and noticed that the driver of the car beside him had done the same. Now he also wished he hadn't gone in backwards, leaving himself no access to the boot so he could load the shopping. Stupid, he thought. So much for being a bright and brainy academic. He could come up with topics affording hours of debate, such as whether Juliet was the one calling the shots with Romeo, or the significance of motherhood as a theme in *Macbeth*, yet couldn't figure out the right way to park at a supermarket. He hoped this wasn't a senior moment. He wasn't ready for those yet; he surely wasn't anywhere near old enough. If

Charles was with him he'd be standing over by the trolleys, hand on hip, tutting and smiling in the quiet triumph that only an older sibling can get away with.

Inside Waitrose was the usual bustle of after-work customers hurriedly flinging goods into trolleys and fuming at the slowness of the schoolkids' shift on the checkouts. Ed, his trolley quickly stocked with smoked salmon, steaks, half a dozen special-offer bottles of Wolf Blass Cab. Sauv. and enough fruit and veg to keep the health police happy, chose his checkout with care. At the end of a working day he didn't particularly want to have to make conversation over the bag-loading with one of his own A-level students, pleasant enough bunch though they were. He could find plenty to talk to them about if the subject was Hardy's take on the Industrial Revolution, but he didn't really want to answer polite questions about what he was doing tonight. Especially as the answer, as too often, was Nothing Special.

Across by the cakes counter, he could see Mimi from next door with one of her schoolfriends, and he wondered what Nell would be doing. There he'd be in his (well, his and Charles's) house and there she'd be in hers, only the thickness of a wall away. He wondered if she fancied going out sometime, just as mates. She might. Most nights there was a band on at the Bull's Head in Barnes. He'd been there several times with colleagues from the college. He'd even been on his own. Maybe she'd like that, not that he had a clue as to what sort of music she liked. She might be a folkie, or have fond memories of punk. He'd ask her. It would have to be in a way that didn't give her the wrong impression, though. He understood from staffroom chat that a newly single woman would be wary of being circled by predators. What was it someone had called it, that approach to a woman who'd been left? Going for the mercy fuck, that was the crude version. That was absolutely not the idea at all.

"God, Mum, what are you doing? It's all dark in here!" Mimi came clattering in through the front door, flung her schoolbag down on a chair and flipped all the light switches on at once. Nell blinked up at her, her startled eyes seeing nothing but silvered stripes and flashes.

"Mimi — hi! What time is it?"

"Mum! It's gone seven! What's for dinner? Where is it? I'm starving!" Mimi opened the fridge and scanned the contents, picking up a half-bar of Fruit and Nut chocolate and biting off a square. "Jeez, you haven't even started cooking. It's going to be *ages*." She crashed around the room, picking up the newspaper, the box of cat food, an empty biscuit pack, slamming them down again, moaning, "What are you doing?" She peered over Nell's shoulder at the screen.

Nell quickly closed down the computer. "I got involved looking something up and lost track of the time. I'll fix us some pasta and salad and stuff. And where've you been till now? Why didn't you call and tell me you'd be late?"

"Like you'd have even noticed?" Mimi smirked. "Me and Tess went to the school play auditions. They're doing *Midsummer Night's Dream*, *again*. They only did it about two years ago, I'm sure. Anyway I'm

Mustard-seed. Tess is Moth. She wanted to be Titania and is *well* fucked about it."

Nell ignored the choice language in the interests of peacekeeping. "Will I have to make a costume? If you need wings, you'll have to buy some from the fancy-dress place where all the hen-party women get them. I can't do wings."

"Yeah, that I do remember," Mimi laughed. "You made rubbish ones from a wire coathanger when I was five. I got laughed at, big-time, at that party. It's probably one of those things I'll have to tell the psycho when I'm being analysed in rehab about my broken home."

"Is that how you think of it? Is this a broken home?" How dreadful that sounded: as if domestic comfort, security, could be smashed like a precious vase. Nell didn't have the sort that was financially valuable in mind; more the type of appealing, clumsy pottery that had deep sentimental attachment, something lovingly squidged together in a school art class perhaps (and which you kept forgetting leaked, until you put a bunch of daffodils in it), or a holiday souvenir invested with the kind of memories that made you smile. You grieved when things like that got broken. With valuable items, you just phoned the insurance company and welcomed the cash as an excuse for glitzy shoes.

"Well . . . no, not really. Not specially." Mimi fidgeted with the strap of her schoolbag. "But years down the line, I don't know, I'll have to blame something and someone if life goes all wrong, won't I?"

Nell hugged her, risking being pushed away with the usual resounding, "God, Mum, gerroff". "Mimi, there's no reason why it should all go wrong. Don't even think about that!"

Mimi allowed herself to be held close for another moment before breaking away, "Yeah, well, I bet you didn't think it would all go wrong either, when you and Dad got together. You must have been a hundred per cent sure it would all be all right for ever and ever or you wouldn't have married him, would you?"

Nell laughed, to put off having to come up with a good reply. "Hey, life's not a fairy tale," she said. "Happy ever after happens, but there's a lot in the middle between the meeting and the long-term living. Give it a chance, don't get bitter because of us."

"Can we have a takeout?" Mimi's attention was back on hunger.

"Yes, good idea. What do you fancy? Indian?"

"Ooh yeah. Sick."

"Huh? Do I take that as a no or a yes?" Youth-speak — it could mean anything.

"No — it's a yes. A top yes. Keep up, Ma. Can it be soon? I only had a tuna melt for lunch, nothing since. I'm *dying* here." Mimi collapsed dramatically into a chair, holding her stomach and making agonized expressions. Nell suspected this was more to do with her being the one of the two of them who didn't intend to go out in the dark, up to the high street to the Delhi Durbar to pick up the food. She needn't have bothered — Nell didn't particularly want her to be wandering up the road on her own in the dark, not with legs that long, hair that blonde, with a skirt that short, with her youth, her beauty and a world full of lions prowling out there.

"OK. Korma? Naan? The cucumber thing?"

"And the big crisps?"

"Yes, I'll get them. I'll phone the order and go now. Warm some plates, find chutney, all the usual."

"Mmm, sure," Mimi murmured vaguely, flipping the kitchen television down from its under-shelf position and aiming the remote control at it. She settled back in her chair, tucking her feet under her, looking certain to be still in the same position when Nell came home again. Nell called the restaurant and ordered the food, then grabbed her keys, her phone and her credit card and headed out of the door. The order wouldn't be ready by the time she got there, but she quite fancied a bottle of Cobra and a quick read through show-biz gossip in a trashy newspaper.

She was halfway through a fascinating piece on best choices for a fantasy royal edition of *Celebrity Big Brother* when Ed walked into the restaurant.

"Hey, we've had the same idea. I did a full-scale Waitrose stock-up tonight and then couldn't face cooking anything," he said, after putting in his order and coming to join her at the table kept for takeaway customers. "Fancy another beer?"

"No thanks, I'm fine," she said. "I couldn't be bothered to cook either. There's a lot to be said for the eighteenth-century days when you didn't even possess a kitchen but just wandered up to the local bakehouse for pigeon and oyster pie and a gossip with Mrs Miggins. I suppose this is the twenty-first century equivalent."

"Could be. One day fish and chips, then pizza, Chinese on Fridays and so on. It could be done, just."

"But only if you live somewhere conveniently urban. I bet you couldn't live like that down at your place in Dorset, could you?"

Ed laughed. "No — not unless you were keen on cold food and a long, winding drive. They only deliver up to five miles so that's not an option either."

"Other things make up for it though, I suppose?"

"Oh yes — the nudist beach over on the Isle of Purbeck has an ice-cream stall that can't be beaten. You should come down one weekend, see for yourself."

"What, the nudists? Not sure it's my thing! Is it compulsory?"

"No, definitely not!" he laughed. "And the cottage is further west, only just into Dorset. It's on the edge of a village; what an estate agent would call secluded but not totally isolated. The perfect bolthole. I'm going down on Friday night for the weekend, to catch up with Tamsin for a bit of father-daughter bonding."

"How's she doing? Is she still writing crime fiction?"

"Oh yes. Still profiting from crime, still living with the same dipstick who can't be arsed to get up before noon on the grounds that he is 'creative' — if you can call it that, welding iron railings together in random form and calling the result something pretentiously poncy like 'a rare peaceful outcome from one tender deed in time of war'."

"Do you think of the cottage or the house here as your main home?"

"Oh the cottage — definitely. I'm a voter there, I take better care of the garden there. It's all done the way I want it, unlike here. This house was our mother's — it feels like an old person's domain and frankly, since she's been dead, Charles has definitely started turning into the resident old person in her place. Now it's six months since she went, I'm thinking of looking for another job so I can live down there full-time. I'll still come up to see him, check he's OK, obviously, but . . . well, this has always been just somewhere I work."

"But you've got friends here. A social life." Ed knew everyone in the road, Nell thought. He went to everyone's parties, and would surely be — if you had to have a ballot on it — the neighbour who'd most be missed.

"I've got all that there too. This is only the half of me. Like I said, you should come and visit. Bring Mimi. Tell her we do have electricity and running water and some rudimentary television reception."

"Maybe . . ." Nell wondered about this. Ed had never invited her and Alex to his cottage when they'd been a couple. What was this? Just a neighbourly gesture? Yes. That would be it. And besides, he probably simply hadn't liked Alex. Which must mean he *did* like her. Well, that was always good to know. Very cheering.

Her order was ready. Nell picked up the bag of food and said goodbye to Ed. She walked home on the better-lit side of the road, her key between her fingers ready to cause serious (but justifiable, according to

Steve) injury to anyone who had thoughts of attacking her. No way would she give up a chicken Madras without a fight.

CHAPTER
SIX

Sunday Girl
(Blondie)

It hadn't been worth checking, as it turned out, but then you never knew your luck. Nell thought this each time she logged on to Friends Reunited. The afternoon before, when she should have been working on the cabbage, she had whizzed quickly through the long-familiar lists of Patrick's old schoolmates and had a look at the Oxford Brookes site, but he hadn't registered either there or with his old school in Hampshire. She wasn't surprised: if he hadn't before, he wasn't likely to now. He'd never been much of a joiner and would almost certainly dismiss those who enrolled as a bunch of sentimental saddos, but even the remote possibility that he might have turned up (or that someone would cheerily report "Hey, just saw Patrick Sanders!") made her heart beat faster.

She had looked at Friends Reunited to check for Patrick a couple of times each year since it was first set up, just in case. Over this time she had met up with old classmates of her own and had had several of those exuberant, "Oh God, you haven't changed *at all*!"

lunches where before the first glass of Pinot G. kicked in they had found that the most they had in common was a hatred of navy blue games knickers and memories of the terrors of trigonometry, too many years ago to matter. After the initial up-and-down inspection to check which looked the older/fatter/more well-worn/frankly gone to seed or unforgiveably gorgeous, there wasn't really a lot to say, and it fast became clear enough why there'd been no contact since they'd walked out of the school or college clutching their locker contents.

One or two had really surprised her, though. There was the feisty queen bee Mo who had been so much at the centre of every naughtiness, every shoplifting escapade, each secret night-time boys-and-booze session, and yet who was now a community-pillar magistrate and golf-playing matriarch. Drab, dull, netball captain Amanda had miraculously glammed up to the max to look as shiny and immaculate as a very classy hooker, and worked as a croupier on a Caribbean cruise ship. How had that come about? As far as Nell recalled, she hadn't so much as played snap at school, let alone learnt all the poker moves and how to do fancy shuffling. Nell's own profile on the site wasn't, as so many were, embellished with girly exclamation marks or shrieky show-off statements. She'd stuck to the boringly factual, simply stating that she lived in south-west London, was married, had two children and worked as a freelance illustrator. She hadn't said she wouldn't mind being ten pounds lighter; still had a weakness for hot-and-dirty rock guitarists; that she couldn't tell if being blonde had bestowed her life with measurably more fun; that the best sex she had always seemed to be outdoors; or that she tended to cook too many potatoes because she was fond of cold, leftover ones (which, she now thought, might have something to do with the extra ten pounds).

So. Patrick. What was it with men? Why were so many of them short of the communication gene? Simply Googling his name produced several versions of Patrick Sanders, none of them him. There was a vicar in Shropshire (a blurry photograph showed a jolly-looking, short tubby man holding a frilly baby, possibly post-christening). There was a fierce-looking motor-trade magnate based in south Manchester and a trumpet player from (appropriately) Tooting, who was available for session work at union rates. As far as Nell knew, Patrick couldn't play more than a bit of Mark Knopfler wannabe guitar chords and had never shown any interest in brass instruments, so that ruled him out as well. And as for Friends Reunited: so few men seemed to be curious about way-back companions, compared to women. Maybe they had other ways of keeping in touch, old-boy networks and rugby clubs and so on. Patrick wasn't at all that type. He'd despised all team sports, saying that they just encouraged the viler aspects of tribalism and how could any thinking person care who kicked a bit of inflated leather into netting or over some big sticks.

Nell had had a look at the profiles of some of her male college contemporaries and these fell into only two categories: first there were the look-how-well-I've-dones. These detailed endless lists of work promotions and sporting triumphs, even sometimes a mention of what cars they drove — Porsches and Aston Martins came up here and there but not Ford Fiestas, which made it all suspiciously like a form of willy-waving. Then there were the ones who seemed a bit down, as if life hadn't come up to expectations. There were those who were divorced and slightly lost, others who hadn't become the next Mick Jagger and minded bitterly, or were between jobs and dropping hopeful hints about "networking", fondly remembering school and college days as if they really were the best times and that nothing had worked out so well since. Nell updated her own profile to include a light and cheery sentence about being newly single, carefully worded so it definitely didn't look as if she was in search of a new partner, and left it at that. She was findable if anyone was looking for her — she couldn't do much more.

"So how far have you got with it?" Kate asked the following day when she and Nell met on the Thames riverbank close to Ham House to walk Kate's dachshund and little Alvin, snug in his all-terrain Land Rover buggy. "Have you got in touch with that missing ex yet?"

"No! He's impossible to find. I've no idea where he is or what he's doing. Last time I heard, he was painting murals for vast amounts of money for the sort of people who stencil underwater scenes all over their bathrooms and want the ball scene from Cinderella in their children's bedrooms."

"Was that his kind of thing?" Kate asked. "Is that what you do an art degree for?"

"God no! He'd have hated it. But we've all got to do something for money, haven't we? I didn't think I'd end up painting ill vegetables and being glad of the work. Patrick would have liked to be more of a Lucian Freud. He used to paint me; I had to lie for hours on his unmade bed with no clothes on, getting frozen while he mixed up the colours he fancied. I only did it because I knew there'd come a point when he'd give this big despairing sigh, say it wasn't going well and we'd have lovely compensatory sex instead."

"Well it would warm you up, that."

"Certainly did."

As she and Kate ambled along the towpath with the dog and Alvin, Nell thought about Patrick's paintings. They'd been huge, oily things that took months to dry and had given his flat a permanent eye-watering stench of linseed oil and turps. He'd been a habitual and shameless art-shop thief, stealing brushes and tubes of paint by the dozen until he had far more of everything than he needed, and each theft was more brazen than the time before. Nell had been shocked, accusing him of arrogantly assuming he was entitled to help himself freely to the means to create works of genius. He'd simply dismissed her concern, telling her she was bourgeoise. He'd been caught more than once but had bluffed it out, never denying, never pretending he'd "accidentally" pocketed the goods but instead pleading dire poverty and arrogantly expecting a sympathy decision on prosecution. With female shop assistants, all he had to do was give them the devastating Patrick smile and return a token half the goods from his pocket back to the shelves. His pretty face and blond too-long fringe never failed to charm.

Did he still look like that? she wondered now. Or had all his hair dropped out and his teeth gone manky and his beautiful long, gangly body filled out and bloated? She doubted it. He'd been quite vain — the first man she'd ever known who was confidently keen to dye his hair. During their time together he'd alternated between highlighted blond and a sort of sandy and scarlet combination, occasionally tinged with purple. Clothes-wise, he'd favoured soft, sensuous fabrics, Kensington Market velvets and silks, and he had an unfashionable lack of conscience about fur. His grandmother's ancient mink lay across their bed and kept them warm when the heating failed in winter. When a girl from their course challenged him about it, he'd simply pointed out that the coat was well over fifty years old. How long did she think minks lived, even in the wild?

"So what do you do next?" Kate asked. "Have you run out of options yet?"

"Well — not entirely. There's the electoral roll. The only thing is, if you really want to look at it properly, you have to subscribe to something. I'm not sure about that."

"In case you get junk mail?"

"No . . ." Nell hesitated. "It's — well, suppose he really minds me looking for him? I'm not sure I want him to know what lengths I'd go to. Suppose . . .

97

suppose he decided I'd really invaded his privacy? I'd rather he just thought I'd accidentally come across him, somehow. If it went completely pear-shaped I don't really want to leave a trail of how I found him."

"Wow! Is he likely to be that furious? Why? Did you two part on a really bum note?"

"You could say that," Nell admitted. "The end wasn't pretty. A lot got said . . ."

"Oh but you weren't much more than kids, really, were you? People get over things. No one can sulk for twenty years. Unless they're . . ."

"Exactly. Unless they're a bit on the mad side. And we weren't really kids. We'd been together close to five years — he was a couple of years older than me, as well. Maybe I'll leave it. Give it a miss and let the past rest in peace. I just think . . . you know, like in Alcoholics Anonymous, where one of the steps is making amends?"

Kate laughed. "Well no, but let's pretend I do. Have you got amends to make with Patrick?"

"Probably. No. Oh I don't know. I just wanted to see how he is, you know? Now that Alex has gone . . ."

"Now that Alex has gone you could start it up all over again with Patrick. Don't say that hasn't crossed your mind. It's written all over you."

"God, I don't think that would happen! He'd probably take one look and think, wow, that was a lucky escape! But I can't pretend I haven't had the occasional fantasy that there we are, casually meeting in a pub for a friendly catch-up and it all ends up as passionate thrashing in a hotel room . . . Wouldn't happen, though. It was way too much of a mess at the end for that."

According to the Sunday morning TV news, New York was many feet deep in unexpected snow and the residents were warned to stay home in case of a sudden blizzard. A jogger had been found dead in Central Park, frozen solid as he leaned on a tree where he had stopped for a breather. He hadn't been found for three days, having been mistaken for an expertly built snowman, and his relatives were choosing whom to sue.

"That'll be global warming," Mimi commented, wolfing down a bacon sandwich.

"Will it?" Nell asked as she poured the cat's food into his bowl. "How does that work then? Shouldn't they all be skipping about in light summer linens?"

"No, Mum, it's slippage of airstreams and stuff. We did it at school. You should learn about it."

Where did teenagers get this superior tone from? Nell couldn't imagine, even now, telling her mother she should learn about global warming, or indeed any other subject. Gillian would give her a look of total incredulity, as if Nell should wash out her mouth for even daring to suggest that her own mother hadn't already learned (and in most cases dismissed as not relevant) absolutely all there was to know.

"I'm sure you're right. But then you've got to remember that when I was your age, we were being told another Ice Age would be well under way before our lifetime was out."

"Yeah well, that was then. The world's changed. I wonder if Dad's all right. I'll email him and ask if he's frozen into his apartment."

Alex hadn't taken his skiwear. He'd be wishing he had, Nell thought. There must be bags and bags of his stuff up in the loft. Perhaps in summer, she'd put some tables in the driveway and have a garage sale. No, what did Americans call it? Oh yes, a yard sale. She remembered being on Long Island with Alex many years ago, towards the end of summer. Driving through the village of Quogue in the Hamptons, they'd passed several season-end yard sale events — all the summer visitors flogging off surplus goods, presumably to each other. If she could have thought of a way of getting them home without the total price sky-rocketing once freight was factored in, she'd have been tempted by a selection of fabulous Adirondack garden chairs. You couldn't get those in the UK back then. She wondered if Alex would remember that holiday — it had been tagged on to one of his business trips. They had driven all over Long Island, taken the ferry back (passing a small fleet of nuclear submarines) to the mainland at New London and driven on up to Boston. He'd be vague about it by now, probably, working on replacing all their memories with new ones that he and Cherisse would make together. It was a sad thought, as if Nell was gradually being erased.

"He might be stuck in the building, sixty floors up with a power cut and no lift and the windows getting icy on the inside," Mimi said.

Nell looked at the TV pictures of this scene of all-American doom and felt immediately cheered. Just imagine, she thought: Alex would get that grey, shivery look he always had in winter's worst depths. His fingertips would go blue and stiff and he would have to ask Cherisse to open bottles and cans for him, a small taster for the care years down the line. And then she thought of Cherisse with her hair tongs, electric home-wax kit, nail buffer and facial sauna, all on the blink. She would feel the cold, too. She wouldn't be able to drift around the flat, being seductively playful in a cute little vest and tiny knickers like something off a Häagen-Dazs ad.

Oh dear. Poor girl. Poor Alex. What a shame.

"I nicked Mum's Oyster card. I hope she doesn't suddenly decide she needs it today. I don't think she will cos Gran's coming over," Mimi told Joel. She was supposed to be at Tess's and now wondered why she hadn't simply told the truth. She could probably have even borrowed the Oyster card if she'd asked in the right way. She had her own, for getting to school and out and around, but she didn't want to use up all its credit on this trip to Paddington.

"Didn't you tell her where you were going?" Joel asked.

Mimi shook her head, feeling a bit silly. They weren't nine years old. Nor were they running away somewhere like a couple of people who weren't supposed to meet. It was only a few hours out and not even at night, which was when all parents thought teenagers were

101

going to have sex. But it was a date, an almost proper one. She couldn't, if pushed, explain why she needed to keep it to herself for now, but it didn't change the fact that she just did.

"Why not? Does she mind you going out?"

"Well . . . she sort of wanted me to be there to see Gran. I told her I had to go to Tess's. She said Gran would be disappointed not to see me. She's only coming up from near Guildford, though, and they're meeting in Richmond for lunch, so it's not as if it's, like, *far* or a big deal. She comes up quite often." Mimi laughed. "And she doesn't usually say when, just turns up. It drives Mum mad."

"So what did you say you needed to go to Tess's for?"

"Maths. And something about the play."

"Two excuses?" Joel grinned at her. "Never make two excuses. It's a sign that you're lying."

"How do you know that?"

"My dad's a psychologist. His speciality is behaviour. I'd never get away with anything. Luckily I don't need to, though; my folks are totally liberal. They just like honesty. Anything else is pretty much a free option."

"Wow." Mimi felt overawed by Joel already. He knew such a lot about such a lot. He knew about astronomy and had, while they waited at the bus stop, told her about red dwarfs and black holes — or at least as much as you could tell in ten minutes. And at the same time he knew stuff about ordinary things like bands and movies and well . . . just about everything. He'd told her he was a polymath, but she was going to have to look that one up when she got home. Just showed, she thought. You really couldn't tell about people. He looked just like any other sixteen-year-old boy who likes music and football and a good time.

". . . the second station he built here. The first one was totally inadequate, with only four platforms. It didn't even begin to compare with what was at Bristol at the other end of the line, and the London end needed to have at least the same grandeur . . ." Mimi had, for a moment, lost the thread. They were now off the bus and walking alongside Paddington station to the steps down to the concourse.

"So where was the first station then?" she asked. She looked around her; there was no space for another, surely.

"Round there, Bishops Bridge Road. A few years ago, when they were updating the roads, they dug up a hidden, original Brunel bridge. It's still there, we'll look on the way back. It's hanging up above the road now, like art, which it is."

Oh God. Was this what happened when you had a boyfriend? You had to be interested in all their stuff? Tess's current boy-of-choice was obsessed by The Klaxons. Now *that* was easy. Not only were they easy to like but everything you needed to know was up there on You Tube and MySpace and other places. Once you'd seen a few videos, downloaded some songs, that was it really. You could read up a few interviews on the Internet and from then on in, talk the talk. With Joel, she was going to end up with a PhD in I. K. Brunel. And all because he'd mistakenly thought she was into engineering. Oh well. He was gorgeous. He had good manners (eeuw, did that sound like Gran?). He liked her and really, he was pretty interesting. Some people, lots of the boys they hung out with, they didn't seem to care about anything much. They just laughed around the whole time and everything, *everything* was a joke except football. The Stuart twins kept bragging they were going to be rock stars, but couldn't even play a note on a triangle. Joel could play guitar, piano and violin. And he was cute as well. If only he'd kiss her . . .

"No Mimi? What a shame. I was looking forward to seeing her!" Gillian Wilkinson kissed Nell and the two women left the station together. It was busy for a Sunday, which was too often the day when track repairs meant the trains were disrupted and few people chose to travel. The station teemed with determined shoppers, subdued morning-after teenagers and linked-up couples who looked barely awake. Nell had been surprised that Gillian wasn't driving. Usually she scorned public transport, considering it an ill-mannered and unpleasant environment (why were people always eating? Who needs to slop coffee around on a short train ride?) and a poisonous pit of viruses, but who knew? Maybe her mother was having a carbon-footprint conscience moment.

"Sorry, she had to go to her friend Tess's. She muttered something about urgent maths." Nell felt slightly guilty, as if it was she, not Mimi, who had come up with the excuse. It wasn't that she hadn't believed Mimi was going to Tess's, but maths had never figured as important enough in her life to come up as any kind of excuse for anything, so there must be some other reason. It probably involved a boy. Mimi would tell her, she assumed, one day, if there was anything she thought a mother needed to know.

"It sounds to me like an excuse," Gillian said grumpily as the two of them walked over the railway bridge towards the town centre. "After you've had three daughters you can sniff out an untruth a mile away. Boys are so much more straightforward."

"Only until they become husbands." Nell giggled. "Then they make up for lost time."

"Not all of them," Gillian scolded, which was a bit rich from a woman whose husband had been a serial philanderer. Perhaps the guilt jewels really had been worth the hassle. "You're just at the bitter and twisted stage. Wait till you find someone else, and don't say you won't, because I know you will in time. As long as you don't let yourself go." She quickly looked Nell up and down to see if her roots were showing or if she'd clearly given up on slinky shoes. "Now where are we having lunch?" she asked, and Nell presumed she'd passed inspection, although the triggered mention of lunch was possibly a clue that her mother had noticed she'd put on a few pounds. It obviously couldn't be too disastrously many, though (so far . . .), as Gillian went on to say, "Because I'd like it to be somewhere with swift service: I want to go to Dickins and Jones after and buy something to wear for spring funerals. I've got one of the bridge club looking unlikely to last the month; you know, that widower at the rectory, moved in after your friend Marcus's family moved away. Remember Marcus?" She looked at Nell and smiled, knowingly. "Yes of course you do. You always remember your first."

Nell briefly closed her eyes and started a one-to-ten count, praying for patience. Details of one's daughter's early (and blush-makingly hopeless) sex life were not something any mother should know about — and especially should not have been organized by her.

"All that was a long, long time ago. Look — here's the restaurant. You'll like Lulu's."

"Ah. Italian." Gillian hesitated, looked into the restaurant and sighed. "Oh well, I suppose one day with pasta won't do any harm. I'm sure I'm developing a wheat intolerance. I'm at a delicate age. You won't know what that's like yet, but in a few years, when you start getting menopausal, well, I'll tell you for now, and I'm doing you a favour, that's only the start of it. The whole lot's downhill from there."

How very *not* cheering this was. Nell studied the menu and looked around for the waitress: she needed a drink, immediately. Would Mimi, in turn, find Nell such hard work, thirty years down the line? She did so hope not. The waitress, a sulky, grubby little girl with smeared eyeliner and huge earrings, who looked as if she'd only slept one hour out of the last twenty-four, came and took their order, writing everything down very, very slowly.

"The trouble with life, Eleanor, is that it's like cake," Gillian was now saying as the waitress returned surprisingly quickly with a couple of large glasses of white wine. "If you save the icing till last, you're too stuffed to enjoy it. You've been too busy concentrating on the sensible, solid bits. Then, too late, you realize the best part was the sweet, gooey filling in the middle, the bit you'd taken absolutely no notice of."

Nell couldn't quite work this out. Was this yet another reference to her own carelessness in not hanging on to Alex? Or was there some regret of Gillian's own in there?

"What exactly are you saying here? I like the metaphor, but I'm not sure how it translates. Is this about you? Are you all right?"

"I'm fine, considering. I'm just saying. Don't leave things too late, Eleanor." Gillian took a delicate sip of her wine and looked hard at Nell. She put down her glass and started fidgeting with a fork. "There's something I probably should have told you. I told Alex instead and that was possibly not quite the right thing to do. It's about that . . . that boy you were with for so long, back when you were young. Not a boy now, of course. No."

Nell felt cold. "Patrick? What about him?" Her voice sounded very faint and far away. She was going to hear something terrible, she knew for certain. Patrick was dead. That must be it. Oh God, this was just wonderful. She was going to be told here in a crowded restaurant, surrounded by jolly Sunday-lunch families, by couples all loved-up in post-coital smugness, by oldies gleefully absconding from the home-cooked-roast ritual, that the one person she wanted to see again more than anyone else was gone for ever.

". . . phoned, he was wondering how you were . . ."
Gillian's words floated past her, joining the increasing
tide of voices all around and barely separating
themselves from the people at the table behind her,
where they were settling a baby into a high chair and
discussing mashed avocado. Don't give it to him, Nell
found herself thinking, turning to look at the infant, it's
too rich — he'll throw up all over his cute Mini-Boden
blue-spotted dungarees.

"Can you say that again?" she asked Gillian. "Did
you say *Patrick* phoned? When was this?" God, was it
recently? Was he psychic?

Gillian smiled, looking strangely relieved. It occurred
to Nell that this revelation must have taken some
courage. Perhaps she'd thought Nell would hit her or
something, for keeping the information from her, or
throw a hysterical wobbler. No wonder she'd chosen to
come out with it in such a busy, noisy, vibrant place.
However furious, Nell was twenty years past hysterics
and she certainly wasn't going to clout anyone in
public. That wasn't the sort of thing women like her got
into the habit of doing, despite having had a
boarding-school education.

"Oh, it was at least four, maybe five years ago!"
Gillian said. "It's only since Alex went, it occurred to
me, oh, he never told her. He knew, you see. I called to
tell you, but Alex said you were out so I told him,
thinking no more about it because he said he'd make
sure you got the message. He didn't pass it on, did he?"

"No, he didn't," Nell said, eventually — thinking,
and neither did you bother to ask me if he had . . . "But

that doesn't matter now. I can't change what Alex did or didn't do. What did Patrick say? What did he want?"

"Ah look — food! I should have gone for the chicken really, but this penne looks delicious!" Gillian gave the waitress her best smile, as if the girl had personally cooked it. "Thank you, dear! And what pretty earrings!" The girl smiled back uncertainly, as if she expected Gillian to add the kind of telling-off a teacher would give, something like "But take them off while serving food, please, those nasty big hoops and beads are germ traps . . ."

Nell could barely look at her lasagne. So much for stress making her hungry. Not today it didn't.

"Just tell me what he said, *please*. And then . . ." Then what? She'd think of that later. It would probably be then . . . nothing.

"Oh, he didn't say much. I don't actually know what he wanted and as you can imagine, after what he'd put you through, I wasn't exactly thrilled to hear from him. He wouldn't leave a number and he didn't ask for yours. He just wanted to know if you were all right, so I told him you were fine. What else could I say?" Gillian shrugged and now looked blank. She had turned her attention to her food, and for her the subject seemed closed. But there was one more thing . . . one possibility . . .

"Just tell me, did he say where he was?" Nell held her breath.

"Oh yes, he did. He was somewhere near Oxford. The place must be crammed to the gills with old students who never quite got away. Not *in* Oxford, in

109

his case. Somewhere nearby. Near Wallingford, I think he said. By the Thames anyway. There isn't enough dressing on this tomato salad," Gillian said, looking round. The waitress with the pretty earrings smiled at her and came over. Older customers could be so generous.

"Why are you telling me about this now?" Nell asked, while Gillian fussed with the dressing and started adding more pepper. "Has it been on your conscience?"

"Certainly not!" her mother snapped. "It's about the cake. Alex might have proved to be the sensible stodgy bit. You are now thinking — and I know you, so don't tell me I'm wrong — that even though you wouldn't have had Sebastian or Mimi or any other children, you're thinking Patrick would have been the icing. You'd be utterly, utterly wrong. All I know is that if you *do* ever speak to him again, he'll tell you he spoke to me. I want you to know right now that if you didn't get the message, it's not my fault."

No, Nell thought. Of course not.

CHAPTER
SEVEN

The Kiss
(The Cure)

"OK! Welcome everybody! Today we're doing home security and then following it up with some hands-on practice at getting out of tight corners. And talking of which . . ."

Steve jumped down from the stage and approached one of the ponytail girls who had arrived at the class late, crashing in through the door with her coat still on.

"Sorry!" she gasped at him, sliding her arms out of her sleeves. "Got caught up at work. *Ouch!* What the *fuck* . . ." Steve grasped the end of her scarf, swung her round and pulled her off balance so she fell against him. She struggled and grabbed at the scarf as it tightened round her neck. Just at the point where Nell and Hell's Angel Mike were looking anxiously at each other, wondering how far he'd take this, Steve let her go. "Sorry, Patsy. I just wanted to demonstrate something and you came in with the perfect opportunity. It's the way you've tied your scarf. What's it called, when you make a loop like that and pull the ends through?"

"It's called a Fulham knot. Because the Sloaneys all used to have it," Abi told him.

"That's the one. All I can say about that is, ladies, just *don't*. As you can see, if someone grabs the ends of the scarf and pulls, there's absolutely no way out. It just gets tighter and tighter. Any other way of wrapping it and you've got a chance of unravelling yourself. But not with that one — it's instant strangulation, no question. Scumbag sees you on the street, grabs the loose ends of your scarf, hauls you behind a bush and you're an intant murder statistic being probed by Forensics under a white tent. Now . . ." he said, returning to the stage as Patsy rubbed her neck. "Where was I? Oh yes. Home security."

"God, he's in a cheerful mood," Abi whispered to Nell.

Nell grinned at her, thinking of Steve's visit and her vision of him hiding in a cupboard. "He'd probably say it was just his way of showing he cares," she muttered back.

"Sure, he's all heart!" Abi replied.

"How many of you have a lock on your bedroom door?" Steve asked. Only two people put their hands up, one of them Hell's Angel Mike, who looked embarrassed.

"It's left over from the last people who lived there," he explained. "I never actually lock it. You don't, do you?"

"Well actually, yes. I do. And you should. Always," Steve told him. "Because . . ."

"But what about if there's a fire?" Wilma interrupted.

112

"I couldn't lock the bedroom door — how would the cat get in?" Patsy protested.

"Or your Darren!" one of her friends giggled. "He'd kick it down!"

"OK, OK, if you'd rather talk amongst yourselves . . ." Steve folded his arms like a cross schoolteacher and waited for them to settle. The buzz of conversation faded and he went on, "As for fire — there's no excuse not to have smoke alarms. And a closed door is a barrier that could even save your life. I just want you to imagine . . . it's the middle of the night. You hear a noise downstairs. What do you do? Do you go down and investigate?"

"I'd send Darren," Patsy suggested. "With his baseball bat."

"OK, so Darren goes downstairs, probably not wearing a lot, definitely half asleep, completely vulnerable, and the burgling scumbag has a knife in his hand. One of yours, that he's helped himself to from your cute All Men Are Bastards knife rack that you keep fully loaded with handy weapons on your kitchen worktop. Do stop me if I'm wrong . . ."

Patsy scowled. "How do you know about my knife block?" she asked.

Steve tapped his nose. "Man's intuition," he told her. "Some of us have it, believe it or not. So there we are. Your Darren's now lying on the floor covered in blood and no use to anyone. If you're lucky, Scumbag does a runner and leaves you with nothing more than a dead boyfriend to clear up. If you're not — and remember he's now got nothing to lose — well, he's halfway up

113

the stairs and you're under the duvet playing dead, rehearsing for the real thing, which will be any time soon."

Everyone was listening closely now. Nell felt slightly chilled by the picture he'd presented, and yet a bit sceptical too. How likely was this to happen? You heard about it on the news, this kind of thing, but entirely because it *was* news. It was surely an incredibly rare worst-case scenario if ever there was one.

"So let's rewind a bit," Steve said. "Let's say you've taken on board what I'm saying here and you've got a lock on your bedroom door and you're lying in bed hearing the noise downstairs. You stay where you are, don't you, and you phone the police?"

"How do they get in?" Abi asked, pertly. "You're locked in your bedroom but you've got to let them in."

"Exactly." He grinned, looking pleased with himself. "When you go to bed at night, you take a glass of water with you, right?"

"Right," Abi agreed reluctantly, "No, make that a last gin and tonic," she muttered.

"And your handbag . . . and your keys. Please tell me you take your keys?" Steve looked mildly despairing.

"I don't take any of those things," Nell admitted. "The keys stay on the hook in the hallway, my cash and stuff is wherever I've left it and if I take a glass of water I wake in the night to the sound of the cat lapping it."

Why had she said all that? Nobody needed to know this. She put it down to having barely spoken all day. She'd concentrated hard on mixing paints, experimenting with colour. Cobalt blue, dulled down with Payne's grey, seemed to work well for the cabbage leaves, mixed with varying amounts of yellow ochre, then the veins added by drawing across the wet paint with a scalpel . . . you really didn't want anyone around chatting and being a distraction for that bit. It could have all gone horribly wrong, but the cabbage was now finished and quite glorious with its colourful selection of terrible diseases and infestations.

"So that's kind and sportingly generous," Steve was saying. "You leave everything conveniently at ground level so when Scumbag's got your stuff together, he can load it into *your* car and take that as well. For the police — or fire brigade, if it comes to that, because it could save time and your life — what you need to do," Steve explained patiently, as if they were nine-year-olds of limited intelligence, "is to keep a spare front-door key in the bedroom in case the police need to get in. You don't just hurl it out of the window to them in the dark, either. You keep it in something that's easy to see, a white sock, a pillowcase, anything so they're not blindly scrabbling on your front path, looking for a means of getting in."

"Um . . . and all this time," Mike was looking puzzled, "the scum — the intruder can't hear any of this going on and is still hanging about disconnecting your telly, with the police car's blue light on the go outside and them crashing about among your flowers and shouting up at your window . . ." There was a ripple of giggling.

"Always one smartarse." Steve shook his head. "Trust me, go home and think about it. You'll work it out for yourselves later — you'll decide I'm right. One more word on this: spyholes. No point fitting a good strong lock on the bedroom door if you then let in any friendly-sounding voice that comes knocking. He might not be who he says he is. You need a proper spyglass in the bedroom door. Cheap to install, any good DIYer can do it. Ladies, if you have doubts about wielding a Black & Decker, just give me a call and I'll be round!"

"I don't think so," Abi whispered to Nell. "I wouldn't trust a man who was so into chains and locks, would you?"

Nell giggled. "He'd be a risky date. I wouldn't want to go back to his, that's for sure. You might never escape."

All the same, she felt impressed. Steve *was* right — most of this added up to top tips for a safe night's sleep, even if she now felt that actually getting to sleep at all was going to be both perilous and extremely hard to do. Every creak on the stairs, every rattle of Pablo's cat flap, each scrape of the lilac tree's branches against the windows would have her reaching for the phone. Perhaps until she'd fitted locks, spyware and a dozen or two sturdy chains, she and Mimi should barricade themselves into her bedroom at night with a selection of house keys lined up in Mimi's school games socks, ready for the various emergency services.

"Right — that's enough theory," Steve was saying. "Now watch carefully: I'm going to show you something simple but effective. I need a volunteer — Mike, you'll do. Just come at me and grab my left arm."

Mike, hefty as he was compared with Steve, looked wary and hesitant.

"Come on, Mike!" Steve taunted, walking backwards in front of him as Mike cautiously inched forward. "Not scared, are you? Just go for me. I won't hurt you — Health and Safety don't allow it!" Mike lunged forward, grabbed Steve's arm and pulled him towards him. With a movement so fast no one could swear they'd seen what happened, Steve twisted Mike's arm behind him, flipped him sideways and sent him spinning towards the mirror wall.

"Bloody 'ell!" Mike gasped, rubbing his arm. "You lied! That *did* hurt!"

Steve gave him a look that suggested the move had been sweet revenge for the earlier crime of flippancy. "Big tough bloke like you? I don't think so! But the serious point is that it was a simple counter-move any one of you can do. It's easy, needs balance rather than strength and it will give you that crucial time for getting away. Into pairs, everyone, quick."

Abi and Nell teamed up together and listened carefully while Steve demonstrated (on pale and terrified Jason this time, but slowly and much more gently) how to do the move.

"Don't you go hurting me now," Abi said to Nell. "And watch the nails. I've just had new extensions."

"Will you say that to your attacker?" Nell asked as she tried to copy Steve's flick-and-twist technique. "I mean, it might be worth a go, talking your way out of trouble. I'm not sure about going straight in with the violence. It'd be sure to be someone bigger and

117

stronger than me, and I wouldn't stand a chance. I'm going to be so wound up at this rate, if someone asks me the time, I'll bloody kill them."

Steve, doing the rounds to see how they were going, heard her. "It's not about beating someone senseless," he explained as he took hold of her hand and rearranged her grip round Abi's wrist. "It's about self-preservation. I'm only trying to equip you, just in case the worst happens. When you go for the talk option, you're assuming you've got a scumbag who's prepared to listen. Or one who even understands your language. OK, now that's it, Nell, just turn and push." Nell did as she was told and Abi went flying.

"Wow! It works! And it's so easy!" Nell felt thrilled, exhilarated. It would be all she could do not to accost the first man she saw on the calm suburban streets and demonstrate her new-found skill.

"OK, my go." Abi floored Nell easily and swiftly and the two women hugged each other in a silly dance of delight.

"Hey, steady. That was just one move. There's plenty more to learn here. And don't forget — this is a long way down the line. First rules, everybody?" He turned to the class, and obediently they yelled back, "Make noise! Get distance!"

"Great. We're getting somewhere. OK, the hour's up. Class dismissed. Usual time next week, folks, and if you've got anything at home that you'd consider a useful blunt instrument, like a torch or Patsy's Darren's baseball bat, bring it in. We'll be doing show and tell."

Abi giggled. "Last time anyone did show and tell with me and a blunt instrument, I got pregnant with my third," she said to Nell. "Must dash, that third is being minded by a teenage babysitter and her boyfriend, and I have a feeling they're up to no good in my bed. I'm going to rush in and catch them at it, that'll teach them."

"Ah well then, it's lucky you haven't got a lock on your bedroom door, isn't it?" Nell commented as she put her coat on. "Do try not to traumatize them!"

As she walked past the bar area on her way to the main doors, Steve caught up with her. "Got time for a quick drink?" he asked, indicating a vacant table alongside the glass wall adjoining the swimming pool. Nell slowed, thinking. What was to rush home for? Mimi would be lying on a sofa, deeply into either a texting session or a gruesome makeover programme that involved extreme cosmetic surgery. She liked that sort of thing, which, considering she was possibly at the stage of looking the most beautiful she ever would in her life, wasn't a good sign.

"OK, that'd be good, thanks. Only a small spritzer, though — I've got the car."

"I know," Steve said. "And I bet you know exactly where you've parked it, too. These classes might seem a bit superficial but you won't forget the common-sense stuff. No one does."

The bar was crowded with after-work gym members. Nell would guess the average age was early to mid thirties. They were younger than her and Steve, anyway. These must be the people who so quickly snapped up the tickets to club events — the Valentine's ball, the quiz nights, the Fake That tribute show, the firework party. It had never occurred to her to join in all these activities and, looking at the mean age of those around her, she realized she probably never would. Where did single women (and men) of her age go to meet people? Oh . . . the answer seemed to be the one coming across the room towards her carrying drinks. You went to self-defence classes. Not that this was like a date. It was just a casual drink with a friend. A rather attractive new friend, albeit in a clean and scrubbed sort of way.

"Here we go, one small spritzer as ordered. And a bag of good, healthy, gym-approved, protein-packed, salt-free nuts."

"Thanks, Steve. It was a really good class tonight. Do you ever teach all this in schools? It's the kind of thing everyone should learn. I'm always amazed at the practical stuff Mimi just hasn't a clue about. She can't change a plug, because they now all come welded to whatever gadget they're attached to, she can only cook just enough to survive and that's only because I let her do some when she was really too little. If I'd left it any later she wouldn't have been interested. I don't think she knows one end of a screwdriver from the other."

Steve laughed. "So she won't be attaching her own lock to her bedroom door?"

"Don't even think about it. Frankly, you don't want teen daughters to be able to lock themselves in. It's bad enough that they race up the stairs in a fury and slam the door on you. Locking it for hours on end would be too much. And I'd never get her up in the mornings for

120

school on those days when the alarm, me shouting up the stairs at her and phoning her mobile just doesn't do it."

"Seriously, if you want help with security attachments, don't hesitate to call. I'm happy to come and help out."

Nell thought for a moment. "Well . . . there is one thing. Not about security or anything. I hardly think I should ask you but . . ." She waited for a bit longer, wondering why on earth she was even thinking of asking this near-stranger. But that was why, really. It was because Steve *was* an unknown. There were no explanations to be given, no need to go through the convoluted ins and outs here. Though he might ask . . . She'd deal with that. Needs must.

"The electoral roll. Do you have signed-up access to it on your computer? I thought you mentioned the other day that you did."

"Sure. It's easy, just a subscription thing. I needed it for work," he said. "Why, are you looking for someone?"

"Sort of. I tried that website that we looked at the other day and they . . . he . . . wasn't there. I know you can opt out of that one, though, so I assume he did."

Steve frowned. "If he's opted out, he must be pretty keen on privacy. Is he famous or something?"

"No. If he was I'd have also found some small trace of him via Google."

"And nothing there?"

"No. Not a mention."

"Unusual. Bordering on the reclusive." Steve looked at her. Nice eyes, she thought.

"Are you sure you want to track him down? Has it been a long time? And let me guess — he's an old boyfriend that you're pretending wasn't *that* important?"

Nell laughed. "Yes! You were good at that detective stuff, weren't you? I'm surprised a bit of gun damage made you give it up. And I haven't seen Patrick for years and years, but now I've been told more or less where he is, or might be, I thought it would be easy. Obviously I tried directory enquiries — he's not listed. Look — don't worry about it. Let's just forget I mentioned it, shall we?" Nell felt disappointed. She had hoped Steve would simply say, "Yes, no problem. I'll give it a whirl when I get home and email the instant results." She hadn't expected him to come up with all the hesitant problems she herself had already thought of. She didn't want that at all.

"I wasn't going to race round to his gaff and bang on the door, you know," she went on. "I do have some sensitivity! I thought I'd send a simple, short letter or a card. Nothing heavy, nothing frightening. Just regular, old-fashioned mail, not anything electronically intrusive."

"OK," Steve said.

"OK?"

"Sure." He shrugged. "I'll have a look. Can't promise anything. He might not believe in voting and possibly isn't even on the roll. But if he is, I'll find him. Just give me a rough idea of the area and your email address. As long as he's not called Smith, it should be no problem."

122

★ ★ ★

Mimi was lying on her bed with Tess alongside her, both girls busy with intense manicure maintenance. Having just finished, between them, a vital and difficult piece of maths coursework, they were feeling entitled to some downtime and were sprawling about, filing and trimming and buffing their fingernails and talking of intimate things. You couldn't do this at school, Mimi thought, you couldn't confide the things that worried you in front of girls you didn't a hundred per cent trust not to laugh at you. Everyone always made out they were so clued-up. It was only on safe premises that you could be honest. Tess could be bossy, and a total pain, but what you told her stayed with her. Mimi wouldn't go into the French class after lunch tomorrow and see Em and Chloe whispering and giggling about her.

"You can't just do it with the first boy who asks you out; it's like, so *needy*," Tess was saying. "We're not even sixteen yet. If you start doing that, you'll end up with a list like some gross slapper by the time you're twenty. Why don't you hang on a bit with Joel? Do everything *but*." She giggled. "Though I don't know why giving someone a BJ is, like, more kind of moral than having proper sex with them. My mum told me that in her youth it was thought, like, some disgusting perversion. I don't think of it like that but I don't actually fancy doing it very much, do you? I think I'd rather just have real sex. Suppose it makes you feel sick or something?"

Mimi laughed. "Well no, I don't much want to either, really. I wonder what that bit of a boy tastes like?

Is there a flavour that you could identify for just about any of them and think, if you did a blindfold test, oh yeah, that's *boy*?"

"Ask Polly Mitchell! If you could get fat giving blow jobs, she'd be the size of a whale. Remember last year, when she did it to creepy Carl at the bus station and Lucy Flynn picced it with her phone? I mean, what was Lucy doing, watching something like that and getting all involved? She was only *thirteen*."

"So was Carl. He must have thought it was Christmas."

"Well, he was still just about young enough to believe in Santa!"

"I was glad they got caught. Lucy shouldn't have shown the photos round the Year Sevens and tried to charge them. They're only kids. They shouldn't even know that stuff yet."

"My dad would say I shouldn't, even now," Tess said. "Probably shouldn't, like, *ever*!"

Mimi got up and went over to the window, looking up the road to where Polly Mitchell lived. You couldn't miss the house — the garden had a row of purple spotlights directed up at the roof as if their particular three-storey Edwardian villa was historically interest-ing, like a cathedral. Pink fairy lights hung in their magnolia tree, a really stupid thing to do, Nell had said, because it upset the blossom so it only lasted a few days, much shorter than the other trees in the road. Which was a shame, because magnolia only looks good for a short time anyway. After that, it's just another dull, small tree, nothing special. It was typical of Evie

Mitchell, though — she liked a lot of show. At Christmas everyone in the road had half expected her to put a lit-up Santa with reindeer on the roof. She'd gone for blue lighting all over the porch instead and twinkling ones in the hedge, that someone had nicked.

"Do you know what Polly's dad said to my mum?" Mimi turned back to Tess. "He told her that when she was older, he'd give Lucy a job in one of his companies. He said she showed a good head for business."

"As opposed to his own daughter, who just has a good head for head!" Tess rolled about on the bed, laughing.

Mimi watched her, wondering if Tess too had someone in mind to be that special first one. She couldn't be considering one of the Stuart twins. For one thing, how could she tell them apart? Duane and Shane looked completely identical.

"Tess?" Mimi came back and sat on the bed. She looked at her nails: cuticles perfectly shaped, no bits of flaky skin. They were ready now for varnish.

"What is it, babe? You look worried. Is it your dad? You must miss him."

"I do a bit. And I miss Seb too. I email him almost every day and he just sends back something really short. Reminds me of when I talk to him in the mornings and he just grunts. Boy-grunt, that's what it is. No, it's not that."

"What then? Come and sit with me and tell me."

Mimi nudged Tess out of the way, turned the duvet back and the two girls settled into bed.

"Cosy," Tess said, cuddling closer to Mimi. "Now tell me."

"I just wanted to ask you. Who would you do it with? What about Duane Stuart?"

Tess shrieked, "Duane? Are you mad? NOOO! I would NOT! I love the Stuarts but . . . no, they're just mates. Good for a laugh and everything, but NOOOO! Aaaagh! They're good snoggers, though. What's Joel like?"

"Are they? You've snogged them both? When?"

"Claire's party. At least, I think I've snogged them both. It might have just been Duane." Tess thought for a moment, then said, giggling, "Or Shane . . ."

"You mean you don't know?"

"Well, that's my point. That's why I can't do anything more with . . . one of them. I'd never know, would I? Which one it was. And suppose I did go out with one of them, and the other thought that just for a laugh, he'd give me a go so they could talk about me. No way. But come on, Mimi, tell me about snogging Joel."

"Haven't," Mimi admitted. "We just talked and stuff."

"Hold hands?"

"No. Not even that."

"Ah. Right. And like, here you are, having this conversation with me about whether you're going to have sex with him or not?"

"At this rate I'll be twenty-one before we get that far," Mimi said, gloomily.

"No you won't, don't be mad."

"Suppose he doesn't even fancy me? Suppose when he does kiss me, he doesn't like me because I do it all wrong? I haven't had enough practice."

Tess looked at her. "I'll tell you if you do it right, if you like."

"What?" Tess was lying back on the pillow, her long dark hair spread out and shiny. It reminded Mimi of Marmite, though Tess's hair was more likely to smell sweet — Bedhead serum.

"It's OK, I won't tell anyone. We'll just kiss and I'll tell you if you're OK. It's no big deal."

"Um . . . well, I think it might be, actually. I'm not a lezzer."

"I'm not a lezzer either. I don't think so, anyway. Aren't we a bit young to tell? Come on, give it a go."

Mimi wriggled a bit closer. "Tess . . . you haven't set up a secret webcam thing in here, have you? I don't want this to be the next thing Lucy has on special offer round the school."

"Come here — just kiss me." Tess reached up and pulled Mimi towards her. Mimi closed her eyes and connected softly with Tess's mouth. And then it didn't feel like Tess — this could be anyone's mouth, anyone's tongue . . . Whoever, it was a sheer, utter delight; she didn't want it to stop. But hey no, she thought suddenly, and pulled away.

"Wow. You're more than OK," Tess said, looking startled. "What do you think?"

Mimi was finding it hard to breathe. "Um . . . yeah. You as well. It's just . . ."

"What?" Tess sat up abruptly. "Tell me!"

"I really don't want to do that again with you, OK? No offence!" She tried to laugh but it didn't sound right. It wasn't convincing. What she'd said wasn't true.

"Nah — me neither! It was an interesting go, but I don't fancy girls. You don't feel hard like a bloke," Tess spluttered. "I don't mean hard like that! I mean hard like your whole body. Girls don't do it for me. They're too . . . squashy."

"Exactly," Mimi said, getting out of bed to look out of the window, check that the car pulling up in the driveway was her mum and not, say, Johnny Depp come to whisk her away.

"Squashy," she murmured, staring into the darkness as her mother climbed out of her car.

It was that simple, that fast: Steve must have gone straight home and got on with the mission. His email was short and to the point:

"Got him! He's very ex-directory — address is, Hanbury Mews, Water Lane, Chadstock, Near Wallingford. Best of luck and stay safe. Steve x"

All Nell had to do now was decide how to use the information. There was no question about any "if".

CHAPTER
EIGHT

Wishing Well
(Free)

"She's off early. It's only just after eight." Charles turned away from the window, picked up the newspaper from the doormat and went into the kitchen. "Where's she going, do you think?"

Ed, who was loading the bird-feeder with peanuts, looked at his brother, wondering if he was really expecting a response.

"First, can we establish who 'she' is?" he said. "And second, do you really think I'm likely to know?"

It sounded a bit harsh, but Charles was used to logic and clear thinking. Or at least he used to be: he'd taught maths for thirty years. Perhaps, now he was retired, he'd deleted all rational thought from his head on the grounds that it, too, was redundant.

"By 'she' I meant Nell from next door," Charles said as he pushed two slices of bread into the toaster. It was nasty bland stuff: no seeds, no husks, no flecks. His digestion could no longer cope with such challenges — another tiny notch on life's worry-stick. "And no, I probably don't imagine you'd be able to tell me, though you talk to the neighbours far more than I do. I suppose it crossed my mind she might have said something to you."

Ed hung the bird-feeder on the hook outside the back door. It was high enough to be well beyond the reach of Nell's cat Pablo, but even so, he sometimes wondered if it was a good idea to attract birds so close to feline premises. Seeds and nuts fell to the ground. Birds would peck on the terrace rather than fight each other for space on the wire feeder, and so were vulnerable. But they were nesting now; they needed extra food, extra energy. He'd risk it.

"No, she didn't say anything to me. She could be going anywhere: doing an early shop at Sainsbury's, off to a meeting with her agent, a day out in Harvey Nichols. Or possibly off for a shift servicing clients in a massage parlour? Who knows? It's none of our business."

Charles needed to get out more, Ed reckoned. He shouldn't be doing all this curtain-peeping and watching other people's lives from a distance. It was turning into a hobby. They *both* needed to do more. Over the past weekend down in Dorset, Ed had been out for supper at Tamsin's scruffy, hippyish cottage, tended his garden and had otherwise done nothing more sociable than say a casual hello to neighbours he'd run across in the village shop. He was getting lazy. If he didn't watch out, soon he would be on a level with Charles in old-man-behaviour terms — content to lie around in the evenings reading old favourite novels and watching football on Sky Sport. This week, up here in

Putney, he hadn't made any plans to do more in the evenings than read through his students' A-level coursework. That wasn't enough. Could do better, as he'd never written on any idle student's report. He rummaged in the recycling box till he found the local paper and turned to the Entertainments page. There was still half an hour before he needed to leave for college today — plenty of time to find something worth going out for, at least a couple of nights this week.

As soon as she arrived at Kate's, Nell realized it would have been far more sensible to make this trip to Oxfordshire by herself. Alvin's equipment alone was going to take half an hour to load. When did babies suddenly need so much stuff that they required the equivalent of a team of roadies in attendance? As she drank tepid tea in Kate's kitchen and watched her persuading the child into his shoes, Nell tried telling herself that after twenty and more years since the last time she'd been anywhere near Patrick, what could another hour or two matter? But the adrenalin was churning inside her and she was trembling with eagerness to get to where she needed to be. She took the Multi-Map printout from her bag again and had a fiftieth look at it, as if there was something new it could tell her. The little arrow marked a spot close to the Thames.

She tried to imagine the house and came up with a Cotswold stone cottage hung with wisteria and clematis. In her picture, these were flowering profusely, a romantic, hectic tumble of purple and palest pink, but of course the reality would be that even if they existed, it was too early in the season for them to bloom. The walls would instead be twiggy and tatty. She had small, multi-paned windows in her vision. Was Patrick a curtain man these days? He certainly wouldn't have net ones, though possibly black lace might feature. He hadn't had any window covering at the Oxford flat. He dismissed them all as suburban, which was fine except in high summer when they'd been woken so horribly early by the sun streaming in. The bed seemed to have been positioned so that by mid-June the day's first light shone directly on their eyes. She'd told him it was like Tess of the D'Urbervilles, arrested on midsummer morning at Stonehenge with the sun blazing on to her at daybreak through the stones. He'd been grumpy and said she was showing off because she'd read more than he had.

"Where's your romantic soul?" she'd teased.

"What is romance?" he'd said, looking weary, then added, "And what is a soul?"

"Obviously he'll need his buggy . . ." Kate was muttering as she ambled around her kitchen, vaguely opening and closing cupboard doors as if the buggy would be found stowed inside. "And something to eat. I'd take a banana but he can make an awful mess with them. The state of your car seats last time . . ."

"Don't worry about the seats," Nell reassured her. "They're not exactly in what they'd call 'as new' condition. An army of slugs have left trails all over the back, from when I took the garden stuff to the tip last week." In truth, much of the reason for the filthy state of the Golf's back seats really was down to little Alvin's delight, from a very early stage, in smearing chewed biscuit on any reachable piece of upholstery. She'd had to take a filleting knife to the wicker chairs at home, the day he'd discovered the joys of pushing half-eaten apple into the weave. The boy was surely either destined to be a plasterer or sculptor, or a rustic soul constructing cob bricks by hand. Nell imagined him at thirty or so, mixing mud and straw out in a Devon field and wondering why he was having flashbacks to blue and grey diamond-check fabric and the scent of organic rice cakes.

". . . and some spare nappies, though he's been doing well lately without, and he is nearly three. Still, you can't stop on the M4 just because he starts shouting. And if you don't stop *right then* . . ." Kate was talking to herself as she assembled the Alvin kit. Into the bag went cartons of Ribena, two bananas, the inevitable rice cakes, baby wipes, tissues, his coat, his bunny, a fleecy blanket, three board books, a bottle of Calpol and a pink plastic toy phone with a frightening array of ringtones.

"We won't be out that long, Kate." Nell was keen to get going. "It's just there and back, a quick recce." She picked up the child's car seat from beside the door and went out to put it in her car, to see if this would gee Kate up a bit. Alvin toddled after her and wailed from the doorway, more, she knew, because he thought she was stealing his car seat than because he thought she was abandoning him.

"I expect he'll sleep all the way there," Kate said as she carried him out and crammed his fat little body into the seat. Alvin instantly did the going-rigid thing that two-year-olds do as a protest against being fastened in. Expertly, Kate squished his middle so he bent and she could secure the strap.

"Right. Now for *my* stuff." She closed the car door on her son.

"Kate . . . are you really sure you want to do this?" Nell's anxiety level was reaching crescendo point. She wanted this trip over and done with. Obviously (and sensibly) there was still the option not to go at all, but then she'd be forever wondering. If they could just get there instantly, preferably by helicopter with a quick in-and-out descent, that would be ideal.

"It's all right! I'm joking! Look — here's me: with handbag, doorkeys, phone! I've even had a last wee! I'm ready! Let's go stalking!"

"Aaagh! Kate, don't call it that!" Nell laughed as she backed the Golf out of Kate's drive. "It's *not* stalking! I only want to check out where Patrick lives so that . . . well . . . I don't know what." There was another uncomfortable rush of adrenalin. She could feel it, sharply pooling into her veins. At this rate she'd have heart failure long before they got to Chadstock.

"*I* know — it's so that you can see if he's got a seductive stately pile for which you could offer your body and soul and eternal love to him all over again. If it's a bungalow with begonias and gnomes and a plastic wishing well, you can creep away and give it a miss and be glad you escaped."

134

"No . . . it's . . . I know this sounds crazy but I want to make sure it's, like, he lives in a kind of normal place. Not somewhere that's a manky squat. Patrick was quite strange in some ways, inclined to depression, you know. He could have gone either way. He might be anything. He could have made it seriously big as an artist — though I guess he'd be using a different name or I'd have heard of him — or he could spend his days hanging around Oxford city centre busking in a doorway with a dog on a string."

"Nothing wrong with busking — it's selling a service like any other. But why would he be doing that? Come to think of it, why would he change his name? Unless he didn't want to be found . . . dare I say it in present company . . . by people from his past?"

"Oh, he probably wouldn't. I'm just surmising, in a ridiculous, nervy, jabbering-mindlessly-through-the-jitters sort of way," Nell conceded as they approached the Hogarth roundabout. "But he wasn't the most stable sort and after twenty years, he could be . . . anything. I just want to be careful. Tactful. If all looks reasonably normal, I'll send him a short hello note and he can take it from there."

"And that's why I'm here. To knock on his door and ask if he's seen my lost cat," Kate chuckled. "I love this. It's going to be fun. And if he *does* have a wishing well, perhaps it's in a spirit of artistic irony."

Nell had even more doubts at this point. What *were* they going to do, exactly? Definitely *not* knock on his door, that was for sure. She didn't want Kate going all giggly, ringing his bell and pretending to be the one

Jehovah's Witness with scarlet and auburn striped hair who wore industrial quantities of mascara, and a low-cut turquoise ripple-frilled top with black bra strap on display. But suppose, as they pulled into the lane where he lived, it happened to be at a moment when he came out of the house and saw them: an unexpected and immediate face-to-face? Suppose she looked at him and he looked at her and there was instant recognition on both sides? And horror? Well, on his side there would be, anyway — he'd be the one with the bigger shock. She knew she risked catching him painting the front door or something. She could just imagine it — the mutual what-to-say agony. And what *could* she say? "Wow! Amazing! Fancy seeing you here!" wasn't going to cut it. They couldn't possibly claim to be "just passing": according to the map the lane was a no through road and led to the river.

"I bet there's a lovely pub in the village — somewhere for lunch," Kate was saying, looking at the map. "Do you fancy that? A pretty riverside place that serves home-made steak pie and chips? I'd have to tie Alvin to a chair leg, though, or he'd be in with the ducks."

"It would have to be a different village," Nell said. "We couldn't have lunch in his local — suppose he walked in?"

She couldn't help adding, in her head, "with someone", as in wife, slinky girlfriend. He wouldn't be with children. He'd been sure about that, always, always sure. Unless he'd embarked on serious therapy, it was very unlikely he'd have changed his mind there.

"Of course we could! It's a perfectly public place! Where's your sense of adventure? There's no point coming if we're just going to have a quick shufti and go home again. I've come out looking forward to causing trouble!"

Nell, now driving through Henley, stopped at the town centre traffic lights and turned to look at her friend, "This isn't *Thelma and Louise*, you know, Kate. *Trouble* isn't what we're here for. I knew I should have come on my own."

Steve might have been a better bet to accompany her, it crossed her mind. Being an ex-detective, he would have been more confident than they were about a possible approach. He really could have gone and knocked on the door with some convincing pretence. He must have done it hundreds of times in his former working life. What was it they always used as an excuse on cop shows? That they could smell gas? Did Chadstock have gas? But she didn't know him well enough for all that, and besides, he might take it that bit too far and inveigle his way in so he could check the fridge to see if the shelves were stacked with bagged-up human heads. Ed, though, he would have been good — quiet, reassuring and unquestioning. He would have been best.

Ridiculously, Nell felt close to tears. This was all a huge mistake. What exactly was she expecting, even if she did find Patrick, even if he was going to be happy to see her? She'd made her choice all those years ago. Nothing had changed — it was like digging up long-dead bones, expecting to see that they'd

137

miraculously acquired flesh, new vitality. What was it Alex had said to her when he'd first started playing away with other women? He'd blamed her for being only a sixty per cent wife. "You and Patrick," he'd said, "you'll never be a closed book." Well, if she was going to get on with the rest of her life without either Alex or Patrick, she had to shut that book right now, and firmly. She should have done it years ago.

As she drove past the sign that said "Chadstock", Nell felt like sinking below the windscreen and keeping well out of sight. She pulled her scarf up over her hair and hunched her body over the wheel. Why were her sunglasses in the kitchen dresser drawer, just when she needed them?

"Hey — you're not going to make yourself invisible, you know," Kate commented, laughing. "He isn't going to recognize you, is he, not after all this time."

"He might . . . though back then my hair was blonder and longer and I had a fringe. And I was twenty-three, thinner. But apart from that . . ." She heard a slightly hysterical giggle. It didn't sound at all like her, but it must have been. It wasn't Kate.

"And now you've got a Vic Beckham bob and multi-stripes like we all have at our age. Hey," Kate patted Nell's arm. "Don't worry. He's a bloke. He definitely doesn't wander the village lanes expecting every other woman to be his great lost love! But if you're worried, go and lie down on the back seat next to Alvin and let me drive. I'll report any sightings of tall, fair, once-gorgeous men of a certain age."

Nell shook her head. "Not a chance! I wouldn't trust you not to pull over and ask him directions or something! And I'm not lying on the seat next to your son — he'd rub banana and biscuit into my hair."

"Yes he would," Kate agreed fondly. "I have great hopes for Alvin. He loves messing about with food so dearly that I just know he's going to be my own home-grown celebrity chef. Not only will he make a fortune but he'll be able to feed me luscious delicacies in my old age. The other two haven't got any practical talents, bogged down in studying law and finance — I'm pinning all my hopes on this little afterthought."

The little afterthought, Nell could see in her rear-view mirror, was asleep with his head lolling sideways and a fine trickle of dribble about to drip from his pink chin. Soon he would be awake and hungry again, in need of a new nappy and some space to run about in. They'd have to be quick if they were to get this mission over and escape from the village. In Nell's thinking, this language of subterfuge and secrecy was perfectly appropriate, but at the same time she could sense how ludicrous Patrick would probably find it. Or not. He might just be livid.

"OK . . ." Kate checked the map. "Water Lane is coming up on the right, past the post office. Or is it a Spar? Whatever happened to villages? They'll end up all Tesco Extra and Starbucks, like Putney . . ."

Nell, her heart pounding, only half listened to Kate's running commentary. She just about took in the pretty mix of old buildings, the cutesy roadside grass verges, protected by low white posts and linked chains. It was the sort of place where a *Midsomer Murder* would be set: an inhabitant, crazed by suddenly revived memories, would run amok in the graveyard and slaughter the keeper of the local archives to stop old secrets emerging.

"And . . . OK, slow down, Nell, we'll be in the river at this rate. Look . . . on the left . . . Yes — here it is: Hanbury Mews! Except . . . Stop the car, you're going too far."

"I'm driving past it, Kate. I can't just park in front of his door. And 'except' what?"

She pulled up in front of a chandlery on the riverbank, beside a small marina and boatyard, and turned the car round on the towpath, facing back towards where Patrick lived. He could actually be there right now, just a hundred yards away. He might be listening to Led Zeppelin and painting; there could be another slender nineteen-year-old lying on his bed . . . Or he could be working in London, a faceless commuter, a completely different sort of person now. What was the least likely thing? Insurance broker. So *not* him, as Mimi would say.

"Except it isn't a mews — I thought it would be, you know, the regular sort, like in Kensington. Lots of old little cottage-things in a row. This is just one house, set back behind the lane."

"There must have been more at one time. Perhaps they fell down. OK, we'll sneak up," Nell decided, edging the car along. Houses of varying vintage lined the lane. Some were clearly Tudor, some Georgian, others had add-ons of later years tacked to them. Many

140

windows were bull's-eye glass and a lot of the inside ledges held collections of sundry pottery items, like the back shelves of musty antique shops. You could almost smell chintz and dust. Older people's homes. This didn't look like Patrick's sort of place at all. Among his decorative items of choice had been three massive sets of buffalo horns hung across the wall, flying-duck style, a tatty stuffed heron that was placed in the bedroom's bay window, from where it oversaw the comings and goings of the neighbours, and, facing visitors as they came through the front door from the far end of the hallway, a life-size black and white poster of Syd Barrett, late of Pink Floyd, his favourite band.

The mews was tucked away up a broad alley off Water Lane. Nell parked behind a black Range Rover and looked along the alleyway to the house facing her. This had to be it: it was the only possibility and looked like something a child would draw — four windows, central door and small, overhanging porch. Nell couldn't help looking up at the chimneys, one at each gable end, somehow expecting to see a row of circular white-cloud smoke puffs painted against the brilliant blue sky. The front door was adorned by a stained-glass pane in some sort of design. She couldn't make out what it was from the car, but it was in vibrant shades of green, something abstract, and was a decider: this was definitely Patrick's place. There was no wisteria, no clematis, no window boxes. Definitely no wishing well, plastic or otherwise. Just a tiny front space of garden with a low wall overhung with leggy lavender that should obviously have been pruned years before. It would never recover now and would gradually become thinner and drier, and its remaining leaves would crumble to curled-up flakes. She wondered if it still bothered even to flower. It probably struggled to produce a few blooms, against all odds. Apart from the dearth of flourishing plants, the building wasn't a million miles from the one she'd envisaged.

"It's very pretty, or will be in summer," Kate commented. In the back of the car Alvin stirred. He grunted and shifted and, in the mirror, Nell watched his big brown eyes open and gaze straight at her, startled. He looked as if he was trying to remember who she was. Patrick would probably look at her in a similar way if he happened to come out of the house right this minute. She didn't think he would, though. The house had an empty look about it, not as if it was neglected or uninhabited, just that right now it was silent, resting, inactive, savouring its solitude.

"And it's a fair size for one person," Kate was going on. "I wonder if he lives with someone? Was anyone listed?"

"On the electoral roll? No. But that doesn't mean he doesn't. She might be ineligible to vote."

"What? Like under eighteen?" Kate laughed. "At his age? Men!"

"No!" Nell punched Kate's arm. "I meant she might be from another country! Or might, I don't know, be an anarchist or something." Or "she" might be a lodger. Or a man. Suddenly, she didn't want to think of him here alone. It was a family-size house; one person surely couldn't fill it. Too many parts of it would be cold, forbidding. There could be rooms where nothing stirred for months. There might be a frozen scene, a Miss Havisham moment in there somewhere. It wasn't a happy thought.

Kate opened the car door. "We really *have* to go and knock. Come on, I can't resist, can you?" She was climbing out.

"NO! Kate, stay where you are, *please*." Nell reached across and hauled her back in. "I already feel I've intruded enough. This was too far, too much and I feel really bad — I should have just sent a card. If he ever finds out . . ."

Kate looked serious. "Something really dire happened with you two, didn't it? You never did tell me why you split up. If doubts have been haunting you ever since, then why didn't you just stay together? I've known you for ten years and you've never let on there was some big secret."

"That's because there isn't," Nell said, abruptly. "Nothing more than a romance from our youth that went wrong. Happens to almost everybody." She would tell Kate about it sometime soon. Just not today.

She started the car and looked down the road before pulling away. As she drove past the end of the mews, she caught sight of something on the wall of Patrick's house. Attached to the wall, high up, was a hoop and net, a basketball net. Would a solitary, determinedly childless grown-up play basketball?

If she only knew it, Mimi was, right now, just a mile or two from her mother. The train rumbled fast over

Brunel's Moulsford railway bridge (which Mimi now knew to be a four-arch, twisted-brick structure) and on to the west. And just as Nell should not really have been snooping in Chadstock, this wasn't where Mimi should have been. At this moment, the rest of her classmates were in school being asked their opinions on to what extent, if at all, Piggy was responsible for his own death in *Lord of the Flies*. In some ways she would have preferred to be with them. She was good at everything, schoolwise, but with English you really got a chance to use your brain, to think things through for yourself and to express these thoughts. You didn't get a lot of that with other subjects: no one wanted you to speculate wildly about the outcome of a photosynthesis experiment in biology — you just learned the facts about it or didn't learn them; end of.

"Lucky it worked — it usually does. But we'd have got well fined and I don't have enough for the fare," Joel told Mimi as they slid into a pair of seats at the back of the carriage close to the buffet car. The ticket inspector had passed Joel in the buffet queue and he'd told the man his father was "back there" with his ticket. Luckily the inspector had better things to do with his time than walk back down the train to check out the story of one seemingly honest teenager. Mimi had hidden in the loo till Joel rapped on the door to tell her it was safe to come out.

"He'll come back again, when other people get on." Mimi hadn't any money with her, either. The fare from Putney to Reading had wiped out all her cash supply. They'd blagged their way on to platform four at

Reading to get this train, and the homeward journey was going to be another terrifying exercise in deception. Mimi wasn't cut out for this, she decided. Having been pretty much spoiled and indulged by her father, she'd never so much as stolen a bottle of nail varnish from Superdrug.

"No he won't — this one doesn't stop now till Bath and we're getting off there."

Joel had thought this through. Mimi admired his thoroughness but did wonder why she was there with him. He had this weird engineering obsession and people like him usually seemed content to enjoy their obsessions alone, not drag some half-interested party along with them — but then he thought she was as nutty as he was. He'd shown her Paddington station, now he was going to get excited about going through the Box Tunnel and on to Bath Spa station. This time he was going to show her how Brunel had managed to negotiate a railway into Bath without damaging the city's stunning Regency infrastructure. "You won't believe the system of bridges and viaducts. It just all fits in, totally," he'd said, with the kind of faraway look in his eyes that other boys only had when contemplating how good it would feel to be fronting a top band, or signing to Manchester United.

"OK, now we're going into the tunnel," Joel said, grabbing (oh, at last! Wow!) Mimi's hand. "You have to listen! You go over points in here. You'd think it was just straight through, but since it was built it's been added to, and a line leads off to what used to be a regional seat of government. There's a secret network of huge bunkers and a depot in case of nuclear war."

Mimi, slyly, had also done some homework. "I wonder if it's still true that on Brunel's birthday you can see the sun shining right through the tunnel? I mean, it might not be true now, seeing as time and the earth and everything must have shifted a bit since Brunel built it, but it's a lovely thought, isn't it?" She looked out of the window at the passing tunnel darkness, and felt Joel's arm slide round her shoulders. She turned back to look at him and he gently kissed the edge of her mouth as they emerged into the brilliant daylight.

At last, she thought.

CHAPTER
NINE

Change The Locks
(Lucinda Williams)

From inside the studio, across the garden, Nell could hear the sound of the drill. Steve had been insistent that, as a man-free household, she and Mimi should have a full complement of domestic-safety devices, and he had turned up just after lunch with a stout chain for the front door and a new lock and bolt for the back one. "One kick and any scumbag would be in, the rubbish you've got on here," he told her, sneering at her back-door security arrangements. "You've got to make more barriers. Burglars are idle bastards: if they weren't, they'd have proper jobs. If they have to work to get in somewhere, chances are they won't bother."

She couldn't fault his logic, gave him a cup of tea and the last of the HobNobs, then left him to it while she went into the studio (surely only a matter of time before he came to sort that door out as well) to deal with her emails and do some more work on painting doomed vegetables. If the noise stopped, though, she would go back to the house and investigate. She didn't want Steve wandering into her bedroom to check whether she was keeping an axe under the pillow. ("Very bad idea," she could hear him saying, as he stood by the bed wielding the thing. "You're just providing a weapon they can use against you.')

Alex had sent four emails, each about ten minutes apart as if he'd done the first one quickly, decided to move on to more pressing business and then kept thinking, "oh yes . . . and . . ." He'd now reminded Nell to forward his mail, to cut up his spare American Express card, see if she could find his old passport (why would anyone want that?) and to find out if the BMW dealer had sold his car and if so, why hadn't the money appeared in the bank yet? So this was now her role, obviously. Once a wife, always a PA.

"*Hello, Nell — how are you doing, ex-darling, ex-love-of-my-life? Are you well/lonely/ecstatically entertaining a string of new admirers who must be queuing round the block, seeing as you're in peak condition and as gorgeous as you'll ever be. Not?*" Nell muttered the words she considered were missing as she sat at her desk in the garden studio and scribbled down the list of Alex's demands. He had never been overprofuse when writing, but surely he could have been a bit more friendly? What was to lose, at this stage? He hadn't even asked how Seb and Mimi were — though she did know he was communicating with them separately. Not only were there a safe three thousand miles between them, but it wasn't as if she was going to interpret any contact as a sign that he was desperate for the two of them to get back together. No — the "it's over" aspect had been amicably mutual, really, all things considered. He just wasn't a wordy, or particularly thoughtful, sort. She thought about the cards and presents she'd had from him over the years — none of them had said anything more than an understated "Love, Alex", and for the last two Christmases and birthdays had, unsurprisingly, been reduced to just "Alex".

Sebastian, now he was different. She'd just read an email from him that contained an unusually detailed account of a party in Truro at which the police had arrested two of his housemates for walking across car roofs and another for making obscene gestures at his own reflection in a shop window. Then he'd gone on to describe how nauseous he'd felt in the morning as, agonized with hell's hangover, he lay on his bed with the whirling-pit sensation, staring up at the nipple-pink ceiling on which someone who desperately needed a more satisfying artistic outlet than home decorating had made free-form swirls of Artex. Luckily he'd stopped short of regaling her with any intimate girl-action details (if there'd been any girl action, the state he was in). If he started on that she'd have to remind him there was such a thing as too much information and tell him that there were times she'd prefer the too-cool-for-contact one-liners that he sent to Mimi. Funny, at home he'd been quite a silent, grumpy sort, quite self-contained. This must be his way of being sensitive — thinking she might need some jolly cheering up now she was husbandless. That level of consideration was definitely a gene he hadn't got from Alex.

Nell got up and went to the bookshelf to fetch her selection of vegetable reference books, ready to start work. On the way, she idly flicked the handles of the football table and scored some goals, very fairly, three at each end. The table had been a quirky present from Alex, five years before when the two of them had been more or less ticking over in mildly stale contentment (or at least she thought they had been: she later discovered that must have been the time of the girl in Germany . . .). Nell and Alex had spent a month having daily football tournaments, best of five games: she'd been Manchester United, he was Chelsea. Mimi insisted on being Millwall and Seb's preference was Accrington Stanley.

Nell usually won, but when she'd attributed her skill to hours of playing the game in the Oxford Poly canteen, Alex had turned sulky and refused to play again, kicking the table viciously and saying, "Even this! You just had to bring *him* into it, didn't you?" As if she wasn't only supposed to have deleted Patrick from her life, but all her college years as well. She hadn't even mentioned Patrick, she'd pointed out, and it had been a girl called Janine who'd been her footie partner, but it was too late and the games between the two of them were over. The table took up too much room in the studio and now often ended up piled with books or housing boxes of paint tubes. She decided, as she switched on the radio and prepared to paint, that she should sell it. Maybe she'd get Mimi to put it on eBay, though that was risky as Mimi might, once she knew it was on its way out, kick up a fuss about getting rid of things that were part of her father.

The radio was tuned very loudly to a vintage music station and the Stones were playing "Sympathy For The Devil". Patrick had been a sixties music fanatic and he claimed to have been born in the wrong decade. He had been very fond of his smelly old Afghan coat that was a genuine sixties relic — Nell had a photograph of him wearing it in a snowstorm on Magdalen bridge. "I'd have made a perfect hippie," he'd told her wistfully as they watched *Woodstock* at the Moulin Rouge cinema in Headington. He so wished he'd been older than primary-school age when Jimi Hendrix was playing small London clubs and — the ultimate wish-gig for him — he'd love to have caught some of the Pink Floyd gigs before Syd Barrett left.

What was she going to say to him in her letter? She obviously *had* to contact him now — otherwise what was the point of finding him, tracking him down to where he lived? She felt a bit guilty about that. She wouldn't exactly be thrilled if she discovered he'd crept up on her like that. Or maybe he already had — it wasn't as if she'd know.

Maybe he too had spent half an hour in his car, perhaps years ago, parked outside no. 14, under Isabelle's overhanging willow, staring at her windows (no net curtains there either) and wondering how she lived and who she lived with and what she now looked like. Perhaps . . . it was possible, remotely, if he had any curiosity, perhaps he *had* seen her. She felt cold at the thought — suppose he'd taken one look, thought, oh

151

Lord, she's put on at least twenty pounds and is wearing a spotty pink frock from Hobbs, and raced back to the safety of the Oxfordshire hills, shuddering at the narrow escape he'd had all those years ago. Maybe he'd despised the colour of her front door (Farrow & Ball's Pitch Blue) or the brazen nasturtiums mixed with out-of-control cornflowers that in summer tangled their garish way up the sides of the path.

But either way, did it still count as intrusive, if he never found out about her recent recce? Kate would say it didn't. She would say it was just human nature, perfectly forgivable; but what, for example, would Mimi say? Teenagers had a very straightforward take on some kinds of morality, real extreme black/white, right/wrong stuff. Not, obviously, that she'd be telling Mimi any of this; which, Nell realized, rather answered her own question.

Work. That was still waiting to be done. She'd deal with the Patrick dilemma later. Much later. Maybe she'd keep him till after a good day of work and an early supper with Mimi. It wasn't as if she didn't have plenty of evening time in which to think through what to say. And the social calendar for the coming weekend wasn't exactly hectic either, featuring a massive stack of laundry to be dealt with and — such a highlight — a silly, boozy Sunday evening at Evie Mitchell's. This was to be an all-women gathering to which they'd been asked to bring "mistakes": clothes, bags, shoes they'd bought in a spirit of either daring, sale-induced madness or that ever-optimistic it'll-fit-when-I'm-down-to-size-ten moment. The idea was to see if anyone else would fall on them in delight and claim they'd always wanted a lilac net micro-skirt or scarlet sequinned shoes. Evie proudly called it recycling. For a woman whose garden electricity would, on its own, run a small town, she had a funny notion of the term "green", but it promised to be a fun way to spend an evening.

Nell opened her copy of Dr Hessayon's *Vegetable and Herb Expert* and turned to the section on tomatoes and their ailments. Blossom End Rot, she read first. It sounded almost gynaecological: some unpleasant ailment resulting from sexual neglect, perhaps. Nell found several photos of the results of this affliction and it didn't look appealing: the ends of the fruit were wizened and leathery. It was, she read (and possibly returning to the sexual neglect theme here), a result of over-dry conditions, as opposed to a condition called Blotchy Ripening, for which one of the causes was too much heat. No chance of that, she thought, as she started sketching a large, bushy tomato plant on which she must demonstrate foot rot, stem rot, eel worm, leaf mould, blight, wilt and a form of hormone damage which no amount of HRT would cure.

It was no good. While the computer sat there alongside her, inviting Nell to play with it, she couldn't concentrate on the right colour to choose to depict Buckeye Rot (raised brown markings in a pattern that resembled crop circles). She pushed the layout pad aside and tentatively began typing a draft letter to Patrick, coming up with what seemed like a reasonable introductory sentence (*Patrick — is this a huge surprise?*), then immediately deleting it. She had

153

another go: *Patrick — I know it's been a long, long time*, then deleted that too on the grounds of feeling she didn't need to state the obvious. He would only sneer at her. This was harder than she'd thought.

In the end, she wrote a brief note about having come across his address by chance, through a friend (well, Steve had been the one who actually found it, and Kate had been a helpful navigator), and that now being so much older, she felt that it was time to catch up with friends who had been important. She read it over again. It sounded spontaneous and friendly and yet . . . did it sound as if she'd got something terminal and was calling up people to say goodbye? Suppose he came rushing to see her, thinking she was about to drop dead, and then felt cheated because there she was, alive and well, simply having a nostalgia-fest and indulging a whim and too much curiosity? Not that he'd be delighted to think she *was* about to go into that tunnel at the end of the light . . . not even Patrick would be so bitter. Not after so long.

Eventually she made a tentative suggestion about maybe meeting up once more, rather than waiting till the time came to meet on the ledge. He'd get this reference to a Fairport Convention song that he'd remember from his brief folkie phase. It was a track he'd played over and over till he'd become haunted by thoughts of his own mortality. Bored by his mood, she'd reminded him that at a healthy twenty-two, his death shouldn't be any time soon. He'd given her a cold look and simply said, "No, it shouldn't." And she'd wished she hadn't said anything. Reminders of too-early death brought him down for days.

She printed out the letter, then decided it looked too formal as typescript and copied it out by hand. It was better like that, more personal, but it also made her feel more vulnerable, somehow. She hoped he'd be happy to hear from her — it could go either way. She kissed the page for luck, sealed it into an envelope and stamped it, then left it on top of the closed laptop while she drew the outline for the tomato plant. She would, she decided, give it a couple of hours before she posted it, just in case.

"Your neighbour's taking a very keen interest in what I'm up to." Steve's head appeared round the studio door, some time later. "He's asked me if I'm a friend of yours."

"That's good, isn't it?" Nell asked. "Aren't you a keen supporter of Neighbourhood Watch schemes?"

"On the whole, yes." Steve grinned. He caught sight of the football table and started casually twisting the handles, positioning the players. "Has he got the hots for you then, that bloke?"

"Who? *Charles?*" Nell laughed. "No! He's close to seventy and what used to be called, in polite circles, a confirmed bachelor!"

"Seventy? No, this one wasn't. He was definitely younger than that. Early to mid fifties? Looked a bit old-hippie-ish, very peace, love and lentils."

"Ah, that'll be Ed, his brother. Much younger. He only lives there part-time. Their mother owned the house and Charles lived with her. Ed's got his own place in Dorset but lives up here in the week. He teaches at the sixth-form college."

"Right. Well, he seemed a bit grumpy to me. *Not* delighted to meet me. Was he a great mate of your ex? He's probably protecting territory or something."

"Friend of Alex?" Nell snorted. "No! I think Ed considered Alex a bit of a tosser, actually. Alex once told him that education after sixteen was a waste of time for ninety per cent of the population unless they were doing something useful or practical. Ed teaches English literature so you can imagine how that went down."

"Hmm." Steve was practising, using the line of five red forward players and aiming the ball at the blue goal. It crossed Nell's mind that Steve might have sided with Alex, not Ed. She didn't know him well enough to be sure, but that didn't stop her suspecting.

"Fancy a game?" Steve looked up and smiled at her. Those blue eyes again . . . She really mustn't think of him like that. If Kate knew, she'd march her out to the local Ann Summers and make her buy that Rampant Rabbit. Or worse, send her a box of condoms, tell her to cook him a seductive supper and order her to get on with it.

"Yeah, OK. Tomatoes with Ghost Spot and Sun Scald can wait a bit longer."

"Blue or red?" Steve asked.

"Manchester United or Chelsea?" Nell said, automatically going to the red players.

"Too obvious." Steve was already carefully lining up his team. "Let's be Liverpool and Everton."

How much later could it have been? It probably wasn't the best moment for Mimi to come crashing into the studio. The tournament, best of ten games, had ended in a draw and Steve was giving Nell a final-whistle hug, nothing more, when Mimi, scowling and furious, stormed in. "Mum! What are you *doing?*"

Nell pulled away from Steve, laughing. "Hi, Mimi! Er . . . this is Steve — he teaches the self-defence classes I go to. We . . . were . . . well, playing football, you know, just having fun!" She felt as if Mimi had turned into her mother and that she was the fifteen-year-old, caught out with a boyfriend. Ludicrous.

Mimi flung her schoolbag on the floor and glowered at Steve. God, Nell thought, it was only a quick end-of-match hug — it's not as if we were swopping shirts or something. Something in Mimi's expression told her it might not be a good idea actually to say this. She was probably hungry: she often came home from school trembling with low-blood-sugar starvation and frantically searched for doughnuts or biscuits.

"I can't get into the house!" Mimi wailed. "It's all locked up and the front door chain's on, even. Why's the back door locked?"

"That's because we're out here," Steve pointed out, bravely, in Nell's opinion. "If it was unlocked, any burglar could just walk in and nick your iPod."

"How d'you know I've got an iPod?" Mimi glared at him, suspicious and wary.

"Because you're an affluent teenager. Of course you've got one."

"Yeah, well, it's not *in* the house. I've got it *with* me, for like lunchtimes and the bus and stuff? So — can I get into the house now, please? I've got homework to do." She gave Steve a look of prim innocence, picked up her bag and stood waiting for them to turn back into grown-ups.

"You'll need this," Steve said, handing her a key. "There's a new lock on your back door, a much better one."

"Thanks," Mimi said, at last cracking into something that was almost half a smile. "Are you . . . coming too?"

"Yes, I'll be right there," Nell said. "I just want to clear up a bit here."

"Fine." Mimi gave her a final glare and stalked off, leaving Nell sure that her daughter suspected that she and Steve were going to fall on each other in a passionate frenzy the moment she was safely in the house.

"A post-match cup of tea?" she offered Steve.

Steve laughed. "No, thanks. It's time I was on my way. I'll see you at the class on Tuesday, Nell. Don't forget your blunt instrument."

"OK, I won't. And thanks, Steve, that was fun."

"No worries. I had a great afternoon. Oh . . ." He picked up the envelope from Nell's computer. "I see you decided to contact him, then?"

"Yes . . . well, it seemed a good idea. I'm still wondering if it really is." A bit of her wanted to rip the envelope out of Steve's hands and tear it up. Another part wished she'd sent it many years ago.

Steve grinned. "I'm going past the post office; do you want me to shove it in the mailbox for you?"

It was a decision that would be out of her hands then, literally, Nell thought. She hesitated only one more second and then said, "Yes please. Thanks."

"So who was that then?" Charles asked Ed. "He's been banging away half the afternoon."

Not a happy choice of terminology, Ed thought. The man was clearly taking the moron's route to Nell's heart. If the old saying was that men could be wooed via their stomachs, modern folklore surely had it that women could be won by way of a big power tool and a firm hand on a screwdriver.

"He's some friend of Nell's and he's been replacing her back-door lock and adding a bolt. Extra security, he said." He'd looked at Ed as if checking out what kind of a threat he'd be on a dark night, and whether he could handle the challenge. Ed was taller and broader but the man's expression had said one thing: a scornful "*Nooo* problem".

"And what was all that hilarity then?" Charles persisted, as if Ed had X-ray vision and as much curiosity as his brother. "All that laughing and yelling in her studio."

Ed shrugged. "No idea. What Nell gets up to in the privacy of —" He stopped. He was sounding like a jealous old grump. He *was* turning into Charles. He really should watch it. After all, it was good for Nell to be laughing like that. It had been far too long since he'd heard that. Yes, of course it was good. Really good.

★ ★ ★

"I shouldn't be coming to this. I'm too young for all your lot and that vile Polly Mitchell will think I'm a saddo, going out with my mum," Mimi grumbled as she and Nell walked down the road towards the Mitchells' house. The purplish lights in their garden were almost fluorescent. It was like the landing spot for an alien craft.

"You didn't have to come," Nell told her. "You could have done what you usually do on a Sunday night and flop out on the sofa with your phone, the remote and a bag of satsumas."

"Don't pick on me," Mimi moaned. "At least it's not crisps."

Nell wasn't going to win, because there wasn't anything to win. Why, then, did this feel like a fight? Sometimes teenagers made you so weary. All the same, she understood it was some kind of honour to have Mimi with her, especially given her loathing of Evie's daughter Polly. Unless, as was likely, there was an ulterior motive.

"Who'll be there?" Mimi asked with grudging interest. "I hope they've brought some good stuff."

Ah — so that was it. This "mistakes" night had the potential for treasures and bargains, though possibly not the sort a girl of fifteen would be interested in. Evie and friends weren't exactly Topshop's target customers — there wasn't likely to be a lot on offer that Mimi wouldn't turn her nose up at as being geriatric.

"I think she's invited about a dozen. Kate's coming, and Isabelle from opposite, just friends, locals and that.

Anyone she knows who isn't a wise shopper, I suppose!"

"Will *he* be there?"

"Who?" They'd now reached the Mitchells' ornate iron gates, and Nell rang the security bell. Steve would approve — Don had got this place rigged up with all manner of burglar-proof gadgets. If he could have got away with broken, jagged glass stuck to the top of his side walls, he'd have had the nearest bottle-recycling bin craned over the gates, bought a ton of cement and made it his weekend DIY mission in the fond hope of severing a villain's artery. Nell shielded her eyes from the glare of the lights and looked at Mimi, curiously. "Who do you mean?" she repeated.

"That bloke." Mimi looked at the ground, mumbling. "The lock man, you know . . ."

"Oh, Steve!" Nell laughed. "No! Of course not — why would he want to come to an evening of women messing about with reject clothes and shoes? I'm sure he's got loads better things to do!"

The buzzer went and Mimi pushed the gate open. "He fancies you, Mum. Just watch him, that's all."

"Mimi — he doesn't, OK?" Nell caught hold of Mimi's arm and stopped her halfway up the path. "But . . . if he did, would it matter so much? I've got to have a life as well, you know. I don't see why all the fun should be Alex's. God knows . . ."

"No!" Mimi shook her off. "No, Mum, it's not that! It's him, just something about the way he looks at you. It's . . ." She shuddered, dramatically overexaggerating.

"It's not *nice*." She shrugged, defeated by her lame choice of adjective.

Sex *wasn't* "nice", Nell thought, not if (to paraphrase Woody Allen) you're doing it right. It could be sleazy, sticky, sweaty, rank, raucous, ecstatically, *blissfully* filthy; anything but *nice* . . . Mimi didn't know all this yet — God, at least she hoped she didn't. Maybe they needed another talk . . . a backup one to the earlier birds-and-bees stuff. Why didn't teenagers, like pedigree kittens, come with a starter pack containing a few essentials? Some comfort reading like Nancy Mitford's *The Pursuit of Love* would be good for those miserable, can't-face-anyone days, a big bag of minty chocolates (for same), some slushy, rom-com DVDs for when he only texts one-worders, skincare that works, zit-zapper stuff, plus condoms and detailed instructions on how to use them in case the school hadn't quite got it covered. A book on how to read boys would be useful too, but no one seemed to have written that one. Perhaps the author of Kate's *After He's Gone* divorce-survival guide could give it a go as her next project.

"Look, please don't worry about it," she told Mimi as Evie opened the door. "Nothing's going on. Steve just teaches the class and he fixed the locks, OK? As you would say, 'end of'. Now let's go and see if I can offload these Joseph trousers and that red jacket that just didn't go with anything. I'm counting on trading them in for some cashmere." An evening out, she thought as she walked into Evie's café au lait hallway. Not quite the defiant, survivalist glitz and glamour recommended in *After He's Gone*, but it would do for a March Sunday.

Evie, as ever, had got everything brilliantly organized. At one end of her long, peachy sitting room she'd put up clothing rails and hangers for her guests' contributions, and she'd set up a table full of didn't-quite-work handbags. There were also many, many of the shoes that all women, deep down, know the truth about: if they hurt even a teeny bit in the shop, they'll always hurt. This will never stop a smitten woman from buying them once they've sent her heart rate skyrocketing.

Kate was there, settled in a squashy chair in front of a coffee table that was covered with delectable Marks & Spencer's party snacks. She was drinking a large glass of white wine and munching her way through the lot.

"I should have brought Alvin to this do," Kate was saying, as she tried to force a lime green wedge-heeled shoe on to her foot. "He was a mistake."

"Just the one, Kate? All mine were," Evie's sister Marie said, looking woeful. "All four of them. Some things I never got the hang of. He only had to walk past the bed and I was pregnant." She snapped her fingers. "Like that."

"I had to do a bit more than that, but even so," Kate giggled, downing the last of her wine and holding her glass out to Marie for another. "Even so, it wasn't hard. Well, when I say *not hard*, obviously I don't mean . . ." She and Marie collapsed with mirth.

Nell saw Mimi and Polly look at each other and raise their eyes heavenward. Such disapproval. Where did

163

teenagers get this from? All the same, she was quite glad when the two girls, putting aside whatever differences they had in the face of mother-embarrassment, took themselves into the conservatory to watch Don's seventy-two-inch TV and a pirated DVD of a movie so new it was barely cold from the cutting room, let alone yet out on general release.

"And you could have brought your Alex," Kate said to Nell, now she was on the far side of the best part of a bottle of wine. "He was another mistake, wasn't he?"

"Well no, not at the time," Nell told her, pulling a pale blue cashmere sweater over her head. It was almost the right size. The sleeves were a bit short, but you could call them bracelet length, pull them up a bit further and it would look all right.

"Well, they never are at the time," said Isabelle from no. 14, a woman who still put lipstick on every morning before breakfast so her husband (a golf-obsessed, dull specimen, by anyone's standards) couldn't accuse her of letting herself go. "It's only later . . ."

"No, really. I don't at all regret Alex," Nell told them. The bright pink shoes were quite nice, too. In her head, though, she could hear her mother being sniffy. "Ankle straps. Tarty." She tried them on. Tarty was good — though she had also heard that straps like this made your feet look like trotters. "If I hadn't married Alex, I wouldn't have Mimi or Seb. I'd have missed out there."

"Yes, but you'd have had some with another one."

"No. No, I wouldn't," Nell said, turning away from them, back to the rack of clothes. "Anyone going to try this Jigsaw dress on? I love this coral colour."

164

"Talking of which . . ." Evie's voice emerged from the depths of Isabelle's never-worn emerald satin off-the-shoulder number, "Mimi looks OK. I heard she'd got some nasty tummy bug. Was it only the one day off school that she had? Polly said something about lucky her — missing a maths test!"

Nell stopped fiddling with the coral dress's zip. "When? Last week? She's been fine! She hasn't been off school . . ."

Even as she said it she wished she hadn't. Because, for some reason, Mimi obviously *had* taken time off. Why? The faces that were staring at her now, with questioning little smiles, were also dying to know. Whatever the reason was, she didn't want the entire neighbourhood wondering about it, discussing how it was all starting to fall to bits at no. 19, now Alex had buggered off.

CHAPTER
TEN

Manic Monday
(The Bangles)

"So. Last Wednesday — where were you, Mimi? Why weren't you in school?"

Eight in the morning probably wasn't the most sensible time to try and get this sorted, but Nell's theory was that if you pounced on Mimi with a really tricky question while she was still warm from sleep, she was likely to come up with the truth, entirely because she was still too dozy to think of an instant convincing lie. The evening before, Mimi had stayed on at Polly's, ganging up in Don and Evie's faux-Gothic conservatory to swop embarrassing-mother experiences, so there was no opportunity to confront her. Nell's evening had turned into a sudden write-off. Apart from loyal Kate's, each of the faces that turned to her after she'd been unexpectedly caught in possession of a lying, wayward daughter, expressed the same gleeful anticipation of trouble ahead. Sweet, clever, pretty Mimi: the one who'd got it all in looks and brains and a potential brilliant future to boot — she was showing early signs, after all, of being a holy teenage terror for her newly single mum. What a result. Every woman's face said one thing: thank you, God! This is happening to *someone else*, not *me*! *I* am a top mother: *you* are a parental-disaster reality show!

Nell felt, though she knew it was an exaggeration, that the baton of thoroughly bad behaviour had been passed from Polly Mitchell to Mimi. Evie was *that* close to shrieking "YESSS!" and punching the air. Nell had gone off the coral dress, suddenly hated the pig-feet shoes, and had gone home soon after, gloomy and empty-handed, to get into bed with the cat and curse Alex for leaving her to deal with everything. How could he just walk away? How could he think that leaving her the house and everything in it was going to be complete compensation for opting out on all teen management? And why did he no longer want anything from this home that they'd made together — did he value so little every item that they'd chosen? He hadn't shipped out to New York so much as a single painting (not even the Patrick Proctor lithos that he'd always loved — or claimed he did), not a book, not a photograph, nothing. She'd lain there sleepless and seething and getting hotter and more furious, calling curses from the most venomous gods down on Alex and all errant men.

"Bath," Mimi mumbled from the depths of the fridge. She emerged with the milk, took the cap off and sniffed warily at the contents.

"You were in the bath? *All day?*" Oh God, Nell couldn't help thinking, was she with a *boy?* While she had been ... ooh yes, sneakily checking out the whereabouts of her own old lost lover?

"Are you mad? Of course I wasn't in the bath!" Mimi sloshed milk clumsily on to her Alpen. It spilt over the sides on to the table. Pablo the cat, waiting on the floor, licked his lips.

"*Bath*. Like, the *place*? Jane Austen and stuff? *Romans?*" Full-scale sarcasm was an expected, challenging defence; Nell recognized it well. The wide-eyed, sneering *derrr?* expression matched it perfectly.

"Bath-the-city. Right. OK, and what exactly were you doing there?" With difficulty, Nell kept her tone calm and pushed a slice of bread into the toaster. Watching Mimi eat made her hungry. She'd thought she wasn't — feeling too keyed up. Trying to sleep the night before, she'd pictured Mimi spending the skived schoolday in Soho, touring the clubs looking for work as a lap dancer (why? Why would Mimi want to do that?). Or having a secret meeting with a top model agency and planning on ditching the rest of her education (also unlikely — Mimi was a beautiful girl but would never grow to the required six-feet height). Or . . . the worst one: she could have been down at the travel agency in the high street, organizing a cheap open ticket to New York, so she could race off to join her father and . . . Cherisse . . . at the first sign of discord in the house. But then she wouldn't do that either. She'd have looked on the Internet for it, surely. Please God, she hadn't.

"'S research. For a project," Mimi mumbled through a mouthful of muesli. "I've never been there and I needed to see it. I'm doing a talk for English — we all have to choose a historic person and give a five-minute talk on them. It's practice for the GCSE stuff, right?"

"All right . . ." Nell recognized that this could be along the lines of truth, but still didn't see where a day's unofficial school absence came in. If all the pupils took off on such flimsy pretexts whenever they fancied, the school would be permanently half-empty. Half? No, *completely* empty. There would be stray teenagers mooching about everywhere you looked, shoving you off the pavements and lurking annoyingly in shop doorways.

"So who are you doing? Is that the Jane Austen connection? Why didn't you say? We could have gone down together one weekend, stayed over, done the whole place. The city has great shops. You didn't need to skip school."

"I'm doing Brunel?" Mimi was looking at Nell as if she was crazy, giving her that question intonation as if this was such an obvious fact that it was clearly beyond requiring discussion. Surely Jane Austen had been a perfectly reasonable assumption? Mimi had read all her books the year before. They'd talked about them, laughed about how Lydia Bennet was as wild and wayward as any twenty-first-century teenager, exactly the sort who'd constantly "wha'ever" her long-suffering parents and have maximum skin on show in mid-January.

"*Brunel?* What on earth do you know about him and what's he got to do with Bath?"

Mimi gave her a glance that clearly pitied her ignorance. "Isambard Kingdom Brunel, born in

London on 9th April 1806. His mother was Sophia Kingdom who was English and his father was Marc Brunel, a French engineer . . ."

"OK, OK, I get the idea." Nell's toast popped up, in a haze of blue smoke. It was overdone round the edges but just about the right side of thoroughly scorched. It would do. Nell spread honey over it and went to sit opposite Mimi.

"And Bath?" And how did you get there, how did you pay for it, who did you go with . . .? Nell squashed down her need to know all this and forced herself to be patient. It would all come out in time, of which there wasn't, right now, anywhere near enough.

"The railway. The Great Western Railway," Mimi said simply. "He built it, and designed the stations at Bath, Paddington, the old Bristol Temple Meads, but now that's not used, 'cept as a museum, and he was a genius. The Box Tunnel was . . . um . . . a . . . pioneering feat of engineering."

Nell gave her a sharp look but saw only wide-eyed innocence. Mimi sounded as if she was quoting someone; this was surely straight from a book. A book would have been the place to find out all she needed. That or by way of the sainted, all-knowing Google.

Mimi returned her stare. "What? That's all. I needed to have a look. OK?"

Well no, it wasn't. They'd have to talk later about the skipping-school thing. Time really had run out now. If Nell kept her any longer, Mimi would triumphantly accuse her of being the cause of more missed school.

Three minutes, max, and Mimi would have to leave to catch her bus.

Now flouncing with a sense of moral high ground, Mimi stowed her bowl in the dishwasher and rinsed sugary milk off her fingers.

"Gotta go . . . I'll be late. I'll just go and do my teeth." And she was gone in a whirl of wheatstraw hair and the scent of coconut shower gel, leaving Nell's "And did you go there on your own?" echoing unanswered down the hallway.

Bugger, Nell thought, crunching through the rigid, charred toast. That didn't exactly go well.

Minutes later, the front door slammed and a casually unconcerned "Byeee!" drifted back to her from halfway down the path. Nell stroked Pablo's furry ears and cursed Alex again for his absence. He should be around — if he came back this minute, even for a flying visit, she would fling herself on him in delight. Another grown-up to share Mimi's misdemeanours with would be very welcome right now. Instead, Nell was going to have to share her thoughts with only blighted tomatoes followed by lettuces that were, literally, heartless. Oh joy.

Mimi and Tess sat silently on the bus. Tess bit her thumb-nail and stared at the graffiti ("Nick's a prick": a direct but pathetically unimaginative observation, in her opinion) scrawled on the back of the seat in front while Mimi gazed out of the window.

"I wouldn't mind but . . . it's not like she doesn't have a secret life as well. I'm entitled. I don't have to tell her everything I do," Mimi grumbled.

"*What* secret life? She's your mum. They don't have secret lives! What secrets can they have? They take care of us and they go down Sainsbury's. End of."

Mimi sighed. "I think mine's getting one. She's got this man sniffing round: her self-defence teacher. She's all sickly-smiley with him, like she's *grateful* or something. It's because Dad's not there — she needs to get male attention to make herself feel better. I read about that in her friend Kate's stupid divorce book. Do you think she's doing pay-back? Is this what they do? God, I hope she doesn't go like Carly Calder's mum." Mimi put her hands over her face, recalling the horror of Carly's mother turning up for parents' night in a mid-thigh black leather skirt, her 38FF breasts crammed into a tight, low-cut scarlet top, the look completed with strappy silver stilettos that someone's dad had sneeringly (and leeringly) described as "fuck-me" shoes. He wasn't wrong. Carly's mum had practically oozed her whole body across the desk at Mr Merrick (maths). You didn't normally feel sorry for teachers — the general opinion was that they mostly deserved all the grief that was coming to them — but in this case, well, if one of the girls got a bit close, he still sometimes had that scared-rabbit look, as if he'd never quite recovered from that terrible night.

Tess put an arm round Mimi. "Shit, babes, there's no way! Your mum's got a lot more class than that. Carly's mum went all needy and weird when the dad went off. Dressing like a slut was just a symptom."

"Yeah," Mimi giggled, "of being a slut!"

"In this case true. A slut. Seriously rough. Poor Carly."

"Can't argue with that. And I suppose I should be glad my mum's not lying on the sofa drinking gin and crying. They were quite OK about the break-up, like . . ." Mimi sniffed. "Like it was something that was always going to happen; time's-up kind of thing. I already think, God, if Joel ends it with me . . . what will I do?"

Tess pulled a pack of tissues from her bag and handed it to Mimi. "Mims, babe, you *can't* be crying over a boyfriend you've had for only two weeks and who hasn't even thought of dumping you yet! OK, he's fit enough, but he's lucky to have you. Get a grip, for fuck's sake. What do you *think* you'd do? You'd be just the same as you were three weeks ago!"

Mimi tried not to think about when she and Tess had kissed. Something about that had sent a zing through her that didn't quite happen when Joel kissed her. Maybe it had been the mood of the moment. Or perhaps it was the scent Tess wore, the feel of her long, soft hair or something. Maybe she and Joel needed a right-time, right-place thing to happen. She was meeting him after school, going to his house. Maybe, for once, they'd talk about something that wasn't hard-core engineering or old-style rave music that he had a thing about too. She now knew more than anyone needed to about Brunel, Thomas Telford, John Rennie, Sir John Fowler, Sir Benjamin Baker, Stephenson, Watt and Trevithick, not to mention bands like Chicane and Leftfield. It was hard to convince Joel that there was

173

more to life than steam turbines, the mechanics of viaduct structure and dance music that pumped at foetal heartbeat rate, but she was working on it.

"Well? Anything?" Kate was on the doorstep at only nine thirty, straight from dropping Alvin at his nursery. She was holding a heap of mail that she'd just grabbed from Nell's postman at the gate. Nell took it from her before Kate took it on herself to rip open any promising-looking envelopes, and, hands trembling as they did at this moment every morning, she flicked through the Visa bill, gas bill, offers from Majestic Wine, a postcard for Mimi from Seb (surfers, Fistral beach) and a cheque from *Top Dogs* magazine for a story illustration. Nothing from Patrick.

It had only been a few days since she'd sent her letter, but Nell's heart pounded uncomfortably each morning when the mail arrived. She'd really thought today might be *it*. She'd imagined him leaving it to the weekend to reply to her, waiting till he had the chance to think what to say in a relaxed setting, with time to get the words right. If he'd posted it on Sunday morning it should be in her hand now. She'd give it another day or two, allow for him choosing a mailbox with no Sunday collection, or for having posted it in the evening . . . or on the way out the following morning . . . or finding it after a hectic Monday and mailing it later that night. So that was the mail covered for most of the week.

On top of that, there was the more likely chance of a twenty-first-century response: every time she switched on her computer, there was yet another hurtling downslide of disappointment as the list of new emails came up in her inbox, showing her usual list of contacts and nothing from him. She checked the junk-mail folder, just in case, and trawled through the offers of penis enlargement, ultimate diets, Viagra, scam lottery wins and fake Rolexes, to make sure he wasn't hidden away among that lot. Whenever the phone rang, she got a surge of adrenalin that scorched her kidneys. She hoped that when (if?) Patrick contacted her, it would be via email or letter. She wasn't at all sure she'd be capable of assembling any words that made sense if she had to talk to him in person, straight off.

"Sweet nothing. Same as every day. I mean, I know it hasn't been long since I sent it, but if he was going to make contact, I'd have thought he'd do it pretty instantly. It's not good if he's having to hang about thinking whether to or not."

"He could just phone you. That would be the simplest. You did give him . . . ?"

"Yes, of course I did! Landline *and* mobile. *And* email address. I'm open to all communication, me," Nell told Kate. "But who knows? Maybe there's a good explanation. Like he'd rather eat chicken feathers than talk to me ever again."

She felt weary, leading Kate through to the kitchen. It was as if having got the mail and the computer-checking out of the way, the day offered nothing more till after school time, when she had the non-blissful prospect of finishing dealing with Mimi. She might as well go back to bed, pull the duvet over her head and sleep all the day's hours away. If she hadn't got a living to earn she'd be very tempted.

"Come on now, be rational," Kate told her. "It's hardly been any time at all. Perhaps he's away somewhere. If he lives alone and works at something arty, he can please himself, can't he? He might be up a mountain getting inspiration from cloud formations or he might be in Australia, staring into the Indian Ocean and wondering how to get the colour of it right."

"I know, I know. I just wish I hadn't started this. I mean, what am I hoping to achieve here? I'm just using it as an excuse not to get on with the rest of my life. It's like some kind of obstacle I've put up, something to be climbed over before I move on and sort myself out. I don't need it and it won't change anything!"

"You should have done it years ago," Kate told her firmly. "It's clearly been an issue."

"Funny you should mention Australia, though," Nell said, measuring out coffee. "Patrick's sister went to live there, not long after her wedding."

And what a strange wedding that had been. On the surface it was the full works, the church, the flowers, the meringue dress, the big white limos, the marquee, the mother of the bride in classic feathery hat and a pale turquoise silky outfit. But there were, quite pointedly, no bridesmaids, and at the reception there was the sad spare place at the top table for the absent sister who was never mentioned. Patrick, until the moment he'd suddenly blazed back into life and dragged Nell into the orchard, had been determinedly drunk and in the morose mood from hell. The bride hadn't thrown her bouquet to a jostling bunch of shrieky friends, either. She had simply walked away by herself and left it, without comment or ceremony, and as soon as the photos outside the church were over, on the little grave in the churchyard where the missing bridesmaid was buried: Patrick and Susannah's five-year-old sister Catherine. And after that, without any further word, Susannah and her new husband had resumed their wedding-day jaw-breaker smiles and got on with enjoying the party.

"You're not on a diet, are you?" Kate was now saying, opening a cupboard and pulling out a pack of dark Ryvitas. "No biscuits? Is this all you've got? You're usually a reliably well-stocked house, especially in times of stress."

"It is, sorry. I really need to go and shop properly sometime. Mimi and I are living like students here at the moment, just grabbing food on the run. We tend to dig out whatever's in the fridge, cook it up with onions and a load of tomatoes and sling it over some pasta." And such a lot of pasta, Nell thought guiltily. Pasta, porridge, roast chicken, anything with mashed potatoes — all you needed for inner comfort. She must come out of this zone, if only in the interests of maintaining her dress size. It was just that eating salad or broccoli or a slab of virtuous salmon — whatever you put with it — didn't make you feel you'd been cuddled.

"You've got to get past that one. She'll get lardy and she'll only blame you," Kate warned, patting her own very substantial hips. She pulled a Ryvita out of its pack and studied it closely, in case it had mould. "I could eat one with some jam on it . . ." Kate was back in the cupboard, moving jars. "I'm always hungry — it's that post-baby thing."

"Post-baby? Alvin's nearly three!"

"OK, I know, but if you consider how time goes faster when you're older, then you have to think that three is the equivalent of six months to the average teenage mother. What's this?" Kate asked, pulling out a pile of envelopes.

"Where? Oh . . . Those are some of Patrick's letters. Shouldn't be in there. I'm sure that isn't where I left them."

They were the ones he'd written when he was away with his family on a ski trip. No emails back then, no mobiles. He'd been bored in the evenings and had written to Nell every night, telling her how many infant-age French children had run over his skis, how much *vin chaud* he'd got through at lunchtime while listening to his parents bickering about whether they should risk going down the most dangerous black run.

"They should be in here with the others," Nell said, opening a drawer and moving napkins and tea towels around. "I've got a box of them — I was looking at them the other day and was sure I'd put them back. I must have left these out on the table by the computer and Andréa moved them when she was cleaning."

"Just suppose," Kate said warily, "suppose he never does get in touch with you. Suppose he just ignores you because for him it's all long, long over and not worth rehashing. What will you do then?"

178

Nell thought for a moment. "Well . . . seeing as according to my mother it was Patrick who was asking about me only a few years ago, I assumed he'd be OK about hearing from me. But . . . If he isn't, well, then I'll deal with that one when it happens. Or doesn't happen."

"Oh good. And don't give it too long. If he hasn't got back to you by this time next week, just give up and forget it," Kate said. "But I hope you *do* get to meet up with him and he's gone old and fat and bald and unattractive. Then you'll feel like you've been set free to find a nice fresh new one, won't you? You need a man without a whole trolleyload of ancient baggage. And look . . ." She pointed at the side window where Ed was passing, on his way to Nell's back door. "There's one approaching now. What with this tasty neighbour and your safety-class man, you can't say you aren't spoiled for choice, can you? They're like buses, men," she said, swiftly grabbing her bag and heading, with helpful tact, for the front door. "None around for years but when they do turn up they come along in convoy."

"I shouldn't really be here," Nell told Ed as they went back into the Bull's Head bar to get a drink at the interval. The John Horrocks Blues Band had played a vibrant first set and her ears were ringing. "Mimi is in disgrace and I should be at home glaring at her and making sure she remembers she's in big trouble."

"If you've got a troublesome teen at home, the least you should do is make sure they see you going out to have some fun. When they're grounded it really rubs it in! What do you fancy? Beer, wine? A vat of medicinal gin and easy on the tonic?"

"Oh . . . definitely not gin; for me, that stuff is even worse than champagne for gloom and misery. Dry white would be good, thanks."

The barman opened a bottle of Sauvignon and poured out two glasses. The place was busy — John Horrocks pulled a fair-sized, though not particularly young crowd. Nell was glad about this — she hadn't made a huge effort with how she looked (plain black wrapover skirt, flat boots, deep rust cashmere and a selection of chunky necklaces), and was grateful not to be surrounded by hordes of sleek, skinny girls in baby-smock mini-dresses and with their endless legs on view. Luckily Ed wasn't the sort who'd expect her to be in full-scale dress-up. As ever he looked comfortably dishevelled, very much in the style (or unconscious lack of it) of the laconic James May on *Top Gear*. She thought of Steve and the contrast with Ed: Action Man versus a well-scuffed teddy bear.

"I haven't actually grounded her," Nell admitted as they went to sit on a sofa on the far side of the bar. "I thought of keeping her in over next weekend, but that would definitely be one for the old "this hurts me more than it hurts you" category. Going out tonight for a bit is one thing, but I wouldn't be able to escape that whole forty-eight hours of watching her pull the moody from hell! And besides, I think she got the gist of the message: skiving school is a capital offence."

"Tamsin used to do it all the time. When the school eventually wrote to ask if the glandular fever was getting any better — something she hadn't actually had, of course — she told me she couldn't give a flying one and said she preferred being educated in the real world. She spent all her time in libraries, devouring books by the dozen, so I suppose she had a point. Not . . ." and he laughed, "not that she was reading Dostoevsky or Milton or anything so edifying, but the amount of crime fiction she got through . . ."

"That'll be the 'real world' she was learning about then, will it?" Nell laughed.

"OK — fair point! All the same, it's stood her in good stead. She got a Silver Dagger award at only twenty-two and she's working on a TV script — a pilot from her first book. If that goes well . . . who knows? Move over Lynda La Plante."

"So, for her skipping school was a canny career move. For Mimi, well, I can't really fathom her. She said she went off to Bath by herself and admitted that she travelled without a ticket, but I think there must be more to it than that. If she was with a boy, why not say so? I'm not exactly the heaviest parent."

"They like their secrets," Ed said, smiling. "Teenage girls like diaries, confidences, whispered things. I bet you remember that."

"Teenage girls and middle-aged men." Nell knew she sounded bitter, but the thought of Alex and his many years of secret liaisons had come sharply to mind. Maybe Mimi would be like him, having to keep something back, having to live in her own head.

"Sorry," she said. "Didn't mean to say that — this is an escape night."

"That's OK — it's not been long since you and Alex split. He's bound to be on your mind."

Nell looked at him carefully, trying to fathom what he was thinking. Why had he asked her out? It had sounded neighbourly and casual ("Just wondered . . . if you've got nothing better to do . . .") and of absolutely no real consequence at the time. Now she wondered, was there more to it than that? Kate would say there definitely *must* be. She'd say, why didn't he just go to see this band by himself, or drag some workmate along? But then Kate was eager to pair her up with a new partner, to keep her friend tidily organized with a love life. Just for once, though, Nell thought, wasn't it lovely to be out with someone of the opposite sex, without the remotest possibility of sex being something you had to consider?

The bar was emptying as the room at the back filled up for the band's second set.

"We don't have to go back in, if you'd rather get back to Mimi," Ed told her, finishing his drink.

Nell hesitated for a moment. "Well, actually . . . I probably should go home. But you don't have to if you'd rather stay — I can go by myself, no problem." She was thinking ahead here. If she went home alone, that would solve any potentially tricky problem about how to say goodnight. This was like being a teenager — would he kiss her? He never had, not even in an air-kiss polite greeting sense, so no, he almost certainly wouldn't. God, why would he even want to? She was surprised to find herself thinking it wouldn't be too unwelcome if he did want to, but she wasn't up on the finer points of dating etiquette. Not that this was a date, not really . . . So much for having no thoughts in that direction. But then he only lived next door. If she was going to practise amorous arts for future use, she'd do better to sign up to some kind of agency and get through a few casuals who wouldn't really count and were safely more distant, geographically. What a ridiculous train of thought! She picked up her bag and started to make a move.

"I'll come with you — I'm ready to go," Ed said, heading for the door with Nell. "Ooh, watch out . . ." Nell had opened the door and walked straight into a stick that an incoming woman was wielding. A ski pole, for heaven's sake — there'd only been two days of snow this winter. What on earth was she doing with it? Ed caught Nell's arm and stopped her from crashing hard into the door frame.

The woman, limping (OK, so she had an injured foot. She wouldn't be the only one if she wielded sticks around like that), and using the pole for support, stomped crossly — if unevenly — past Nell into the bar, ignoring her apology, followed by an equally bad-tempered-looking man, bulked up in a North Face quilted jacket.

"They were a cheery pair," Ed laughed as they went out into the chill air. "Do you think she really hurt herself skiing? I bet she didn't."

Nell looked back at the pub. Through the window the woman was glaring at her as she leaned the pole against the bar at an angle guaranteed to trip up the next unlucky punter.

"She'd like us to think so," Nell said, feeling cheerily malicious. "But I think she just fell off her front doorstep or something. You know," she said as the two of them walked along the road towards where Ed's car was parked, "it's funny round here, isn't it? It's so typically south-west London that if you need a walking stick for a while, a person would immediately look around their house and pick out a ski pole. Not an umbrella or a golf club. And can you imagine they might, say," and she giggled, "unscrew the mop head from a Vileda and use the stick?"

Ed laughed. "Certainly not! That would be far too downmarket! Imagine passing up a chance to be a show-off! Come on," he said. "There's a gap in the traffic — we can cross here." He grabbed Nell's hand and they crossed the road, which didn't, Nell decided, feel at all strange, or challenging or problematic, merely friendly and perfectly normal. Just so long as he didn't kiss her and complicate things. She really wasn't ready to deal with anything like that.

CHAPTER
ELEVEN

Sweet Wine
(Cream)

"I felt a bit iffy coming here tonight with this." As they walked into the candle-smoked Body and Soul studio, Abi opened her bag and showed Nell a big chunky hammer. "D'ya think that's blunt enough to please Steve?"

"I don't know about pleasing Steve, but I'd have thought it was blunt enough to slaughter a rhino," Nell told her. "Can't you get done for carrying something like that around?"

"Probably. If I got pulled up for it I could say I was a carpenter, or on my way to help a friend who had a couple of pictures to hang. What have you got?"

"This." Nell showed her the two-foot-long Maglite torch she'd brought for Steve's show and tell. "It weighs a ton and isn't exactly handbag size. I keep it in the car, so I suppose if someone got in and tried to hijack me I'd be ready for them . . . except," she laughed, "I'd have to tell them to hang on a minute while I climb across to the back to get it off the floor behind my seat. That would work."

"Aha — the trusty Maglite!" Steve said as he whizzed into the room alongside them. "I wondered how many of those would turn up tonight! A classic mistake — weapon too big for the user. OK, everyone . . ." He leapt on to the stage. "Register first, then violence. Who's here?" He went down the list — there was a full class complement except for Patsy.

"She's got an aroma-stone massage with Leonie in the spa. She booked it ages ago," one of her friends told Steve.

"A *massage*? She's missing out on saving her own life for a *massage*?" He put a cross by her name on the list and shrugged. "Oh well . . . if she wants to be murdered . . ."

"Bit harsh, that," Abi whispered to Nell. Possibly it was, Nell was inclined to agree, but this time she'd put it down to his having an off-the-wall sense of humour.

". . . Being ready in case of trouble, getting the stance right . . ." Steve was talking about body language and called Mike, the Hell's Angel, out to the front to help demonstrate. Mike looked terrified, anticipating at any second to be hurled across the floor. Nell had noticed in the last class that he kept to the back of the room, trying not to be picked on. Being so easily flung around by a guy half his size couldn't be doing his personal esteem as a well-'ard biker any good. He was leaving his huge shiny Harley very close to the gym doors too, she'd seen as she arrived, as if he was avoiding having to walk across the car park and risk being ambushed by Steve, whose idea of "just testing" could be to wrestle him into a painful armlock over by the Parent and Child bays.

"Why do you always pick on me?" he asked now, with what Nell thought was quite reckless courage, given Steve's speedy skill at the top end of assorted martial arts.

Steve gave him a cold stare. "I'm only . . . OK, you win this time. I'll save you for later, wuss. Abi? You'll do instead. Come up here for me, darling." Abi stepped on to the platform, giving an apprehensive glance back at Nell.

Steve smiled. "Don't look so worried! All I want is for you to make like I've approached you in the street, as if to ask you a direction or something. OK, now just walk towards me."

Abi did as she was told, then waited when Steve stopped her and politely asked her where the post office was.

"Now don't move, Abi, not an inch," he told her; Abi obediently froze, grinning at Nell and waiting to be thrown to the floor.

"Mistake one," Steve said to the class. "Look: she's face on to me, feet together, with maximum exposure of her softest and most vulnerable parts." He indicated her front. Abi stuck her tits out, page-three style, and pouted provocatively. Steve frowned at the resulting wave of laughter. "One push and she'd be over. Make your own jokes there, if you must, but this is serious stuff. You see it all the time, even police taking witness statements — they stand too close to the suspect, looking down and writing. Amateurs. No readiness for attack; like grazing antelopes again, you see. Any scumbag that's been apprehended by that kind of idiot could give one hard shove and leg it, no problem, before the dumb plod has even noticed." He sighed. "Now, Abi, feet slightly apart, OK, stand a bit more sideways on . . . You're only half the target that way, see? And you're ready to fly if you need to. Simple, isn't it? Just common sense."

He sent Abi back to the floor. "Right — let's see what toys you've all brought from home," he requested.

Out came an assortment of potential self-defence items: two baseball bats (Wilma and Jason), a piece of chain (Mike), several torches, an umbrella. Steve picked up Abi's contribution and laughed. "What the . . .? Did you walk the streets with *this*?"

"Yeah? And?" Abi challenged. "It's only a little bitty hammer. Every home's got one."

"*Only?*" Steve spluttered. "This, my love, is a full-scale lump-hammer. You could break up pavements with it. A light tap on a head with this and the road would be sticky with brains. Probably yours." He handed it back to her. "I'd get a cab home with it, if I were you, for your own safety! Now let's look at these torches," he continued, taking hold of Nell's Maglite.

"If you must use one this big, hold it like this." He held it by his shoulder, like a javelin. "Ready to swing it down on your target if you need to. But you'd do much better to invest in a police light." He showed them a small, ordinary-looking torch. "You see, it's tiny; very portable, very innocent-looking. You can't be arrested for carrying one of these little things. But look . . . it's got this crenellated edge. On the blurb, they say it's a 'strike bezel, for enhanced personal protection' which just means it's useful for jabbing hard into an attacker's face if you have to. They'd feel it." He poked it towards Mike, who flinched and jumped a metre backwards. Steve smirked. "And don't accidentally leave the light switched on in your handbag — it's not only strong enough to blind temporarily and have a no-good bastard staggering around wondering where the hell he is, but it'd also burn a hole through your leather. It's called a Surefire light, about ninety-five quid, give or take. Well worth the investment."

"Ninety-five pounds for a torch? What's in my bag isn't worth that!" one of the ponytail girls said. "I'd rather just hand the whole thing over and buy shoes with the cash!"

"It might not be your bag the scumbag is after," Steve told her, ominously. "We'll be doing sexual assaults next week. After that you might just decide ninety-five isn't bad — there are versions of this that go up to well over three hundred quid. It depends if you want to put a price on your life. Your choice."

"He's very persuasive," Abi said to Nell as they left the class sometime later. "If he'd had some of those torches with him, I'd have been writing a cheque there and then."

Nell rubbed her sore wrist — they'd spent a long time practising twist grips and moves for getting out of holds, and she'd pulled something. She'd been partnered with Jason, who'd turned out to be a hard little sod, well into the roleplay and making no allowances for her being either a woman or old enough to be his mother, but then she supposed he had a point: it wouldn't be any kind of picnic if a vicious stranger pounced on her.

"He *is* very persuasive. I feel like getting on the Internet right now and buying a top-of-the-range torch, then going out and daring someone to go for me. I can just see it, I'll be in Richmond town centre, Saturday at midnight, shining this blazing beam around and shouting, 'Bring it on; what are you waiting for?' to all the drunk hordes."

Abi laughed. "Yeah, but you know what would really happen: you'd buy one of those little torches, right, and then you'd put it down somewhere in your kitchen and it would vanish. You'd be three hundred quid down and someone would have taken it up to the loft to look for something and dropped it in the water tank."

"Or I'd leave it switched on in a drawer and it would burn the house down."

"Either of you two fancy a drink?" Steve caught up with them and got between the two women as they walked through the gym bar. Nell felt his hand lightly on her shoulder. She could, jokingly, consider this as molestation, grab, twist and bend his arm, trapping his elbow on the floor, show him she'd learnt a thing or two. But maybe he wasn't the one to practise on. And possibly not here in the bar area, where he'd enjoy an audience as he flung her to the ground, half broke her thumb and put his foot on her neck like a hunter with a slaughtered leopard.

"Can't, ta, gotta dash, Olly's outside, picking me and the lump-hammer up," Abi said, nudging Nell as she left her. "See you next week!" and she was gone, leaving the two of them in the bar.

"And I can't either. Sorry," Nell told Steve, reluctantly. "Mimi's on her own and I was out last night too."

"Oh? Where did you go?"

Nell hesitated: his tone was very inquisitive. It reminded her of her mother. Was he going to ask her who with and what time she got back and did she wear a skirt that was a sensible length?

"To a pub, to see a band. Just with Ed from next door."

"Oh — yeah, that one I met. And . . ." Oh here it comes, she thought, ready to be as defensive as she'd been in her teen years. When did you really grow up? she wondered; then considered, maybe she *was* being the grown-up here. It was none of his business.

"I just wondered. Did you hear anything from that old flame of yours yet?" he then asked, throwing her off track.

"Um . . . no. Nothing. I don't expect I will now — I mean, if you were pleased to hear from someone after so many years, you'd let them know pretty much immediately, wouldn't you?"

She wished he hadn't asked. Now she'd put into words what she'd been trying not to believe, it seemed there was no chance of a response from Patrick. It wasn't remotely fair to blame Steve, but she couldn't help feeling that by asking, he'd jinxed any contact possibility.

Steve smiled at her. "Well, possibly. Don't give up."

"Oh I won't," she lied, to be polite. "I won't."

Was there no end to the troubles of vegetables? *Home Grown*'s editor was so far highly pleased with Nell's depictions of diseased cabbage, tomatoes, lettuces, beans and potatoes. It was now the turn of onions and Nell intended to draw several of these, as there were far too many ailments to be able to cram them on to one. In the studio, she placed a row of onions on the window ledge in front of her, consulted Dr Hessayon's trusty book and made a rough plan of a neatly planted row of afflicted bulbs all lined up like battle casualties, with the name of each one's disease pencilled in beneath. Maybe she could give them tiny temperature charts as well, and a selection of nursing notes ("Onion no. 3 had a comfortable night but an attack of Downy Mildew rendered him unfit for storage"). She'd be surprised, after a potential grower had seen the results of the many infestations and disfigurements, if any readers of *Home Grown* would be tempted to try to raise them. One look at this lot and they'd decide it was much safer to stick to nice healthy ones in a net bag from Sainsbury's.

Nell finished the sketches and then painted for an hour with Fleetwood Mac playing in the background. She became completely absorbed in what she was doing, having mentally divided the onions into those that were simply unlucky (Saddleback, Bull Neck, Leaf

Droop), and the wayward ones that should be attending the equivalent of a sexual-health clinic (Smut, Shanking, White Tip). The morning had flown past, and when the sun's rays shone through on to her painting she realized this was the first day she hadn't given any thought to Patrick and his lack of communication . . . except that, of course, she had now. But all the same, he hadn't been her first thought when she'd checked her emails that morning and she hadn't gone back into the house to see what the post had — or hadn't — brought. This was good, she decided. If she wasn't to get any response from him, she could live with it. She'd done what she could to make contact — she'd be able to move on.

Feeling hungry now, she stretched her cramped limbs, washed the brushes and headed for the kitchen. She flicked the kettle switch on and then Radio 4 to catch the grumble of the day on *You and Yours* (the price of cat litter) and glanced into the hallway. A heap of mail, mostly polythene-clad junk at first sight, was strewn around on the doormat and she went and gathered it all up, happy to see the spring Toast catalogue had arrived. She put a tea bag into a mug and poured boiling water in, then went through the post, weeding out items to be sent on to Alex along with offers of bargain-price insurance and a brochure for a swanky spa. Patrick's letter was in a long white envelope, which was handwritten (though with a blue ballpoint pen, not with the deep purple ink he'd liked back in his youth), and simply addressed to her as Nell Hollis — neither Mrs nor Ms. She was slightly surprised: although Nell Hollis had been on her own letterhead, she'd signed off as Eleanor. Apart from her mother, Patrick was the only one who had habitually used her full name, and it had been a small intimacy between the two of them. At school, college and in her grown-up life, she'd always been Nell to everyone else. But it had been such a long time since the word "intimacy" could have applied to her and Patrick, nor was the envelope the important thing.

Nell put the letter down on the table while she added milk to her tea, conscious that she seemed to be moving at half-speed, reluctant to let this moment of heart-thumping anticipation go. Contact — wow! She'd found him, he'd responded: it was hard not to think ahead to what that envelope contained — he might want to meet, might be on his way right now — no, that would be ridiculous! A case of imagination running riot. What was she thinking? That he'd know when it would be delivered, and that he was waiting round the corner, ready to whisk her away to the Soho Hotel for an afternoon of reunion passion? That couldn't happen on the outside of rom-com movie-world, sadly. The postmark was north London, and she wondered where exactly he'd been at the time he'd dropped it into a mailbox. She pictured him wandering in the sunshine through Highgate Village, or maybe about to return to Chadstock after trailing through the Wembley Ikea. Perhaps he'd forgotten he'd got the letter with him, or had been carrying it around, agonizing about whether or not to send it. She thought of him finding it in his pocket as he walked through the lighting section. Would he regard the Knappa lightshade as a piece of cheap-and-nasty tat (Alex's opinion), or as an iconic design classic (Nell's)?

Nell sipped her tea, which was still too hot, and scalded her tongue. Then she picked up the envelope and slid her finger under the edge, carefully opening it, savouring the moment. There was only one page — he hadn't written a lot. She smiled at the sight of his writing. It wasn't quite as it used to be but was smaller, more cramped, somehow. And strangely, it had a very wide left-hand margin, as if he needed the space for something else, an afterthought maybe? A drawing, even? But as she read, her smile vanished, the heart-pounding increased and the excited anticipation evaporated instantly.

Nell — After all this time there is no point us having any contact. I don't know how you found me but I consider that you have invaded my privacy in an unwelcome and unacceptable way. If you do so again I shall feel obliged to take legal action. Patrick (Sanders)

The shock of these formal, hostile words was searing and sharp. Nell dropped the sheet of paper on to the far side of the table and felt clammy and sick. He couldn't have said that, not Patrick. Not even after all that had happened, surely. How vile, how spiteful was that? Nell looked across at the paper and read the words again, as if this time they'd say something different, contain at least one tiny hint of warmth. Nothing. Carefully, she

195

put the letter back in its envelope and opened the dresser drawer, pulling out her box of Patrick's correspondence from the happier times so long ago. This couldn't be him, it just couldn't . . . She took out the top one, written when he was twenty-three and in Wales painting a bacchanalian scene on a restaurant wall near Caernarvon. The writing wasn't the same, but was too similar for her to have any doubts that this lovely, loving Patrick was the same as this bitter, spiteful Patrick. How deliberately vicious this was — and for what? What could he possibly get out of knowing how hurt she would be?

Trembling and with tears flowing, Nell picked up the phone and tapped out Kate's number, only to remember that this was one of her work days and she would be sitting behind the reception desk at the Richmond Hill Medical Practice, far too busy to give any attention to a distraught friend. Nell put the phone down and it rang immediately. Ridiculously, her heart scudded again, her overcharged brain somehow thinking surely this must be Patrick, telling her he'd got it all wrong, that he'd been writing to someone else and got confused. She picked it up and mumbled a barely coherent greeting.

"Nell? It's Steve. Um . . . are you all right?"

Steve? Oh Lordy, she thought, what does he want now? More lock-fitting? She wanted to tell him to go away, or actually not to say anything at all, just hang up.

"Yeah. I'm fine," she told him, as abruptly as possible without actually telling him where to get off.

196

"You don't sound it. You sound . . . really miserable. Is it anything I can help with?"

Nell sniffed, and made a supreme effort not to sob down the phone at him. He sounded so kind, so concerned. Sympathy was making her feel worse, if that was possible.

"No, not really, Steve, but thanks for offering. It's . . . I just had some sad news, something a bit unexpected, that's all." ("All?" Right.)

"Oh. I'm sorry to hear that. Look, I only called up to tell you next week's class had to be rescheduled for Thursday, not Tuesday but . . . I'm not far away, I don't suppose . . . would you like to come out for lunch with me? Say no if you'd rather not; I'll understand. But it might cheer you up."

Nell looked at Patrick's letter, still lying on the table. She didn't much want to share house space with it, although she knew she couldn't yet throw it away, if ever.

"I'm not very hungry," she told him. "But . . . it's a really sweet thought and actually, yes, it would be good to get out for a bit. I don't want to be too long, though. I've got work to do and I want to be here when Mimi gets back."

"Oh, that's OK, no worries — how about just a quick bite round at the Italian on the high street? Would that be all right? If you want to tell me what's wrong, fine. If not, we'll talk about absolutely anything else. See you in ten minutes? Deal?"

"Deal. And thanks," she told him.

★　★　★

Nell had had one glass of Prosecco while looking through the menu and had drunk it down fast in an attempt to feel more like a normal human, then with her *penne amatriciana* she had had a glass of red wine which was a lot larger than she'd thought it would be, and now the waiter was offering her a refill to the glass of sweet, sticky limoncello that she'd had with her espresso. Steve had turned out to be welcome therapy, entertaining her with stories about his detective days (a dawn raid on a convent, incompetent cocaine dealers cut off by the tide on a Thames island), and never once questioning, however obliquely, whatever it was that had made her so tearful on the phone. He didn't even, she acknowledged with gratitude, do that careful, treading-on-eggshells thing that most people would, didn't once say, "I won't ask . . ." or make any clumsily curious attempt to get her to confide. She was grateful for his tact and his lack of intrusiveness.

"Steve, thanks so much for this. I've really enjoyed it," she told him as she sipped the oversweet liqueur. She feared for her tooth enamel, but it was irresistible: sharp yet syrupy at the same time, probably highly potent but for once, so what? After the shock she'd had that morning, she deserved a few hours of irresponsible escape.

"For what, that sticky drink?" he laughed.

"For the lunch, for thinking of asking me!" she said. "It was almost like —" She stopped abruptly, oh she'd so nearly blown it. She'd almost said, "like a proper date". That wouldn't have been a generous thing to say.

Maybe he thought of it like that, though. She hoped not
— she'd insist on paying her share, make sure he knew
she understood this was just a friends thing. Her head
felt a bit muddled. She wouldn't be putting paint to
paper this afternoon, that was for sure. Workwise, the
day was clearly a write-off. It was probably just as well
— if she started thinking about Patrick again she'd be
too shaky to paint.

"'Almost like a real date' was what you were going to
say, wasn't it?" Steve looked at her, amusement in those
knowing blue eyes. She smiled nervously, acknowledg-
ing how truly he'd spoken.

"So if it's nearly like a date, would you *nearly*
consider coming back to mine for . . . well, some more
coffee, maybe? It isn't far."

"Only if you've only *nearly* got honourable inten —
no, I mean *dishonourable* intentions towards me," Nell
told him, half-hearing herself as if from a distance.

"*What the hell are you saying here?*" an inner voice
— a spoilsport guardian angel — asked her. The angel
bossily accused her of flirting, told her to go home
immediately, drink tea, sober up and think about what
to cook Mimi for supper. Nell, in her head, slapped the
angel and told her to sod off, and, what seemed like
minutes later, found herself in Steve's second-floor
apartment, in a new and classy block close to the river,
nestled into a creamy leather sofa with her shoes off
and her feet curled beneath her. She felt comfortably
woozy, and while Steve was in the kitchen making
peppermint tea, had been close to falling asleep. Now

199

she reached across to pick up her cup from the leather-padded surface of the table in front of her.

"That's a very strange piece of furniture," she commented. It had a black leather top and bars all around it instead of legs. It reminded her of prison windows.

"It's a sort of puppy cage," he told her, showing her a door at one end that opened. "And no, I haven't got a dog."

"Well no, you wouldn't, in a flat, I suppose. Unless," she giggled, "you could have one of those handbag ones, but then you wouldn't need a cage for it. It would fit in a cat basket . . ." She could hear herself, rattling on pointlessly. The angel chimed in again, telling her to stop right now, it was time to go home. This time she listened.

"Steve, I should go — this has been lovely. Exactly what I needed, thanks so much. I should be able to pick up a cab on the high street." She stood up, swaying slightly. Steve was quick — he caught hold of her and steadied her.

"I'll drive you back. I can't have you wandering the streets."

Oh God, he thought she was as drunk as a skunk. It crossed Nell's mind that she really hadn't drunk that much — sure, she wouldn't have been safe or legal to drive, but it shouldn't have affected her that much. It must be down to the Patrick thing. Stress.

"That's really sweet of you," she said. "But . . . before I go you must show me what security arrangements you've got here. I'm so hoping to find that all the stuff you teach us doesn't actually apply to you. I bet you haven't really got a spyhole on your bedroom door!" The angel tried to tell her something else here . . . but she waved it away.

Steve took her hand and led her into the corridor, then into a large, dark-walled bedroom, pointing out the Banham lock, a bolt and the spyhole.

"Man colours," Nell commented, looking at the deep magenta walls, the chocolate bed-coverings, plum suede cushions. "Not sure about that leather headboard."

"Oh thanks! I bring you here to show you my locks — which you have to admit makes a change from etchings — and you diss my decor!"

"Well . . . it looks weird. How unusual to have those studs round it. And what are those metal D-rings for? Are they to hang your police-issue torch collection from? Or handcuffs? Oh . . . you've actually got some! How amazing . . . are those police-issue too?"

For there were a set of them, scarily real, sitting on the table beside the bed, exactly where you'd normally expect to find an alarm clock and a book. Well, she thought, he must have loads of things like that . . . being an ex-detective.

Steve pulled her hand and led her back into the hallway. Nell, caught off balance, felt her elbow painfully nudging a cupboard door which swung open, revealing a row of hooks on the door's inside from which hung an array of truncheons, black leather whips (arranged in size order), a riding crop and a selection of silky ropes. The display reminded her of her late father's shed in which he'd hung all his hammers and chisels so neatly, and in a similarly grouped size-order pattern.

"Oh! How . . . um . . . tidy," Nell giggled.

"*Out of here. Now,*" ordered the angel.

"Mum . . . wake up! Why are you asleep? Sorry I'm late, we had play rehearsal and my mobile needs charging so I couldn't call. What are you doing? Are you ill or something?"

Nell opened her eyes and saw Mimi standing over her, looking puzzled. "Mum? You look *well* weird. Kind of messy. Have you got a headache?"

Something told Nell that "messy" wasn't a look Mimi approved of. She was surely right. Nell sat up on the sofa and smoothed her crumpled skirt down. Her foot, which had been underneath her, had gone numb. "Mimi? Oh God, it's nearly dark. What time is it?"

"Six o'clock. Are we having proper food tonight? I'm starving."

Nell yawned. Mimi's guess was right — she *did* have a headache. A blinder. Bits of the day began to reassemble themselves in her slowly waking brain. The wine. The handcuffs. The leather gadgets. Then Patrick's letter. Its arrival seemed an awfully long, long time ago.

Nell's mouth felt parched. She got up and followed Mimi into the kitchen to get some water. Even from the back, Nell could sense the expression of deep disapproval on her daughter's face. Mothers weren't supposed to be found asleep on the sofa, headachy, hung-over and dishevelled.

"I'll see what's in the fridge," she told Mimi. "There's a lot of leftover chicken — I'll do a risotto. Fancy that?"

"S'pose so. I suppose that in your state I should be glad you can cook anything at all. You're *drunk*."

"No. I'm not, actually," Nell corrected her, running her hands through her tangled hair. God, she must look like death. She certainly felt like it. "I *was* drunk. A bit. Now I'm just mightily hung-over."

"Oh — and that's better, is it? Some kind of big improvement?"

"I didn't say it was better," Nell told her as she took a pack of rice out of the cupboard. "It's just more accurate. I went out for lunch with . . . a friend. It's no big deal. I haven't been sitting around here on my own drinking, if that's what you're worried about."

"No. I wasn't worried." Mimi yawned, picking up the pile of unopened mail that Nell had abandoned. Patrick's letter was safely stashed in the box with his others. Nell didn't think she'd be looking at it again any time soon. Perhaps it was time to throw out the whole lot of them. Alex would have said that was long overdue. She almost felt like phoning him, telling him that the Patrick book that he'd said would always be an open one had slammed shut, very very hard.

"Anything interesting in the post?" Mimi said, flicking through the envelopes.

"No." Nell washed her hands, then started chopping an onion. "Nothing important."

CHAPTER
TWELVE

Midnight Rambler
(Rolling Stones)

"Can you get out of the house extra early one day soon?" Joel asked Mimi as they sat on the bench outside Tesco Metro before school.

"I suppose." Mimi pulled a face. "But that would also mean getting *up* early. I'm not very good at that."

She could do it perfectly easily, especially now it was light quite early. If he'd asked her in January, it might have been different. It would have been a test: do I love him enough to leave my lovely warm bed when it's not even light?

All the same, she was savouring the look of wanting on Joel's face. She loved it that he asked her to do things like this. It was like having a secret life. And she deserved one. Why should her parents be the ones in this family who did stupid, immature things? That was what teenagers were for, surely. Your dad shouldn't take off to live with some *girl*. You shouldn't have to be finding the Nurofen for your own mum's hangover and *in the middle of the day*, for heaven's sake, or worrying about whether she was going out with really odd men. Mimi didn't like Steve. He looked at her funny.

"Come on, Mimi, for me? It's just a one-off." Joel looked so anxious, she thought, as if she just might not want him enough. Oh, but she did. She did, especially when he looked at her like that. She'd do anything, just about, when he looked like she was all he wanted in the world.

"Maybe. I'll let you know later," she conceded, treating him to a teasing smile. "But what's it for? Will I need money? I haven't got that much." And what she had was soon to be on its way into Topshop's till in exchange for a cute dress and some strappy wedges.

"Bring what you can. And . . . can you tell your mum you've got something on after school? We'll be really late back. It's a long way."

"Another train trip?" she giggled. "I don't believe it! Can't we stow away on a big ship to America or something instead?"

"Do you want to go there?" Oh, was he serious? If she cried a bit would he come up with a ticket? Or would he give her a lecture about how Brunel (and she'd done some very efficient Googling) had come up with the design for the SS *Great Britain*?

"Course I do. My dad's in New York, isn't he? I'm going in the summer, though, with Seb. Mum said we can. I sort of want to and I sort of don't. Dad promised *she* won't be there at the time, it'll be just him and Seb and me, but I bet she gets in on it somehow."

Joel took a pack of mints out of his pocket and offered them to her. She took one, even though they were the really strong sort that made her go breathless.

"She must want to meet you," he said. "Does she have a name?"

She gave him a sharp look. Was he ripping the piss? He didn't seem to be — he just looked like it was a reasonable question.

"She's called *Cherisse*. Minging name, no?"

Joel laughed. "Wow. Nice one!"

"Er . . . not! You know . . . maybe I'd want to meet her one day, but she's not my *family*; I don't want to meet her and have her think that just cos I say hi and have the manners not to hit her, that means it's OK. It's like she's trying too hard, already. You know what she did? On Sunday I opened an email from Dad and it wasn't from him, it was *her*! Can you believe that? And it wasn't a new one; she'd pressed Reply to something I'd sent, which means she'd been reading my private stuff — I'd asked him about my Amazon account and was he still paying it. There she was, all like: '*Hiiii*', all American and chirpy." Mimi laughed. "She was, you know. Have you been to America, Joel?"

"Yeah, fly-drive holiday, Florida. Nightmare for parents, fun for us," Joel said, smiling at faraway memories.

"Right, well, you know how the waitresses all go? Like, all singy-songy and trying too hard, it's, '*Hi guys I wanna welcome you to Bart's Restaurant my name is Cindy I'll be your waitress for today can I get yous all something from the bar please go visit our delectable salad cart.'* Well, she was like that. Like it was a script."

"She said all *that*? And didn't you say she was called Cherisse?" Mimi closed her eyes and sighed. Sometimes, boys were just so *literal*.

"No, of course she didn't, idiot!" She punched his arm. "She said something like, '*Hi I'm Cherisse and I'd like to say hello here and maybe get to know you, so please email me and do you want fries with that?'* No, not the last bit. That, Joel, was a joke. Anyway, I just wish she hadn't used Dad's address. She'd gatecrashed our thread and read all my private stuff. Made me hate her."

"And all she was doing was trying for the opposite."

"Yeah. Failing badly then."

"So one day soon? I want to take you to the seaside." Joel slid his arm round Mimi and nuzzled her neck softly.

"The sea? Mmm. Candyfloss and chips. Excellent. Just let me know which day and I'll tell Mum there's a play rehearsal after school. No problem."

Alvin was supposed to be awake. This afternoon's outing was meant to be a treat for him. Instead he was head-back in the buggy, pudgy little nose pointed skywards and his eyes firmly shut. His breath was huffy like an old man's, and in spite of being directly beneath Heathrow's landing flight path he wasn't showing any signs of wanting to return to reality on this warm afternoon in Syon Park.

"I could prod him, I suppose. But then he'd wake up in a state and none of us would have any fun," Kate was saying as she and Nell took their time strolling from Nell's car towards the Aquatic Experience building, where lived a wildlife collection that was surreally exotic for south-west London.

"Let's go round to the pond-dipping section and sit in the sun for a bit," Nell suggested. "A breeze on his face might do the trick. And the squawking of the parakeets." On cue, a flock of them swooped overhead, screeching, landing in a beech tree.

"He's used to those. They're in our garden all the time, nicking the blossom, the buggers. They need culling."

Kate wheeled the buggy past the circular pond where a couple of mallards swam, watched by a big black and white cat, past the cage from which Ossie the Siberian owl glared moodily, and round to where an excited crowd of primary-school children were wielding fishing nets and plastic boxes and trying to catch examples of pond life for identification.

Kate and Nell chose a bench out of range of the wet, flicking nets and swathes of blanket weed that the children were hurling at each other. No one seemed to be in charge; a young woman who could have been a teacher, but who looked more like a terrified teenager, was concentrating on the finds of a small group of easy, studious pupils and their neat array of netted bugs. Nell didn't blame her for keeping out of the way. She'd have done the same. Any pond life with a brain cell would do well to consider choosing a big pebble to hide under until this crew left.

"Poor tadpoles," she commented, watching a boy holding one up by its tail while his classmates squealed and laughed. "They must be a very long-suffering lot to survive here." The boy threw the creature at one of the girls, who screamed and ran.

"Oy you!" Nell shouted to the child, just about managing not to add "you little shit". "Treat the animals with respect!" The boy gave her a look that was way too old for his years and went chasing after the squealing girl.

"I suppose Alvin will be doing that in a few years," Kate said, looking round and glaring at the oblivious keeper of the unruly mob. "He'll be a holy bloody terror. In the garden the other day, he'd put together a little collection of snails — got them all lined up, really neatly, about thirty of them. They looked like a solitaire board, you know — the real sort where you had marbles, not solitaire the card game. And I thought, aah, he's fond of animals; that's so sweet, maybe one day, twenty years from now, I'll be watching him presenting a wildlife telly show and remembering this moment. And the next thing, there's this crunching sound and he's laughing like a demon and I go and look and he's stamped on every last innocent one of them, loving the sound of the shells crushing."

"I could tell you it's just a phase," Nell said, looking at the cherubic just-waking face of the snail-murderer, "but you've been there twice already, you know." Alvin yawned, stretched his hands out towards the group of children who were now trying to catch a dragonfly in their fishing nets. He looked as if he'd love to join the bad kids.

"The other two didn't do things like that. They wouldn't have had the nerve or the imagination. Maybe it's partly because this time round I don't give him the attention. Too old, too tired, too jaded. Blame the mother, as ever. Nothing new there."

"Hey, he's awake now. Let's go and show him the crocodiles," Nell said. "See if he fancies his chances stamping on those."

They went round to the front of the building, paid the entrance fee and were given small pots of food for the koi carp, then went in through plastic swing doors, almost knocked over by the steamy jungle heat inside. It was other-worldly: the light was low, thick tendrils of damp creeper hung from the ceiling, monkey cackles sounded, there was a lazy swoosh from waterfalls and an earthy, reptilian scent. And all this, Nell reminded herself, in a worryingly rickety prefab, only three miles from Heathrow.

"I don't give Mimi the attention she needs either," Nell told Kate. "I've been distracted and weird since I got Patrick's letter, and she looks at me as if she thinks I'm losing the plot. I'm not really surprised. I got a bit pissed when I had lunch with Steve and she came home from school and found me asleep on the sofa in the middle of the afternoon. I cried last night for twenty whole minutes over some stupid thing that happened on *EastEnders*. And over supper last night I asked her

210

if she thought I should try emailing James May off *Top Gear* and asking him out."

"James May? Do you fancy him?" Kate asked, looking foxed.

"Yes, of course I do — he's very tasty in that dishevelled, don't-care way! You should be pleased — you keep saying I need a new man. Not that he'd look twice at me, but even thinking about it is a start, you've got to admit. But poor Mimi, she's being the grown-up and she shouldn't have to at fifteen. She keeps looking at me as if she really disapproves. It's so unnerving."

She knelt beside Alvin's buggy and pointed through the glass wall. "Look, Alvin, look at the crocodile — he's called Elvis. Isn't he lovely?" Alvin blinked at the long, olive-coloured creature which was safely behind floor-to-ceiling glass, lying on a slab of rock in the centre of his pond, surrounded by lush foliage. Beneath the water, close to the wall's edge, giant catfish were swimming around, along with another, far bigger crocodile which was — according to the sign on the wall — called Houdini. Nell didn't want to speculate on how he got his name, and hoped there was no chance of him showing them why he'd been given it. Houdini swam closer and gave them a close-up view of his terrifying teeth. Alvin pointed at him, shouted "tummies" at the fish, laughing at their pale silvery undersides as they swam into the glass and turned, rolling idly away.

"Wow — impressive creature, that croc," Nell said, backing away as Houdini swam so close he was nose to nose through the glass with Alvin.

Kate giggled. "I wouldn't fancy his chances against my boy. Maybe you should bring Mimi here for a bit of mother-daughter bonding. No, second thoughts, she'd surely prefer a Topshop gift voucher. That might take the 'could do better' school-report-look off her pretty little face."

"Too right. And I *will* do better," Nell laughed. "Yep, that's me: I'll get right back to whatever kind of normal it is when your husband's gone off with a young American slapper and the only man who fancies you keeps a cupboard full of S&M gear in his hallway, but, hey, I've finished the vegetables and I've got an artist's impression of a holiday complex in the Cotswolds to do next. It's so boring, but it's architectural and complicated enough that I won't be able to think of anything else while I'm doing it."

"So — you've thrown that letter from your nasty ex away, haven't you?"

"Er . . . no. I was thinking . . ." Nell walked on through the tangle of trailing lianas towards the python pit. It possibly wasn't the best moment, she thought, from Alvin's point of view, as one of the Aquatic Experience assistants was dangling a dead rat from a stick in the direction of one of the snakes.

"Shall we move on to the turtle pond so this doesn't blight his life?" Nell whispered to Kate, anxious about the effect on the child of seeing what looked like a cuddly toy being slowly devoured by a massive python. If he could stamp on snails, it was anyone's horrible guess what he might do to any future pet gerbil if he watched much more of this.

212

"No, look — he loves it." Alvin's eyes had gone wide with delight, watching the snake's huge mouth engulfing its lunch, inch by furry inch.

"Quite. That's what I'm worried about."

"No, it's fine, it's keeping him quiet. And don't panic, I'll keep a careful eye on any future furry pets we're ever daft enough to get." Kate then turned to confront Nell. "Now, you — don't you even think of saying you were planning to write back to that man after what he said! Have some dignity, woman!"

"Yes, but . . ."

"Yes but *nothing*! He's a *git*! You were together *five years* and he can't even scrape up enough respect for a barely human response? All he had to do was tell you *nicely* and *politely* that it's good to hear from you but no thanks, he'd rather not see you. It would be basic good manners. Legal action! Who the hell does he think he is, Madonna?"

Nell giggled. "Maybe I was just a crap shag!"

No you weren't, her inner voice told her. They shouldn't be talking about this. It made something painful stab at her soul. She would almost prefer to take her chances in Elvis's compound than have this conversation with Kate.

"It must have ended really badly," Kate said slyly, looking at Nell.

"It did — but not badly enough to deserve that. That's why I wanted to write again — let him know how hurt I feel."

"And then what? Suppose he sets his lawyers on you?"

"Yeah — maybe I'll end up with an ASBO. That'd go down well with Mimi, wouldn't it? The shame of it: ASBO Mum in Stalking Ban. I could be excluded for ever from Oxfordshire. Well, bring it on, Patrick, bring it on."

"Quite possibly." Kate sounded serious. "You'd definitely get at least a lawyer's warning shot. He sounds that kind of bastard."

"Oh, he never was a bastard, though, Kate; something really strange must have happened since. But I've thought of the lawyer one. I'd just write them an equally up-yours note, something like, *Dear Sirs, Thank you for your letter. I suggest you deal with Mr Sanders and his ludicrously pompous overreaction by telling him to fuck off. Yours faithfully.* You see? I can do ludicrously pompous too." She laughed. "It might be fun to see him in court, though. I wonder how he's looking these days? He was so beautiful. I can't imagine him any older, greyer, balder, fatter, whatever."

"Please tell me you're not serious," Kate said, pointing Alvin's buggy in the direction of the koi carp pond. He leaned out sideways, reluctant to lose sight of the fascinating python-and-rat scenario.

"OK, I'm not serious about court. I'd rather see him in a restaurant or a bar."

"Or in a bed," Kate said, wryly.

"No, not that. Not any more." And she meant it — if she'd had even the slightest secret for-old-times'-sake fantasy in that direction, he'd killed it.

"You never told me how it ended."

214

"Ah, the end . . ." Nell sighed. "It ended how these things always end. Tears and blame and all the angst that goes with it. I got pregnant."

"Well, you'd been together so long, how could that be such a disaster? These things happen." Kate unstrapped Alvin and let him out, holding his hand as he happily scattered the entire tub of fish-food pellets into the carp pond. The fish splashed and snapped and shoved each other aside to get at the food. Alvin giggled and pointed at them, slapping at the water and shouting "Silly fish!" Nell reached across and gripped the back of his jacket, tightly. The pond was very deep and dark.

"Oh, Patrick saw it as a disaster. He went berserk. He didn't ever want children, you see, not *ever*. He said I'd always known that was the deal, blamed me, all that."

"But men do change their minds. They all think that way when they're young. Sean did, and now look. Mind you, he was slightly amazed each time I said I was pregnant. Aren't they funny? Why is it always our fault? I sometimes wonder if they actually know how babies are made. We are merely flowers to them, mysteriously pollinated by bees."

"Patrick would never change. He had his reasons. I suppose deep down I assumed that one grown-up day he *might* change his mind, but it wasn't going to be *that* time. It came down to a simple choice — babies or him. And as it happened, this accidental baby didn't stick and I lost it about six weeks in, but the big damage was done and something else beside the baby had died between us. I went home to stay with my mother for a while to recover, and . . . well, she'd never liked Patrick really, always thought he was way too off the wall for me. She kept saying I'd be better with someone more *balanced*, that I'd always wish I'd had children and that I'd regret it years later. She gave me this scenario, that I'd get to fifty-something and have regrets, and that he'd leave me then and go off with someone young and new and have children after I no longer could. It was horrible. I was vulnerable: I'd lost a baby and I grieved for that and I thought, hey, you know, she's right: I will want them one day. And with Patrick it simply wouldn't be an option. So that was that."

"Didn't he fight to keep you?"

Nell laughed. "What, go all romantic, come and chuck stones at my window in the night and beg me to come back? No. He wasn't like that. If I said I didn't want to see him, he'd just take that as what I meant. He went into one of his depressions and stayed quiet for ages. And then, somehow, he just . . . slid out of my life and vanished."

"And Alex slid right into it."

"Eventually, after a year or two in which I behaved like a stupid slapper with one-nighters I can barely remember. But that's best forgotten! Yeah, Alex felt safe, easy, comfortable, reliable. Huh!" She tried to laugh but it sounded a bit like the little caged marmoset that Alvin was now studying closely.

"You know what?" Kate said, putting an arm round Nell.

216

"No — please don't say anything. I'm feeling wavery. All those schoolkids are just coming in here and I don't want to be crying like an idiot! They'll take me apart, especially tadpole boy."

"OK, I won't say anything about all that. It's just . . ."

"What?" Nell felt impatient. Just leave it now, Kate, she wanted to snap.

"You know when Alvin grows up?" Kate said. "And when people mention Elvis and expect you to know exactly who they're talking about?"

"Elvis will be very old history by then," Nell told her.

"Oh, he'll be remembered . . . except by Alvin and all the kids who visit this place. They won't be picturing some overweight singer in white spangly spandex, will they? Just some big, dozy crocodile."

"Bless. OK — let's go and do the difficult bit. I can see they're rounding people up for a show and tell. Let's go and stroke an iguana."

There was something about the pre-dawn hours that made you think far too clearly, in Nell's opinion. The clock beside her said three forty-five a.m., but her brain's activity-rating was more at the mid-morning level of powerful. What was that phrase, she wondered . . . something like "Don't get mad, get even"? She switched on the lamp beside her and sat up, pushing the cat off her feet. Pablo opened an eye and gave her a wary look, annoyed to be disturbed at the wrong time.

Bloody Patrick, Nell thought, pushing her tangled hair back from her face; why couldn't he be the relaxed, casual sort of person who said hey, let's have lunch and catch up? But the thing that was bugging her right now wasn't just his cold hostility. She'd done the hurt-and-angry stage and was now, in the middle of this night, wondering *why* he was still so angry with her. It couldn't be just about her . . . no one could sulk for over twenty years, surely. That cramped handwriting, the strange spacing, it just wasn't like him. Perhaps, she thought, it *wasn't* him. Suppose a jealous wife/girlfriend/boyfriend/enemy had got hold of her letter and had actually sent the reply instead of him? No . . . that would be ridiculous. And besides, it was too close to his writing, just . . . older, or something.

Nell pushed the duvet back and got out of bed. She wasn't going to get any sleep while she felt like this — her thoughts were going round and round in her head and getting mixed up with the excruciating half-dream she'd been having that involved being trapped, naked, in Steve's so-called puppy cage. There are, she thought, some very bizarre people out there. She didn't intend to stop going to the Stay Safe classes — there were only two more in the course anyway, but, having written a card to Steve and thanked him for lunch, she wasn't overkeen on having more one-to-one contact with him. Right now, what she needed was a cup of tea and a biscuit; that was the other downside of being awake for hours at the wrong time of night. Once your body woke up you got hungry and, in a jet-lagged kind of way, you needed the day to get going. How annoying it was that the rest of the population out there were sleeping peacefully as they were supposed to. Probably the only others pacing the floors of their own homes and waiting for the world to wake up had the excuse of small squalling babies.

In the kitchen, Nell switched on the kettle and took the HobNobs packet out of the cupboard. There were only two left. Mimi and Tess had been in after school, munching through the new pack and leaving only enough to show reasonable manners. They were like those women who drink almost a whole bottle of wine, but leave an inch in the bottom to kid themselves it was only a half-bottle. The awful evidence can then be dealt with the next day, when sobriety shows up the truth that there isn't enough left to get a budgie drunk, let alone go down well with a prawn sandwich at lunchtime, but all solvable with a personal promise that this was just a one-off and wouldn't ever happen again.

Nell hadn't given up on replying to Patrick. That was what had really been stopping her from getting back to sleep, the mental planning of a response. She'd sorted the tone (cutting yet wounded, *deeply* wounded), but needed to see it all written down to work out the order of what she wanted to say. It didn't have to be long and rambling, in fact the shorter and more concise the better. She could draft it out on a notepad, but really she wanted to play with it on her computer, and that was locked in the studio.

She went into the hallway, shoved her feet into her old Ugg boots and picked up Mimi's long, black, hooded coat from its usual place, flung over the post at the bottom of the stairs. She collected her keys from the kitchen table and unlocked the back door. The cat startled her, sliding out into the cold air and skimming his body under the coat against her legs, his warm tail on her bare skin making her tingle. The air in the garden was very soft and still at this time of the night. There was a chill and a silent tension that made her feel as if time wasn't ever going to move on from this moment. Nothing stirred, and with thick cloud cover there was barely any light other than a thin shaft from her kitchen window. All the nocturnal activity of animals, plants and insects seemed over for the night, and she felt she was intruding into a secret, suspended vacuum that came before the dawn.

With the hood of Mimi's coat pulled up against the cold air, Nell crossed the garden as silently as she could, reluctant to disturb so much as a breath of the air, unlocked the studio door and went inside. The computer was recharging on her desk and she reached down to the floor to unplug it, knowing the layout too well to need to switch on the light. Quickly, she pulled the door shut behind her, relocked it and made her way back towards the kitchen door.

"OK, give that to me! Now!"

Nell gasped as she was grabbed from behind by someone strong and overpowering who was trying to wrestle the computer from her. She immediately dropped it on the grass, relaxed against her attacker's body and heard a gratifyingly pained curse of "*Shit!*" as she scraped her boot down from below his knee. She then squeezed out from beneath his grip by wriggling downwards and backing him away in the way Steve had taught the class. He recovered, hissed, "No you fucking don't," and grabbed her right hand in his left. Somewhere inside her head, Nell wondered why she was finding it impossible to scream. She didn't seem to have the breath spare. Surely it wasn't a politely pathological fear of waking the entire street? It should be the one easy thing she could do to save her life, but it just wasn't happening. What she could do, though, was sidestep this man, twist his arm back and . . .

"*Fuck!* That *hurts!*" he shouted from down on the grass as she leaned on to his awkwardly skewed arm. Oh thank you, Steve, Nell thought, wondering where to go from here. This should be the point at which she did the screaming. Had she won yet? Who was this bastard?

"You sure picked the wrong house . . ." she began, knowing this wasn't the thing to do. She mustn't give him time to fight back. The back door was only steps away — she should be in there by now, forget the computer.

"Nell?" came a muffled voice.

"Huh? Who's that? Oh God — Ed!" Nell let go and Ed stood up, rubbing dew and grass from the front of a sweat-shirt that listed Led Zeppelin's US tour dates in 1973.

"Why are you in my garden?" she asked.

"Why are *you*?"

"God — I thought you were a burglar!" she told him.

"I thought *you* were! I was up and about — wandered into the kitchen and saw you through the window." He looked her up and down and laughed. "You must admit, you look the part. Big hooded coat, dark boots, stealthy creeping."

"I wasn't stealthily creeping!" She hit his arm and he flinched.

"Hey, no more violence!" he pleaded, hands raised in surrender. "You definitely won there. I'll think twice before challenging an intruder another time, that's for sure."

"Oh Ed, I'm so sorry. Look, come on in, let me make you a cup of tea. You can have the other biscuit. Mimi only left me two. In fact you can have both of them . . . you deserve it for being brave enough to come out and defend my property like that."

"Sure, even if it was only from yourself," he commented wryly, picking up the computer and following her into the warm kitchen. "And I should be apologizing to you for pouncing on you like that."

"Oh, I don't know," Nell said. "You can hardly go up to a villain and say, 'Excuse me, I hope you don't mind me asking, but I was wondering if you are up to *no good*.'"

And when Mimi came into the kitchen, rubbing sleep from her eyes, she found the two of them sitting at the table over mugs of tea, giggling together.

"Er . . . what's going on?" Mimi said. "And, God, Mum . . . er . . . like, *clothes*?"

"Oh Mimi! Sorry, baby, did we wake you?" Nell asked.

"Er . . . yes? And *Mum* . . . Both of you, you're not . . ."

"What?" Nell looked down at herself. She'd taken the big coat off and was down to an all-enveloping extra-long, extra-large T-shirt with a picture of Björk on

222

the front. She'd thought it went rather well with the Ugg boots.

Mimi ran the cold tap, hard, and filled a glass with water. "Mum, you're just not *decent*," she hissed.

"No. I'm probably not, entirely," Nell laughed. "But I'm decent *enough*; it'll do. OK?"

CHAPTER
THIRTEEN

Big Wheel
(Tori Amos)

"So that's one more thing I have to leave out of emails to Dad," Mimi grumbled to Tess as they walked across the bridge towards the shops. It was lunchtime — Mimi wanted to get a birthday present for Joel and needed Tess to help her find the right thing. What did boys of sixteen want? Girls of twenty-two, at a guess.

"I tell you, Mum's losing it, for sure. It's getting like Dad sends me one and says, tell me what's happening and that, and all I can say is, 'Hi Dad. I'm all right.' I wish he was back here. She was normal then."

It sounded disloyal. Her mum might have been "normal", but that had been normal as in not very happy. She might be strange, just now, but you couldn't say she looked all that miserable — just . . . manic.

"She's still not at the Carly's mum stage though, is she?" Tess tried to reassure her.

"She's not going around in a studded biker jacket and red patent stilettos with the Perspex heels." Mimi thought for a moment, remembering the time at Evie Mitchell's when Nell had been eyeing up the pink shoes. Well, at least she hadn't bought them . . . but she'd been thinking about it, definitely thinking. It was the next, dreadful stage. After that would come the little baby-doll smocks from Topshop and mad purple hair. She hoped she'd stop short at things with frills or a pierced lip, or tattoos. Mothers. What could you do?

"Last night she was hardly wearing *anything*. After that I couldn't sleep properly. I kept listening in case she and Ed-next-door started creeping up the stairs together," Mimi said, shuddering at the memory.

"And did they?" Tess asked, in a mildly interested tone that suggested it might be a perfectly normal thing to do. Mimi wondered which of them was out of line here. This was her *mum* they were talking about. Didn't Tess get it?

"No, thank God. And don't make me start thinking about sofa-activity possibilities, please."

She stopped walking and looked down at the river. Below her, there were several people working on the moored restaurant barge, putting up pink and white flags and hanging baskets of flowers. It must be for a wedding at the weekend, she presumed. Would she have something like that one day? Would some lovely man ever ask her to spend the rest of her life with him? She couldn't imagine anyone would. Did people really see more than a few months ahead? She definitely couldn't. Even the summer holidays seemed a faraway blur, and it was already nearly Easter.

"She had this big old T-shirt on and knickers — well, I suppose she did . . . I *hope*, but possibly not. She was being like she wouldn't care either way. And Ugg boots and bed hair, and that was it. *It!* She probably thought the look was all Kate Moss at Glastonbury but really she just looked half-naked. And she's sitting there in the kitchen with him from next door, not the old one, the hippie one with the hair . . . Oh God." Mimi shook her head hard, trying to erase the image. "I really thought they'd like, been, you know . . . and had got up for a cup of tea before he went home or something. Do old people do the sex stuff? When do they stop? And, if they *do* have to do it, they really should keep it well away from us. I'm at an impressionable age."

She turned away from the sight of all these people working so hard on someone's happiest day, and the two of them carried on walking into the town. It was busy — the pavement was clogged with cross mothers with double buggies and small whiny children overtired from a busy morning at preschool.

"Don't even go there," Tess giggled. "My mum and dad only have to get close to each other on the sofa and I'm like, *stop it, now.* Sex is only acceptable when it's young and beautiful people like us. Except we haven't done it. I knew there was a catch."

"No . . . well . . ." Mimi looked around. You couldn't be too careful. Half the school would probably know by the next day if you so much as whispered anything secret in any part of this place. If Polly Mitchell heard what she was about to tell Tess, she'd probably blackmail her for months.

"What do you mean, 'no, well'? Mimi . . . you haven't, have you? With Joel? *When?*" Tess looked surprisingly distraught. Mimi had second thoughts about telling her, deciding to backtrack and keep her half-formed plans to herself for now.

"No I haven't! Yet. But I was thinking, maybe sometime . . . soon. But only maybe. You know? We really like each other, Tess. And . . . he says he's got special plans for Friday night." It sounded so lame. And when Tess asked her, she'd have to admit that so far they hadn't done any more than full-on snogging. It could be a big leap, from that to the whole way. She didn't even know how to do the bits that came in between. Did Joel? And suppose there was stuff that everyone but her did and she didn't know and he looked at her in a *don't you even know THAT?* kind of way. No, that wouldn't happen. He was such a sweet one — he'd be fine.

"You could give it to him for his birthday," Tess said grumpily. "And if you decide you wanna do that, we could just go home right now. Then we don't have to trail round the shops looking for some old tat for him. Just get him a card and make it into a gift voucher, why don't you? You could write 'IOU Mimi's virginity. A one-off special offer.' Every boy's wet dream."

Mimi laughed and pulled her arm. "Tess! Whassup, babe? Why are you being like this?" They were now outside Gap. Mimi had a quick look inside, just in case her mother (or Tess's) was in there. Or worse, Polly Mitchell and her slapper posse. If the posse heard the word "virginity" being used out loud, she and Tess would never hear the end of it. At school there were girls who looked down on you if you'd lost it, and girls who looked down on you if you hadn't. It was better not to mention all that. And "virginity" was a funny word, she thought. So ridiculously like it was from another age, like "petticoat" and ... and ... "sanitary".

"It's nothing. You're a bit young, that's all — a few months off legal. It's that conversation all over again like we had before, on your bed. Nothing's changed, has it, you know, since ... that time? You're just the same, you're still not sure what you want really, and if you're not sure, then you shouldn't do anything." Tess was looking at the passing traffic, avoiding Mimi's eyes.

Mimi thought back. Mostly what she could recall from that night was the all-over electric feeling of kissing Tess, of savouring her tongue with her own and how too-shockingly good it felt. She couldn't at all remember what they'd talked about, but the scent of nail varnish was in the mix somewhere, with the warmth of Tess's silky Marmite hair twined in her fingers and their soft bodies pressed together.

"No. I'm not the same," she said, sliding her hand into Tess's and pulling her close.

"Mimi!" Tess glared at her. "We're in the middle of the town? Like, anyone could be watching?" She pulled her hand away from Mimi's, eyes wide with shock.

"I was only going to hold your hand, Tess. I wasn't, like, going to snog you up against the shop window or anything!" Mimi yelled. Now people were looking. A man cleaning the windows next door at Oasis yelled, "Go for it, girls, don't mind me!" Two old ladies with wheeled shopping bags turned and gave them the big glare.

228

"Oh, weren't you? Well that's a big disappointment! Not!" They looked at each other and started giggling, heading into the sort of hysteria that was going to make their insides ache. This was better, thought Mimi, trying to get her breath and stumbling around on the pavement with Tess while they shrieked and howled helplessly and got in the way of people trying to walk by. It meant they didn't have to talk about this for a while. Perhaps they never would have to again.

"Tess?" Eventually Mimi needed to stop laughing long enough to get an essential question out.

"Yeah, what?" Tess spluttered. "I don't even want to guess what you're going to ask me . . ." And she went off into a fit of giggles again.

"No, really, Tess, listen . . . On Friday Joel wants me to go out somewhere after school. I don't know where it is because he won't tell me, so I don't know what time I'll be back and . . . can I, like, tell my mum I'll be at yours?"

Tess stopped laughing and frowned. "Why can't you just tell her you're going out with Joel?"

Mimi looked across the road, focusing on the window display in Monsoon. "Um . . . I dunno. Sometimes you just want to be sort of . . . private. I don't want her asking questions and she hates it when I say I don't exactly know where I'll be, even though I've got my mobile. It'd be easier if she thought I was with you. It's just in case." Did it need spelling out?

"I'm not stupid, Mimi." Tess glared at her. "It's in case you do something you don't want to have to tell her about when she *does* ask you questions. What kind of mother do you think you've got? Do you really think she'd want full details?"

"I don't know," Mimi muttered glumly. "I used to, but she's weird and different now. I don't know what she might say to me or want to know. Or what she might *not* want to know."

"OK then. I'll cover for you this time." Tess hit Mimi hard on the arm and ran off, squealing, "But after you've done whatever you do with Joel, I'll make you answer all *my* questions instead!"

"You look different," Charles told Ed. "Older, younger, I don't know. Different, anyway."

"Spring, that's all," Ed replied. "Just warm air and longer days. Spring lifts the spirits. Or did you mean it in a negative way?"

"Well, if I did I could hardly say so, now that you've obviously taken it as a compliment," Charles said, sniffily. Ed looked at him, wondering why he was being so waspish. Was this a sign of grumpy-old-man territory?

"So it wasn't, then?" Ed teased.

"It was just an observation," Charles told him. "It meant nothing either way, though you have obviously chosen your own interpretation."

They were out on the terrace with an early lunch (Marks & Spencer chicken Caesar salad), watching the birds. A blackbird, fearing for its nest, was sitting on the fence making the kind of furious warning racket that told them Nell's cat was somewhere around.

230

"Bloody cats," Charles commented. "They all need shooting. Is it Korea where they eat them? Or China? Wherever it is, they've got the right idea."

"I don't think anyone eats cats," Ed told him. "But I could be wrong. I know they get skinned, alive and horribly, somewhere. You wouldn't wish that on any creature."

"I expect they taste like chicken, or maybe like lamb. No, not like lamb, because cats are meat-eaters. They'd be more gamey than chicken, wouldn't you say? Possibly like pheasant, then. Well-hung pheasant. And stringy. There's not usually a lot of fat on a cat. They'd be tough, I'd imagine, to eat. They'd need long, slow cooking. Casseroled for several hours with shallots and bacon and tomatoes could work, and plenty of thyme, a bay leaf and some decent claret in there too."

It was Charles's afternoon for his Classical Civilization class. Ed guessed he only went so that he could pounce on any mistakes the class tutor might make. Charles, all-round scholar and widely read bibliophile, could outwit any upstart teacher-type presumptuous enough to think they knew anything at all about the political intrigues of Ancient Rome. Ed wouldn't have minded an excuse to be in the room, spotting the other class members exchanging glances as the know-all geek with the half-moon glasses chipped in yet again with an alternative opinion on the events leading up to the downfall of Nero.

"What are you doing after this? Haven't you got some kind of meeting?" Charles asked.

"Yep. About marking A-level papers. It's just a refresher — I went to the one last year and it'll be much the same, but they like you to make the effort. I'll see you later — I'll be back in time for supper. It won't be cat, though."

The District Line platforms at Richmond were deserted, which meant a train must have just gone and another one, even if it arrived in the next few minutes, wouldn't leave for ages, this being a terminus. Nell muttered "Bugger" to herself. She was supposed to be meeting her agent in Kensington and would now be late. She started to walk further down the platform to wait on a bench and her foot slipped on half a crust of soggy bread. She said "Bugger" again, but not quite quietly enough, and earned a glare from the bird woman, who was throwing chunks of bread and handfuls of corn to the pigeons from a super-size bag on wheels.

Which was more anti-social, Nell wondered, glaring back, a murmured curse or the wilful fattening-up of a thousand feathered vermin? She'd seen the woman before. She was a well-known local character who seemed to be everywhere, trundling her sack of corn and loaves of stale bread and distributing them wherever pigeons gathered. They probably followed her like the Pied Piper's rats by now, knowing a soft touch when they saw one.

"At the risk of being karate-chopped to the floor, hello, Nell, and could the old bat get an ASBO for doing that?" a voice whispered in her ear, startling her.

232

For a moment she thought of Patrick and his legal-action threat, and imagined she was being followed by his lawyers. She hadn't yet written her letter to him. The night-time events in her garden had lightened her mood to the point where the fury was now downgraded, in the manner of stormy weather on the Beaufort scale, from "anguished outrage" to "disappointment". Today, she hadn't had time to think about it. Patrick could wait.

"Ed! Oh, hi! An ASBO for feeding pigeons? I expect so — even if it's only on grounds of littering. It would take a braver woman than me to challenge that woman, though," Nell told him, moving the two of them further along the platform, safely away from the swooping pigeon flock. "She's half-barking and comes out with a tirade of abuse if you dare suggest maybe they're undeserving, disease-ridden pests. In her opinion, it's people who are."

"Well, in some cases, I suppose she's not wrong. I expect she sees it as her mission in life; somewhere between the bird woman in *Mary Poppins* and St Francis. Where are you off to? Somewhere fun?"

"Not really, I've got a meeting near Gloucester Road with my agent about some more work. I need to up the amount I do if I'm going to keep the house. The mortgage is all paid off but the bills don't get any smaller. I sometimes think we should move, but I can't face the hassle. I'd rather see if I can keep the place going — otherwise I'll feel that Alex has kind of . . . well, won, I suppose. What about you? A fun date with a foxy sort?"

Nell and Ed sat on a graffiti-scribbled bench, well out of the way of the pigeon woman, facing a poster advertising free chlamydia tests for under-25s. "Not for *you*," the poster seemed to be telling her. "*You're* way past having the kind of frenzied sex life where you might catch something. *You're* way past having one *at all*." Great, she thought — remind me, why don't you, that I'm heading fast for a celibate lifetime of sensible knickers and old cronedom.

"Hardly! I've got a catch-up session on exam-marking techniques somewhere near Paddington. I don't know why they bother. It's the same old pep talk every year and soon they won't need any more than a basic computer to sort out the grades. It'll be nothing more demanding than some random multiple-choice stuff, like: Duncan was murdered because: a) he had it coming; b) Macbeth fancied himself in a big crown; c) Lady Macbeth was a bit pre-menstrual and told her old man to show her what he was made of."

"Tricky! If you got a chance for that good old word 'discuss', I'd go for a). I know I'd be wrong, but over six sides of lined A4 I could make it really, really convincing."

Ed looked at her admiringly. "I don't doubt it. But soon there won't be any room for a well-argued case. Depressing, isn't it? Everything's got to be cut and dried and incontrovertible."

"Like biscuits," Nell said, vaguely.

"*Biscuits?*" Ed laughed. "What have biscuits got to do with it?"

"Oh nothing, really. I was just thinking last week, when I was eating four in a row, the way you do when you need a sugar-fix cheer-up, how guilty you're now supposed to feel about something that used to be just a harmless little snack, and I quite enjoyed that feeling. It was just a pleasant little dose of sin, innocent — if that's not a contradiction. But then I read on the side of the pack that they were low in salt, full of fibre and only two per cent sugar, and I suddenly didn't want them at all. Because if I'm going to have something that's supposed to be bad for me, I don't want the luscious guilty edge taken off it by the nutrition police." She glanced up the line to see if the signal had changed. "Where is this train? Shouldn't there be one here by now?"

As if on cue, a muffled voice coughed down the PA system and, sounding barely awake through boredom, announced that the District Line would be suspended for several hours because of an "incident" on the line at Turnham Green.

"Ah! Result! That means I don't have to go." Ed was gleeful. "Not that I don't feel sorry for any poor desperate sod who's fallen or jumped under a train."

Nell sent up a quick prayer for any possible suicide's soul. "Me too. But hey, let's hope it was really only a bomb scare." The two of them got up and walked back towards the station steps. The pigeon woman glared at them and chucked a handful of bread in their direction.

"No thanks, I prefer stoneground!" Ed called to her, then said to Nell, "But definitely not a real bomb. No bomb, no one jumping."

It wasn't even half in the spirit of making an effort to get to where they were supposed to be going by alternative means that ten minutes later Ed and Nell were on the fast train to Waterloo, with both their meetings cancelled and without a plan as to how they were going to spend this unexpected free time. If Nell had had to analyse how they came to be on this train rather than on the way home, she would have found it hard to decide whether to blame a fifty-strong school party hurtling down the steps that led to their exit, or the fact that bus travel to their original destinations would have involved a long, complicated trip towards central London. Whichever it was, the Waterloo-bound train was just pulling into the station and they were close enough to catch it without making any effort.

"This is fun," Nell said as they watched the allotments of North Sheen whiz by. "I don't know where we're going but I love this adventure feeling. It's like when I was a teenager and I used to hitch to places. I knew it was dangerous but it was worth it, just for the feeling that nobody knew where I was. And it shouldn't only be schoolkids who get to skive, should it? I know that being grown-ups we can more or less go where we want, when we want, but sometimes it feels great being *not* where you're supposed to be."

"And we've each got an excuse, an alibi," Ed added. "In fact, two — one for the people we're supposed to be seeing and one for those back home who might need to know where we are. It couldn't be better. Where shall we go? Did you bring your passport?"

"To go to Paris? Sadly I didn't."

"Never mind, next time."

"Hmm. Sounds good, but will planning it kill the spontaneity?"

"It depends — you could decide that bringing your passport along simply extends the range of possibilities rather than making Paris a foregone. And if you really want to keep guessing, there's always Lille or Brussels for that last-minute decision."

Nell smiled, thinking how lovely a slow, delicious lunch at the Café de Flore would be with Ed. They could play at being Simone and Jean-Paul.

At Clapham, a group of Italian students got on the train. The three boys and two girls hung around by the doors, even though there were plenty of spare seats. Nell watched the smaller of the girls as she worked her charm on the boys, teasing them for her favours. Her skirt was tiny and she swung around the centre pole between the doors, never still, seemingly swaying about in time to her iPod but watching slyly as the boys jostled and joked and kept their eyes focused on her legs. Soon she had singled out the best-looking one, although the others were still hopefully including her in their banter. The chosen one responded to her as he was meant to, upgrading from the chat, grabbing playfully at her long hair as she twisted away from him around the pole. She kept her graceful balance easily as the train lurched, always just out of his reach. Then he was touching the skin on her neck, trying to still her, trapping her hand on the pole and leaving his there, over hers, claiming her.

The other boys visibly backed away, defeated, sullen but not yet willing to start again on the taller girl, who now leaned silent against the doorside panel, waiting for the fallout. Oh, the awful competition of lust, Nell thought. Why would anyone who'd been bruised by it ever want to enter that fray again?

"Kate gave me this book when Alex left, called *After He's Gone*," she told Ed. "It's about dealing with the aftermath of divorce."

Ed laughed. "The title sounds more like it's for after someone's died, if you don't mind me saying."

"It's probably not dissimilar — for some the misery must be even worse, really. If someone who loved you has died, it's terrible, but at least they *did* love you. You've got that, even if it's not a huge comfort till much later. With being left — well, you haven't. As you know."

"When Alicia left me it was a relief all round, frankly," Ed told her. "She was a natural-born bolter, practically scratching her way out of the door from day one. She's on her fifth now, Tamsin says. Tell me about this book."

"Well, one of its suggestions is that to lighten the general misery, you should do one thing every day that makes you feel specially good. It doesn't have to be anything big; some women get a kick out of going to Tesco in their funkiest shoes that they'd usually only wear to a party. Or putting turquoise streaks in their hair, or eating doughnuts and sod the diet. Any small thing to get you through a day — like getting on a train on a whim, like we just have. What would you choose?"

Ed thought for a moment. "I quite like the odd sneaky cigarette in the garden," he said. "A crafty Gitane after a rubbish day can do it for me. Or reading one of the tabloids from cover to cover — one I've bought, not just found covered in someone else's ketchup in the college canteen. It makes a jolly change from the *Guardian*." Ed glanced out of the window as the London Eye came into view. The train had slowed now, approaching Waterloo.

"There goes our train," Nell commented, watching a Eurostar slowly pulling out from its platform.

"Ah well . . . Paris another time." Ed smiled. "Never mind — for today I've had a better idea . . ."

This early in the season and on a weekday, there was hardly any queue for the London Eye. Nell and Ed bought their tickets, were patted and scanned for weapons and explosives and in no time were being ushered towards the constantly moving pods. They waited their turn to board for what was rather unnervingly described as a "flight", and Nell looked down at the scarily insubstantial netting, there to prevent any accidental plunging into the Thames. A couple dithering with small children behind her and Ed meant that they were the only two in their capsule, and the door closed behind them.

"Hey, that's lucky — you have to pay a fortune to book this space to yourself!" Ed said. "We should have brought champagne with us, made out it was an anniversary or something."

"Ah yes, but if we'd done that, it would have turned out differently. We'd be sharing it with six Japanese tourists and a drunken hen party from Newcastle."

"And two of those would feel sick with vertigo. You don't get vertigo, do you? Have you been on this before?" Ed looked nervous, possibly picturing her becoming faint and panic-stricken. He was eyeing the door as if to check it couldn't be prised open by a hysterical screamer when they were two hundred feet up in the sky.

Nell laughed. "No and no!" she told him, though as they were now on a level with the roof of the derelict Shell building, she wasn't so sure about the first "no". There was something mildly unnerving about the way the glass walls of the capsule curved at the bottom, as they became part of the floor.

The day was a clear, sunny one. They could easily see the arch of Wembley stadium, the slaty tower blocks of the Roehampton Estate, the radio mast at Crystal Palace, Hampstead Heath. St Paul's, the Gherkin, Canary Wharf all looked squashed together as if there was no real distance between them, and on the other side of the river, quite close, there were intriguing glimpses of the hidden inner quadrangles of the Houses of Parliament and into the Treasury.

"We must do that another time," Ed said, indicating the parliament buildings. "We should go in and see what they all talk about. I've always meant to."

Nell watched a tourist boat turning round at Westminster pier. Did he really mean they should go out again, properly, not just on this kind of daft, spontaneous whim? Paris and parliament? It was close to . . . Well — Kate would get excited and call it dating. The "D" word that she hadn't wanted to think about when she was with Steve. But no. It wasn't that, they were just friends and neighbours with nothing better to do. And in spite of being the only people in the pod it wasn't remotely "romantic". It was almost as if, having been pushed in here alone together, they were keeping a polite, no-complications distance. Nell tried to imagine how it would have been if, instead of being so icily hostile, Patrick had agreed to meet her, and if it were him she was with in this capsule instead of Ed. Would he have been laughingly scornful about her choice of rendezvous, mocked her for choosing something so cheesy? Or would he have raved about the scale of the view, the colour blocks of London's most distant vistas? She couldn't even begin to guess, not after all this time. Perhaps they wouldn't have had anything at all to talk about. Or possibly she wouldn't have been able to stop looking at him, silently trying to find the clues to the former Patrick inside the carapace of someone so much older, so lived-in, so . . . well, the word now could only be . . . *unknown*.

As the last minutes of the circuit passed, Nell sat on the long padded seat in the centre of the capsule and wondered if all such long, leather-covered benches would forever remind her of Steve's peculiar puppy-cage table. She pushed the thought out of her mind and instead watched the railway far beneath her, a layout that looked like the kind of train set her own father

241

would have dreamed of, with an endless dance sequence of trains going in and out of Waterloo station.

The wheel had almost turned its circle and a voice that sounded weirdly electronic told them to keep clear of the doors. Ed stepped out first on to the pier and took Nell's hand as she left the moving capsule. It was only as they entered the crowded, rush-hour chaos of Waterloo that she realized she still had her hand in his. Ahead of them on the station concourse were the five Italian students again, and the alpha boy who had earlier pursued the smaller girl was now walking with his arm round the taller one. They looked very happy together, very comfortable and relaxed, as if this had always been the way it was going to be. How had that happened, Nell wondered, had both sensed they would sooner or later get together, if they simply waited for their time to come? What a strange thing love was.

CHAPTER
FOURTEEN

Angels With Dirty Faces (Sugababes)

"Where are you going? Are you going out *again*?" Mimi was curled up in a corner of the sofa in a nest of cushions, watching as Nell dashed around finding her car keys, her coat, her bag. Andréa had been in cleaning that morning and she had her own favourite places for putting keys that she found lying around: sometimes on top of the microwave in the kitchen, sometimes on the piano, even on the stairs — anywhere but the hook in the hallway where Nell kept them.

"I told you this morning, it's my safety class — put off from Tuesday. Look, it's only a couple of hours. Unless . . ." Nell hesitated, wondering if putting Mimi first would be a good enough reason not to go to any more of Steve's classes. Of course it would. That was what you did with children — you used them as a blatant excuse. The image of the handcuffs beside his bed kept coming to mind — the whole bedroom did. If she had to, Nell could slosh together a quick gouache mix in the exact colour of the walls of the room, draw the patterns of the cushions on the bed, add the shackle points on the leather headboard. It was all stuck there in her head like a picture. She so wished it wasn't.

However much she told herself that what people got up to in the privacy of their own premises was their business, and that as he was an ex-detective she shouldn't be surprised that he owned a set of handcuffs, it still wasn't a comfortable image. Then she told herself off for being prudish. The "hey, don't knock what you haven't tried" factor kicked in. Back when she was twenty-one, if Patrick had suggested a little light beating with a soft leather paddle, she'd have given it a go, no question. She smiled at the thought — what would that have been like? Ludicrously funny, she concluded. It would have felt so contrived, so staged, that neither of them would have been able to keep a straight face. Had he really become so humourless?

"Would you rather I stayed in? Will you feel lonely?" Nell went and sat beside Mimi and put her arm round her.

Mimi shrugged her off, almost growling. "Er . . . no?" She hunched further into her cushions, flipped the remote, changing channels. "I'll be fine. I was just surprised because suddenly you go out *all the time*. I mean, you weren't home the other day when I got back from school. I'm a latchkey child."

Nell felt a small guilty flicker, even though she knew that if at any time *she* dared use the world "child" when talking to Mimi, she'd get the sharp end of teen scorn. She wasn't sure why the omission had occurred, but somehow she hadn't got round to telling Mimi that she'd spent an afternoon on the London Eye with Ed.

On the day, Mimi had had a crisis of homework to be dealt with, next day a late play rehearsal, and since then she'd been anatomically welded to a new set of must-listen iPod downloads, and unavailable for chat about anything that didn't involve basic information regarding the presence of food on the table. It was now as if the event had a life of its own and could make its own decisions about whether it came out into the open or not. Days later, and it still hadn't got itself mentioned, so it would seem peculiar to bring the subject up now. Mimi would have questions to ask about why she hadn't told her before. And worse, Nell would have to think about that herself.

"You're nearly sixteen, Mimi! Or would you like me to get you a babysitter? I know . . . I can ask Charles and Ed if you can go and sit with them next door till I'm back. You'll like that."

"Aaagh noooo! I'm not going in there with two old men. They'll make me play chess or something!"

"Well, that wouldn't hurt — it's good for the logical side of your brain. It might help with your maths. Though I doubt it's what they'd do. Ed's more likely to initiate you into the finer points of the Jimi Hendrix catalogue."

"Oh, I already know all about Hendrix. Joel says he's —" Mimi suddenly clammed up, shifting about, re-arranging her cushions and leaning forward to take an intense interest in a car-parts rip-off scandal on *Watchdog*, leaving Nell, who was now running very late, storing away the existence of "Joel" for discussion another time.

As she left the room, Nell caught Mimi giving her a sly sideways look, as if assessing whether her mother had clocked the reference. Daughters, Nell thought — did they imagine mothers were born yesterday? Of course she'd clocked it.

"It feels all wrong, coming here on a Thursday," Abi grumbled as she and Nell approached the Body and Soul studio. "It's Olly's darts night and he didn't take kindly to coming over to mine to keep an eye on the evil brood." She pushed the studio door open and recoiled. "Phew, it's whiffy in here!"

The studio definitely wasn't perfumed with lavender-candle smoke today. The class before theirs had been something called Hyper-robics. All the women leaving the class had muscle definition that rivalled Madonna's. They were panting, pungent and glistening, and left an aroma of bodies that were in obvious, post-exertion need of the showers.

"Hmm. Bring back Advanced Yoga and scented meditation," Nell agreed, sniffing the air. "And I know what you mean, it sort of puts your week out, doesn't it? Somewhere in my head I imagine I've got three more days to get this week's work quota done." She'd got diseased fruit to do now; *Home Grown*'s editor had called to say that following on from the identification of vegetable ailments, they were *branching out* (peals of laughter down the phone) into soft fruit.

Abi and Nell sat on the bench at the back of the studio. Nell kept an eye on the doors, waiting for Steve to arrive. She felt a bit churned up inside, wondering if he'd look at her and sense that she was thinking handcuffs, cages, chains, whips — all of which he might not be into at all. It might just be an interesting collection of confiscated police items . . . hmmm. The last part of this class was going to be a women-only session about fending off sexual attackers, but surely that must apply to men, too — didn't they get sexually assaulted sometimes? If Steve had a hands-on demonstration in mind, she'd make sure she kept well out of range when he asked for volunteers. And suddenly there he was — as ever she'd watched the wrong door and he appeared as magically as if he'd materialized through the mirrors. How did he do that?

"Right! We're having sex today!" he announced cheerily. There was a ripple of sniggering from the ponytail girls and groans from the more world-weary. "We'll start off with car safety. Now, you do all lock your cars when you drive, don't you?"

Steve didn't look at Nell once as he spoke. She concentrated hard on taking notes about what he was saying and found nothing to argue with in the common sense he was dealing out to them, although she did wonder how her car-insurance company would take the news of a collision that was somebody else's fault, when she hadn't stopped to take the collider's insurance details on the grounds that the shunt might be a hijacker's ruse.

"And you do keep your handbag locked in the boot? Please tell me you don't keep it on the seat next to you, in full view as you're in a traffic jam down the high street?"

Patsy squeaked, "In the boot? What about . . . well, my mascara and my phone and stuff?"

One or two of the other women muttered agreement. "Definitely phone," Wilma pointed out. "I mean, if someone runs into your car you're going to need that for calling the police, aren't you?"

"Yes — and it might be your phone they're after, if you've got some state-of-the-art all-dancing gadget," Steve told her, with seen-it-all patience. "In a car, you're best with some old pay-as-you-go thing that nobody in their right mind would think of nicking, just for this eventuality. And even then, you don't want it in full view. Just sit on it."

"*Sit* on it?" Abi said. "Are you saying I should have a special phone just for the car and that I should *sit* on it?"

"Yeah right, that'll be safe," Patsy giggled. "If you've got it on vibrate, you could definitely cause an accident, all on your own!"

"You may laugh," Steve said. "But this could save your life." He waited patiently for all the female hilarity to settle.

"OK — we've more or less covered car travel. What about when you're out? It goes without saying, or it should, that you never lose sight of your drink if you're in a bar."

"Never been known to let the glass out of me hand," Abi whispered to Nell.

"And then there's if you get lucky . . ." Steve glanced down at Nell and she avoided his gaze, feeling her face getting warmer.

"I can teach you everything I know about self-defence, you can be a black belt in karate, judo, t'ai chi, but it could all be for nothing in a date situation if you don't stay sober enough to take care of yourself. Basics . . ."

Nell concentrated hard on her note-taking, having more than a vague suspicion about what was coming.

". . . well they're obvious, but worth repeating. The things you don't do. I'm not talking like those old-school judges who used to think that you were asking for it if you wore a short skirt —"

"Well, good," Patsy's friend interrupted. "Because girls like to have fun, you know? And if you can't get a bit dressed up for a night out without some git saying you're gonna get what's coming . . . I mean this *is* the twenty-first century, no?"

"Indeed it is," Steve agreed, "and have you ever been the one who needs to get home on her own and you've got in a car because the driver has pulled over and asked if anyone needs a minicab?"

"Er, like no?" she said. "Obvious, innit?"

"Or met someone you fancy and gone back to their place just for coffee . . ." There was a ripple of knowing laughter. ". . . and not, as it happens, actually known exactly what his address was once you're in there?"

Nell looked up. Steve was staring straight at her. What was *his* address? She didn't know now and hadn't known then. She bit her lip, conscious that she was being told something here. Mimi should be hearing this — it would surely be a good thing if her daughter didn't wait till she was in her forties to do this kind of essential learning.

"And maybe decided that a tour of the apartment might be interesting?" Steve's voice became slower, quieter. "Did you notice how the door locks worked or refuse another drink because, actually, you'd had enough?"

The room was silent now; everyone was listening intently. Nell could have sworn she heard her own heart thudding. According to what Steve was saying, she was lucky it was still beating at all. She deserved to be lying under his floorboards, stone dead and trussed up in a bin-bag. "*You've only yourself to blame.*" She could hear her mother's voice; it was what Gillian had said the time Patrick had told Nell to get rid of the baby or forget about long-term life with him. *Why* did she have herself to blame? Being on the pill wasn't fail-safe. Well, it was, so long as you didn't cop a nasty dose of food poisoning. Here, though, would she have had herself to blame if Steve had persuaded her that a demonstration of the handcuffs would be fun? All those D-rings on the headboard — plenty of choice to clip the cuffs to . . . She had no reason to think he'd have hurt her but . . . it was a sharp lesson in the dangers of risk-taking, of not having a clue if your date's idea of fun could turn out to be a long way from your own.

To be fair, Steve did offer the men the chance to stay for the physical fight-him-off section of the class. None did, and none moved out of the studio faster than Hell's Angel Mike, who raced away as if he was terrified

Steve would change his mind and insist on him hanging about to play the part of the Second Attacker.

"Right — now this is where it gets serious," Steve said as soon as the door was closed. "Sexual crime, rape by a total stranger, the sort you read about in the worst-case events, they're pretty rare, but whether it's someone you know quite well who doesn't understand the word no, or a nutter who's followed you off the train, this'll all come in useful. Now a volunteer. I want one of you girls to come and get on top of me, pin me down . . ."

There was nervous laughter. Steve lay flat out on the floor on a gym mat and looked at the faces above him.

"Well, come on then! One of you's got to pretend to be the attacker so I can show you how to preserve your virtue! Nell?" He was grinning at her, provokingly.

Nell frowned at him. What was he playing at? Why couldn't he have picked Wilma or Patsy? They'd shown a finer line in brass nerve in the class than she ever had.

"No, not me," she said, simply.

Steve sat up abruptly. "No? As in, 'No, I'm not interested in learning these techniques that might keep me alive'?"

"No, Steve, it's no as in, no, I'm not going to do it. Not this time. I'll watch, I'll pay attention and I'll practise with one of the girls but I'm not volunteering."

"Right. And why not?" He gave her one of his best, most disarming smiles. She smiled back.

"I'm doing what you're always telling us," she told him with calculated sweetness. "I'm saying no and meaning it. Being assertive. Defying the lion. You should be pleased with yourself — it shows you've taught me something."

"OK, Nell. It worked — you win. Nice one!" he laughed. "What about you, Abi?"

"Oh thank you, God!" Abi squealed, sprawling herself across him almost before he'd finished asking.

"What was all that about? What's going on?" Abi pounced on Nell as they were leaving the building. "You've been seeing him, haven't you? I knew it! I could tell from *day one* that he fancied you." Abi looked very pleased with herself.

"Once. I went out for lunch with him once. And before you get all oooh-er about it, nothing happened!" Nell laughed.

"Nothing? How disappointing!" Abi patted her shoulder. "Not even —"

"No, really," Nell interrupted. In the light of what she'd learned in the class, he more than deserved a top reference. "Steve was a perfect gentleman."

"So where are we going? What's all the mystery?" Mimi had never been on the Silverlink rail line before. In her experience, Richmond station's London trains went to Waterloo or were the District Line towards Hammersmith and Harvey Nichols. Now they were past Gunnersbury she was in unfamiliar territory and hadn't a clue where they were heading. She felt nervous. How many hours this time? Were they going to end up in Scotland or something? This surely wasn't the seaside trip? He'd said they'd need all day for that, not just a few hours after school.

"I told you, we're going for a picnic," Joel said. He put his arm round her and hugged her close to him. "It's not far, not by train. Just up to north-west London," he said reassuringly.

He might as well have said the North West Frontier. Mimi recognized how pampered she'd always been, driven everywhere by her parents, who had been safety-conscious enough to ensure that wherever she was going, she got there safely. Or they had been, until her dad went. It all seemed to have fallen to pieces a bit since then, and her mum's attention was definitely in a different place. But then, to be fair, Mimi's social life so far had occurred in quite a small, restricted area, if you didn't count Joel's train habit. Being fifteen was strange: you sometimes felt as if you knew so much, that you were digging your way out of the burrow and could go anywhere, do anything, but then other times, you felt as if you'd love to be all cosied down in the back of your mum's car, listening to music or playing some silly kids'-type car game, taking no notice of where the roads led and depending on someone else to get you to where you were heading. Here with Joel, she was in danger of doing that toddler thing and saying every few minutes, "Are we nearly there yet?"

"Look up there on the map." Joel pointed above the carriage door. "Kensal Rise is only two more stops and then we walk a bit."

Mimi had never heard of Kensal Rise and felt even more confused as the train pulled into Willesden

Junction. Weren't picnics for fields and country, birdsong and sunshine? Here they were in what looked like an endless industrial jungle. And she had the wrong clothes — what she'd planned to wear (cute bell-sleeved grey-blue dress, blue footless tights) was with her, but uselessly, pointlessly in her bag. Somehow this was all going horribly wrong. The scenes of near-sex in Joel's bedroom that she'd tentatively rehearsed in her head hadn't involved her school uniform and an endless vista of railway container-truck sidings.

But after the industrial greyness of Willesden's rail yards, Kensal Rise looked reassuringly domestic, similar to her own suburban area. Joel took her hand and they walked along a tree-lined avenue towards . . . where? He still hadn't told her. He just ambled along happily, smiling and pleased with himself.

"Joel, this is mad. *Please* tell me where we're going. I mean, suppose my mum phones me and asks where I am?"

Joel looked alarmed. "You told her you were at Tess's tonight, didn't you? I told mine I'd be at Duane Stuart's. It's cool."

"OK, I was just . . . I feel lost." Mimi also felt sulky. Her feet hurt. She'd got all her weekend homework in her bag along with what she'd planned to wear, and it wasn't light to carry.

"We're going over there." He pointed across a broad main road. She couldn't see what he meant. On the other side of the road there was nothing but a massive brick wall, for as far as she could see. Was it a prison?

254

They crossed at the lights and approached an ornate iron gate and a sign that read West London Crematorium. Great, she thought, peering through the gates at a seemingly endless cemetery.

"The dead centre of Kensal, then," she muttered, hesitating by the gates. Was this an ideal picnic spot? She didn't think so.

"Come on, it's great in here. This is Kensal Green cemetery." Joel took her hand and she felt as if she was stepping into another universe. "It's historic, famous, it's got atmosphere. You'll love it."

"Will I?" Mimi wasn't so sure but it was his birthday, she had to give it a go. They were walking along a rough pathway, past bizarre mini-temples that looked weirdly modern, like hideous holiday chalets. She'd never seen anything like them in a graveyard — they looked peculiarly incongruous among ancient, leaning gravestones and traditional angel statues.

"Those are horrible." Joel read her mind. "But there are brilliant old ones further in, you'll see."

"OK — but . . . why are we having a picnic in *here*?" Mimi didn't want to hang out with the dead. This was wrong, like wishing for bad luck. She'd never even been to a funeral before.

"Ah . . . you'll see. Come on."

Deeper into the cemetery the graves were densely packed together: new ones, heaped with flowers and fresh earth, were like tiny body-length slivers squeezed in between long-forgotten weed-strewn mounds. Three women were sitting on the grass beside a grave, busy with trowels and lupin plants. Mimi thought of slugs and worms, and wished she was home watching *Neighbours*.

They came to a group of weather-worn ancient monuments, ornate church-like buildings draped in ivy, rustling with nesting birds. Gargoyles leered at them from roofs that were only just above head height and windows were bricked up — though whether to stop body-snatchers getting in or souls getting out, Mimi dared not speculate. She just imagined being trapped in one, walled in alive. All around them, marble columns and angels with missing limbs cut into the vivid blue skyline. Some graves had chunks of shattered, collapsed stone revealing deep, dark caverns beneath. Mimi couldn't look at these, fearing to see bones and coffin splinters and feeling the neglect was almost an obscene disrespect, leaving the occupants so vulnerably near-exposed.

"It's all right, they're long rotted." Joel picked up on her unease.

"Oh thanks, Joel, that's a comfort." Mimi shivered. She stopped in a patch of sunshine by a low white picket fence that enclosed a strangely modern grave. It was an unusually big plot, containing a triptych of plain grey granite, each panel elaborately scrolled with gilt flowers, and with a sepia photo of a young, smiling woman set into the central one.

"I bet she didn't look like that when she died," Joel said, leaning over the fence. "Look at the dates, she was ninety-eight when she went."

"It must have cost a bomb. She's got more space than just about anyone," Mimi commented.

"Yeah and what a waste. I bet they didn't spend that much on her when she was alive and old."

"Oh, they might have. Look at this lot." Mimi pointed to a collection of ornaments, little plaster cats, hedgehogs and squirrels, lining the edge of the fence. "They've made a sort of garden for her. In a way, it's sweet, but it's also strange, as if they really cared but didn't know what to do to show it. I bet her house was full of ornaments too. They wanted it to be like home for her."

"Yeah, OK, but just don't ever do that for me, promise?" Joel laughed nervously, backing away from the grave plot. "It gives me the spooks. And anyway, it's ugly. I mean, look at the old ones." He pointed to a pink marble obelisk. "Now that's fabulous; all that skyward stuff, it's . . . it's . . . *aspirational*. It means something, like the broken columns, they represent life cut short. And then look at this slab tat — is this the best of twenty-first-century grave design? It looks like my mum's kitchen worktop, up on end. Let's go." He pulled her away from the fence. "We're nearly there."

Again, Mimi wondered where "there" was. It was getting colder now. No one else was around. Did this place close at night? And if it did, at what time?

"Here!" Joel plonked his bag down on top of a table-like slab of pale, mossy marble. "*This* is . . ."

"Oh, I get it . . ." The truth at last dawned on Mimi. "Brunel's grave!"

"Brunel, father and son and more." Joel pointed to the list of names on the inscription: "Come and sit here

257

with me. Fancy a drink?" He pulled a bottle of champagne out of the bag along with a couple of plastic mugs, using the grave like a table.

Mimi hesitated — it didn't seem right to sit on someone who was all powder and bones. Joel's phrase "long rotted" came back to her head. So this was the big treat. A picnic on some dead geezer. Great. She wasn't sure whether to feel disappointed or strangely flattered that whatever Joel wanted her for on this special day, casual disposal of her virginity wasn't part of it. That was one thing to be thankful for, she supposed: he didn't expect to do it with her on this cold marble. Or did he? Maybe that was for later, like dedicating the event as a sort of sacrifice to his hero. It wasn't a very impressive grave, either: among monuments that were so show-off this was like a simple, grubby, marble box, really, pockmarked from moss, chipped, shabby and plain. It wasn't even that *big* — just . . . grave-sized. Surely this great man deserved better?

"It's very ordinary, isn't it?" Mimi stroked the engraved lettering. "I mean, considering what he did, you'd think someone would have organized something much more like those swanky monuments that people we've never heard of have got. Shouldn't there be something to show what amazing things he made? A huge carved ship, maybe? Or a tunnel that he could be symbolically buried beneath?" She felt quite upset on behalf of Isambard and his family. Perhaps this was the absolute best they could afford. She'd look it up again on the Internet, check how Sir Isambard had left the family finances. Joel's obsession must be catching.

"I don't agree — the thing is, surely his designs stand for themselves. Perhaps the man he was, really, was quite a humble sort. Maybe he was a bit like those rock stars who deep down like fly-fishing and cats. Or maybe his family thought that everyone's equal in death — monuments are just not important?"

"Well, humble or whatever, it still doesn't seem right just to sit on it, or to use it for a table."

"OK — I know what you mean," Joel said, picking up on Mimi's reluctance. "Come round here then." He took her hand and led her under a low-branched tree. "This is better. And I've got this . . ." He pulled out from the bag a tartan, plastic-backed rug that Mimi recognized from the summer before when her mum had got one as part of a free offer from the Marks & Spencer's food store.

"You've come prepared for everything, then," she said, accepting a glass of the champagne and sitting beside him, leaning against the tree's substantial trunk.

Joel slid his arm round her, pulled her against him and kissed her. "Pretty much everything, yes," he murmured.

Email would have been easier. Letter-writing was definitely becoming a lost art. Nell played about for a long, indecisive while with the order of the sentences she'd come up with, working out how to tell Patrick what she wanted to get across in the most concise way possible. Eventually, she got it into shape.

*Patrick — Your letter was vile, hurtful and
completely over the top. I know we didn't end well
but five years together was a long time, and I'd
have thought enough mutual respect would be left
over for at least basic politeness. As for legal action
. . . surely a crazy overreaction? Don't worry, I
won't intrude on your privacy again. I'm really
sorry that I did and that you feel this way. Have a
lovely rest-of-your-life. Eleanor.*

He'd be in no doubt from these few short, sharp
sentences that his hostility had left her shocked, hurt,
and frankly furious. Before she could change her mind,
she quickly added her email address after her signature
in case she'd guilt-tripped him into apologizing for his
previous attitude, stuffed the page into an envelope and
took it down to the postbox, delighted to see that she
hadn't missed the last collection.

"Goodbye, Patrick," she muttered, kissing the
envelope before she dropped it into the box. It was only
on the way back that she realized it was nearly dark.
Mimi had said she was going to Tess's after school, but
hadn't said what time she was coming home or whether
she'd be needing food. Why was she so vague? As soon
as she got back to the house, Nell phoned Mimi's
mobile, but she'd either got it switched off or it was out
of battery. She'd give her another hour, then phone
Tess's house, see if Mimi needed a lift home. Teenagers,
they didn't want anyone nagging and checking on
them, but offering a comfortable ride home usually

went down well. It was, as ever, a simple matter of timing.

"My mum will kill me!" Mimi was close to tears as well as feeling a bit wobbly and drunk. "What are we going to do now? Isn't there *anyone* around?"

"Wait here, I'll go and check in the big chapel."

"NO! Don't leave me!" Mimi grabbed hold of him. "I don't want to be by myself!"

Joel laughed, though nervously. "Nothing's going to hurt you in here, is it?" he teased.

She didn't think this was a good moment to try to be funny. "Just, like, *don't*. OK?" she warned. "I'm scared. I'm more scared of my mum than of ghosts, but right now she's not here and they might be. Got it?"

Mimi peered across the graveyard at the terrifying silhouettes, pointy pillars, bits of steeple and the endless angel hands and wings against dirty-dusk sky, which, thanks to the Harrow Road streetlights, would not get really dark tonight. This wasn't a comfort. It might have been better if it turned to pitch, moonless black, then she wouldn't have had to see anything at all in this spook-ridden place. The cemetery gates were locked and had been from 6p.m. Somehow, giggling and champagne-heady, loved-up and kissing beneath their tree, the two of them had managed to miss closing time. There was no way out. Joel knew the place fairly well — on one side was the high, unscalable wall, on the other a steep and dangerous bank down to the canal. It was vandal-proof from outside, escape-proof from inside.

"Better phone home, I suppose." Joel shrugged. "I haven't got mine — I left it in my room this morning."

Mimi stared at him. "But . . . mine's out of power!" she said. "I put it on the charger last night but Andréa had switched the plug off!"

"Shit. That's it then. We're stuck." He looked at her and smiled. "Looks like we'll be spending the night in here."

Mimi glared at him. Why didn't this bother him? She might be drunk but she wasn't stupid. He had to be joking. Didn't he? "Don't be ridiculous, Joel! We *can't* stay here! There must be . . ." Her voice faded away. Ridiculous it might be, but . . . it looked like he was right.

"You didn't plan this, did you?" she accused him.

"No!" He looked hurt and she immediately regretted what she'd said. "Why would I do that?" he asked. "I mean, yeah, sure I'd love to spend the whole night with you, Mimi, but not bedded down among the dead, OK?"

"Yeah. Sorry," she conceded. She dropped her bag on the ground, put her arms round him and cuddled up close. She loved the warm strength of his body against hers, even though this possibly wasn't the best moment to be thinking like this. She could put it down to the alcohol, or to the hormones that cascaded through her teenage blood-stream. She just hoped they'd keep her warm in the coldest time of the night. Could they freeze to death? Would a freebie M&S blanket keep them alive?

"Come on, we'd better go and find somewhere to be, while there's still a tiny bit of light," Joel said, leading her away from the locked gate. "The Anglican chapel has got covered archways, like cloisters. It's about as good as it'll get and if it rains we'll be dry. Unless . . ." He looked along one of the main avenues, at the graves in the fast-fading light. "One of those big tombs might have a broken window?"

"No! I couldn't! And besides, it'd be . . . wrong, surely?" He couldn't mean it, no one could climb into what was really a grave and expect to spend a *whole night* there. Freezing would be a better option. She shuddered, and he stopped and hugged her close to him again. Over his shoulder she eyed the statues and the obelisks. She was, for a moment, sure she saw one of the angels turn slightly.

"It moved," she said, pointing. Was it the champagne? Hysteria? Terror? Or . . . real?

"What did?" Joel turned to look, peering into the gloom.

"The angel. I'm sure she swayed. Maybe she's drunk like me," she said, laughing nervously.

"Don't say that. It's just a trick of the light."

"Do you think they all come out at night?" she asked Joel as they wandered hand in hand towards the Anglican chapel.

"What, the dead? No. Definitely not."

"No, not the dead people." Mimi's voice was tired, slurring slightly. She giggled. "I meant the angels, the statues and stuff. Like that big horse one, that we saw earlier, and the stone lions and stuff. Maybe they all come to life. Maybe they party." She shivered again. "I'm scared, Joel." She wasn't sure what she expected him to say — something big-strong-blokey along the lines of "It'll be OK" or "Hey, don't worry, I'll sort it". How pathetic was that of her? How girly? The one thing she didn't want to hear was what he said next, which was, "Yeah, me too, Mimi; me too."

CHAPTER
FIFTEEN

Weekend Without Make-Up
(The Long Blondes)

It was just Nell and Mimi now, circling each other like angry cats. Nell had done the thank-God-you're-alive bit; Mimi had done I'm reeaaaallly sorry. The kind but seen-it-all-before police officer had gone. Evie Mitchell (who had heard by way of Polly and the ever-busy text grapevine) and Tess's mother Louise, who had turned up early to sympathize on the traumas that teen daughters put parents through, had hastily finished their coffee and left Nell's kitchen clear for the inevitable fallout, of which there was an immediate explosion.

"*Grounded?* But that's not *fair!*" Mimi wailed her reaction to Nell's verdict. From the look of utter devastation on Mimi's face, anyone would think the girl had been sentenced to several years in a hard-labour camp, no remission, not to a week confined to her own perfectly comfortable home. The no-going-out regime was hardly a massive deprivation, either — one weekend out of circulation wouldn't mean eternal banishment from teen society, and it wasn't as if Mimi was in the habit of midweek partying. She was to come straight home from school each day during the next week; no going to Tess's, no hanging around outside Tesco Metro with the St Edmund's boys, no staying on for play rehearsals, genuine or otherwise: the absence of a three-scene fairy wasn't going to disrupt the drama department's schedule significantly.

"Oh it's fair; it's *more than* fair!" Nell shouted back. "And it's not as if you'll be feeling like going out *this* weekend anyway, is it? You must be exhausted. I know I bloody am!" And she was, she was. She was too old for staying up the whole night with only a few drifted moments of half-sleep on the sofa; you could hardly go to bed when your daughter had gone missing and could, for all anyone knew, be lying in a hedge, naked, raped and strangled. She didn't need to thank Steve for these worst-case visions, either — any mother would have had them. Thank God she wasn't one of the tragic few who were proved right.

"But I told you; we didn't *mean* to get locked in there! It was an *accident*! Why don't you ever *listen*!" Mimi stormed out of the kitchen, slammed the door and thumped up the stairs. Nell counted to ten: here it came — the music at full blast, The Killers, if she wasn't mistaken — not the most subtle choice. If Ed and Charles were the complaining types they'd be banging on the door insisting that *some people* liked a bit of peace and quiet on a Saturday morning, if it was all the same to her. If only Ed *were* there, it crossed her mind. He'd have been just the person she'd have wanted to be with during that last terrible night. If he

266

hadn't been at his Dorset cottage for the weekend she would, without question, have knocked on the door and wept out the worst of her fears all over him.

Nell hadn't the slightest doubt that spending the night in Kensal Green cemetery *was* accidental. Even in the worst spirit of sheer devilment it wouldn't have been Mimi's idea of a good time, for she was a girl who cherished her home comforts and each morning had almost to be surgically separated from her 13-tog goose-down duvet. She'd never spent so much as a night under canvas, and had refused to join the school's Duke of Edinburgh scheme for fear of having to trek agonizing miles across freezing moorland in unsightly shoes. A year before, she had come home from three nights in a hostel dormitory on the school's geography field trip so appalled at being deprived of her usual facilities (rainstorm shower, Aveda products, underfloor bathroom heating, bedroom TV) that anyone would have thought she'd been condemned to the most primitive Third World prison cell. Gillian had been in the house at the moment she'd returned, and hadn't helped matters by sympathizing profusely as Mimi shuddered and trembled and lay on the sofa weakly pleading for tea and croissants.

"Oh you poor darling!" she'd crooned to her granddaughter, "surely not a *communal bathroom?*" leaving Nell incredulous that this was the same woman who had guiltlessly packed off her own three daughters to five years of boarding school.

If a sense of humour ever returned, Nell knew the thought of the woefully spoiled Mimi shivering all night among the graves with nothing more comfortable to lie on than damp ground or icy marble might one day make her smile. Perhaps (oh please) a bit of domestic appreciation would result. And it wasn't the staying-out that Mimi was being punished for. *Of course* Nell knew she hadn't intended to do it; no — it was the lying. What on earth had made her say she would be at Tess's? What secret, underhand deeds had she planned that would need an elaborate cover story (and as it involved a boy, as if she couldn't guess)?

It had led to all sorts of muddle and confusion and ultimately to sheer bloody panic, the involvement of police and some frantic calls to Alex who — though he couldn't do much from three thousand miles away — was at least the one person who could be relied on to worry about Mimi as much as she was doing. It must have been around four in the morning, his time, when she was finally able to call and tell him, in a rare intimate moment of absolute empathy, that all was well. She wondered what Cherisse had made of it all. Had she stayed awake, pacing and imagining the worst alongside him, or had she calmly gone through her usual night-time maintenance routine and meticulously cleansed, toned and moisturized (and anxiously inspected for new lines and wrinkles) before getting into bed, mildly resentful that men of a certain age came fully loaded with complications?

Nell switched on the kettle again for about the fifth time that morning, and sat down at the table. Exhausted, she laid her face against the wood, feeling its rough but comforting grain against her skin. The

268

tears that threatened could be from relief or sheer bloody misery, either would do. When the doorbell rang she could barely make herself move from the chair through weariness.

"My God, you look terrible!" was Kate's greeting. "So ... the naughty minx is back, then. I saw Evie outside Waitrose just now. She told me what happened. Evie says Tess is in big trouble for covering up, too. Why didn't you call me last night, Nell? I'd have come straight over and stayed. You shouldn't have had to go through all that by yourself!"

"Thanks, Kate; I thought of it, but Louise came over for a while as soon as she'd dragged the truth out of Tess, and the police were great. I also thought, well, you've got Alvin to deal with, and besides, if it hadn't been a good outcome ..." Nell's voice faltered. "I'd have ... well, it would have been today I'd have needed you."

"Another time, though, promise me," Kate said, hugging her. "Though God knows, let's hope there isn't one! Now sit down," she ordered, marching Nell into the kitchen, opening the fridge and pulling out a pack of bacon, "you need food. How do you switch this grill on? I bet you haven't eaten a thing, have you?"

"No, not since lunch yesterday," Nell admitted, flicking one of the oven's switches. She was suddenly ravenous for a bacon sandwich, smothered in ketchup — oh, that deep, eternal comfort of well-loved food. "Mimi has, though. Can you believe, she and Joel had a full-scale breakfast somewhere on Ladbroke Grove before they slunk back here? The kind man in the

269

cemetery office let them use his phone — I bet they aren't the first idiots he's found shivering by the gates when he unlocked it — so I thought, hey, they'll head straight back, but no!"

"Oh I can believe it, *no* problem. I've had two teenage boys, don't forget. The food thing won't be Mimi's fault — once they'd let the parents know they were all right, Joel's mind would have turned straight to food."

"I hope Louise isn't too hard on Tess," Nell said as she made yet more tea. "I mean, when you think of it, covering for each other is what fifteen-year-olds do. We'd have done the same. I just wish . . . well, she held out till past ten last night, not saying who Mimi was with, only that she was sure she was OK. And then when she and Joel weren't at his place either, that was when even Tess realized it was serious."

"I know," Kate sympathized. "You imagine the worst — it's only natural."

"I thought at first — and I know this is mad — I had this idea they'd gone on some silly mad trip to New York to see Alex, a big crazy adventure, but Mimi's passport was still in her room. I almost wished it wasn't — then I didn't have to think something horrible had happened to them. Mimi doesn't have such a terrible life, either — she's got no reason to start lying or running off."

"They do get into all sorts of muddles, though, honestly. One of the boys in Matt's year got arrested once for doing something stupid like peeing in a shop doorway," Kate said as she assembled the bacon sandwiches. "Hmm . . . maybe I'll just have a little one, to keep you company." She then continued, "He was as drunk as a skunk, so they put him in the cells and rang his folks, who were out. And when they got back they didn't bother picking up their messages so the poor boy was in there for twelve hours. By then, of course, his parents thought he'd been knifed and left for dead in some alley and were going mad. It was only when *they* got in a panic and called the police that a cop who was using the communal brain cell put two and two together."

When Kate had gone, Nell fell into bed and drifted in and out of sleep for a couple of restless hours. Eventually, realizing that proper sleep wasn't likely, she went and had a long, reviving bath and washed her hair. On the radio as she lay drowsily soaking, *Weekend Woman's Hour* had a feature about orgasms in which Jenni Murray led a brave man and a giggly woman in intense discussion on clitoral stimulation. Although the woman enthused about Practising Alone, no one suggested the pink plastic Rabbit as recommended by Kate. Nell snarled, "Oh *shut up*," to the earnest lot of them and thumped the radio's off switch, feeling grouchy. Then, remembering the advice in *After He's Gone* about going for as near-happy as possible, she made a special effort to blow-dry her hair the way she most liked. If the rest of the weekend with Mimi was going to be like treading on eggshells, she might as well have at least one minimal aspect to feel good about while having to pace this domestic cage with a moody daughter. Following the same train of thought, she chose a newish dress (a silky blue one from Whistles) and put on her last-year Prada-sale boots, reflecting (though without much regret — for there was many a classy bargain in the Tesco Florence and Fred range) that there probably wouldn't be any more footwear of that elevated calibre in her life. Well, that was OK — it would neatly match the lack of orgasms. Terrific.

There was no sound from Mimi's room as she passed the door on her way back down the stairs, and she envied teenagers their ability simply to fall into a deep sleep at any time of the day. Her fury had now abated and she wished better dreams for Mimi than the potential graveyard horrors that the previous night's sleeping companions might well trigger.

Back in the kitchen, Nell opened her computer and read a brief email from Seb describing yet another surf session. She hoped he was finding time to fit in some work and sent a reply aiming to put this across without being too bossy-mum. Just before she switched off, she checked the Junk Mail folder as she always did, in case something work-connected had mistakenly been routed there. There was the usual pharmaceutical selection promising to gee up her non-sex life, and some requests to update account details at banks she never used. At first she almost overlooked an unfamiliar sender's name: "Tricksand" looked like any made-up trash name, maybe inviting her to lose her entire income playing online poker, but the subject heading, "Hallo Eleanor", caught her eye just before she pressed "delete".

Nobody on the Internet knew her as Eleanor. With a rising sensation of prickly nerves, she clicked the message open. And there he was — "Tricksand" — Patrick Sanders. OK, she thought, despondently clicking the "not junk" icon and putting off the moment where she read the next instalment of dry-frozen fury, what was he going to throw at her this time? What delightfully over-the-top reaction to her last letter? A writ? Threats of sending The Boys round? Just when she'd thought the weekend couldn't get any worse . . . Expecting yet another complete heart-sink moment but deciding she might as well get it over with, Nell read the message.

> *Eleanor — I got your bizarre note and I'd say it was great to hear from you but I'm completely mystified. What letter? I haven't written to you since about 1984! And if I had, I wouldn't have been "vile and hurtful" as you put it. Why would I? What's going on here? Let's sort this out and then do the how are you/what's happening bit. If you want to, that is. Patrick xxx*

Eleanor read it at least five times. What on earth was he talking about?

"So — what happened? I got into big trouble because of you so you owe me the goss. *Every detail.* Starting with *why a cemetery?*" Tess sounded scary, like a threat. Mimi wasn't properly awake and was snuggled down with her now-charged phone under the duvet. She had an unreal feeling, as if whatever had happened the night before had been something she'd dreamed. A dampish, woodsy smell in her hair told her it was all too real, as did the bruise on her shin where she'd banged it on a piece of broken-off gravestone when she and Joel had raced away towards the chapel in a panic, thinking there was someone (or something) creeping in the dark towards them. Joel had told her it was probably a fox and maybe it was. Or maybe it was the ghost of Thackeray, whose grave she had sat on earlier. Either way, Joel had sounded just as petrified as she'd felt. *Not reassuring* — which he should have at least tried to be, seeing as it was all his fault.

"The cemetery is because Joel is mad. His hero, the great Brunel, is buried there and having a birthday picnic on his grave is Joel's idea of a fun day out. Me, I'd have settled for a kebab and a movie. And . . ." She could hear Tess breathing down the phone. She knew what she wanted to hear and was going to disappoint her. "And nothing happened." Mimi rubbed her eyes and sat up in bed.

"*Nothing?*" Tess's voice was screechy. "I don't believe you! You were out *all night* with him! All alone among the scary spooks! *Something* must have happened!"

"I'll make stuff up, if you like." Mimi yawned. She wanted to have a long, steamy shower, put her pink velour trackie on and her big furry Garfield slippers (Christmas present from Seb — for the sake of mutual credibility they'd agreed to pretend they were ironic but she loved how soft and snuggly they were) and just lie

274

on the sofa all evening watching trash TV. She wanted to make it up with her mum. They could watch *Casualty* together and some easy comfort telly like six back-to-back reruns of *My Family*. They should eat something lovely like her mum's lasagne. Or just chips. And oooh she felt a sudden deep longing for fish fingers, like an overtired six-year-old. Fish fingers with ketchup.

"No, don't make stuff up. That's no good. You know what I want to know . . . did you . . . you know. Did you *do it*?"

Mimi felt slightly sick. "Tess, do you know how much like some old perv you're sounding?"

"Oh really?" Tess snapped. "You'd know, would you? OK then, don't tell me anything, and don't bother to ask me how much trouble you got *me* into. It's not all about *you*, you know. Just don't ask me — not *ev-ah* — to cover for you again. Alibis are *not* us, got that?"

"Got it," Mimi told her. "But, Tess . . ."

"What!"

"I'm sorry. I'm *really* sorry. And, OK, I'll tell you. We had a bottle of champagne and we got giggly and felt really pissed. We did a bit of snogging under this tree and it got really uncomfortable and we were getting a bit further on . . . like . . ."

"Like what? Did he . . .?"

"No . . . he got under my clothes a bit, that kinda stuff, but by then I was feeling slightly ill from the drink and it was getting dark. It was freezing too and I kept thinking hey, everyone else here's dead. It doesn't exactly make you feel sexy, that."

Tess giggled. "You are *so* mad. So you haven't done it. Not even close to."

"That's all you wanted to know, isn't it?" Mimi laughed. "No, I haven't. I'll probably end up ancient, like nineteen or something, and still a virgin. Even Joel went off the idea once we realized we might be locked in. In the end we spent the whole night shivering under this picnic rug under some chapel arches. I thought I'd *die*. And we kept hearing weird noises. It was, like, for *ever*? Never, ever again!"

"You're still going out with him, though?"

"Suppose. He's still talking about going to the coast but I'm grounded for a week. Maybe when it's warmer, but I don't know."

"So it wasn't worth it?"

Mimi laughed again. "Er . . . no? Good snogger, though." She just about managed to stop herself adding, "Almost as good as you."

"Better than me?" Tess whispered down the phone.

Mimi bit her lip and wondered if being friends from seven years old really made you psychic.

"Nowhere near, babe." She giggled. "But if you lend him that lipgloss you wear — that'll help."

There was one conclusion that frightened Nell, out of the only two logical ones to choose from. If Patrick hadn't had her original letter he couldn't have sent a reply, which meant that someone else had. So Patrick hadn't had the letter because either someone who lived with him had intercepted it, *or* it hadn't been posted, and the person who hadn't posted it could only have been ... Steve. Nell's brain kept going round in confused circles and had been doing so since she'd received Patrick's email. She hadn't yet replied to it and was still working out what on earth to say to him. And of course she might, depending on what he said back to her, have to tackle Steve. But today was Sunday and she and Mimi were now on their way to Guildford to have lunch with Gillian. She hoped that getting some distance from home would mean she could put both Steve and Patrick out of her head and simply relax a bit.

"Did I really have to come ...?" Mimi was still grumbling, even though they were now on the A3 and well past Wisley. She was slumped down in her seat twiddling with her iPod, feet on the dashboard.

"Yes of course," Nell told her, "and it's not part of your punishment; it's just a nice family lunch with your gran."

"She'd rather it was Seb," Mimi said, with some justification.

"She loves you both," Nell said. "And she'll be thrilled to see you. She doesn't often, these days. You're always busy or out."

"I'm *supposed* to be out; I'm a teenager. Wouldn't you worry if I had like no *friends*?"

"No danger of that being a cause for worry — you never seem to be short of friends." Nell sighed. How many minutes had Mimi *not* been on the phone or computer since she'd woken up late on Saturday afternoon? She could probably count them on one hand. News of Mimi's graveyard adventure must have reached every person she'd ever met in the whole world and her whole life, and it had been elevated to the kind of major drama that, in the retelling, had become highly enviable and hugely glamorous. Mimi was gleefully delighted to relive the entire event for anyone who asked. Even being confined to home made her some kind of star among her peers, and the words, "It's like *so* not fair" were the refrain of the day. Nell was half-inclined to give up on the going-out ban, in the interests of getting back to normal and depriving Mimi of glorying in victim status.

The driveway to Gillian's house was overhung with drooping laurels and leggy hydrangeas and was clearly becoming too much for the once-a-week gardener. Thanks to Steve's classes, all Nell could think was that the overgrown shrubs offered too much cover from which a lurking burglar could case the place. At some point she'd have to bring up the subject of security — Larchfield would be such an easy-peasy target with its simple Yale locks and fragile single-glazed windows. As well as feeling some despair about the house's exterior, Nell felt mildly uneasy inside this house where she'd grown up. It wasn't connected with reverting to childhood and unwelcome parental authority, but more to do with noticing small signs of her mother's advancing age and incipient frailty. Gillian would not take kindly to being incapacitated even in a minor way (well, who would?) and Nell wondered how on earth, when the time came, she would be able to persuade her that there were easier ways of living than in this rambling, out-of-date, draughty house that must be ruinously expensive to heat.

Each time she was here, worrying new evidence of domestic decay and shabbiness presented itself. Last visit, she'd noticed the window frames looked rotten. Where paint had chipped off at the corners, damp had got in and the wood felt soft and spongy. A burglar wouldn't need to concern himself with locks — he could just punch the wood away. Gillian had dismissed that as being down to a spell of wet weather, certain it would dry out and somehow mend itself. This time, too, the stair carpet had newly loose threads that would soon become dangerous. Gillian had a stalwart "it'll see me out" attitude to her home, an attitude that she wouldn't dream of applying to her wardrobe, and Nell knew that a suggestion she get a new carpet would be met with a derisive dose of "don't be so silly". It was contrary in a woman who, only a few weeks ago, was delightedly buying an expensive outfit for a spring funeral for which the potential corpse had yet to stop breathing.

Now, in the kitchen, the fridge had a strange smell that told Nell that either cream or yogurt had spilled and gone mouldy in some essential tubes at the back. Gillian simply said, "Oh, I'll put half a lemon in — that'll get rid of it." Nell resolved to mention all this to her sisters, make sure they kept up to speed about how things were in the old family homestead, see if they would back her up on the matter of security. They didn't turn up in Guildford very often; Sarah (the clever one) was busy being a GP in Scotland. Claire (the pretty one) lived a Wirral-society whirl of charity events, forever in cocktail dresses and a laser-white smile for the *Cheshire Life* photographer. When they made it back to Surrey they overlooked the creeping tattiness in the interests of not having to do something about it, somehow certain they could leave all that to Nell (the arty one).

"Darling, you look terribly tired," Gillian said to Nell later, as she handed her a massive slice of tarte tatin. "Have you been working hard?"

"She's been going out," Mimi told her, giving Nell a triumphant look across the table. They'd gone through the story of Mimi's cemetery stop-out over the roast lamb, with Nell underplaying the fear aspect of it in favour of amusing her mother. Mimi hadn't seen the funny side and minded very much being laughed at. Revenge, Nell now realized, was on its way.

"*She*'s been going out with *men*." Mimi poured cream all over her pudding, smirking at her grandmother. Nell gave her a warning glare.

"Have you, darling? So soon?" Gillian's eyebrows were up to her hairline.

"What do you mean, 'soon'? Soon after what?" As if she didn't know.

"Soon after Alex . . . went."

"What am I supposed to do? Give it a decent period of mourning? Anyway, I wouldn't call it 'going out with men'. That's a bit of an exaggeration." Nell could feel her voice becoming higher, defensive. Why did her mother still make her feel like this? Did it ever stop, or would she have to wait till Gillian reached her second childhood and it was all the other way round? Lord, would this be her and Mimi one day?

"Shall I go and make some coffee for you both?" Mimi asked sweetly. She was smiling now; the grenade had been lobbed into the arena — job done. Nell could see her eyeing her bag, which contained her Gameboy. In ten minutes from now, the kettle would be boiling away (its automatic switch-off was long defunct — another cause for concern. She'd bring a new one next time, even if Gillian told her off for needless profligacy) and Mimi would be feet-up on the sofa, obliviously tap-tapping away at some daft game.

"Oh please, darling, that would be lovely. And there are some minty chocolates in the fridge — bring those as well."

"Ooh great, I will." Mimi collected up the plates and sauntered out of the room.

"Such a sweet girl," Gillian said as soon as Mimi was out of hearing range. "Now this boyfriend of hers, do keep an eye on him. I hope she doesn't get too involved too young. It can only lead . . . well, you know what it can lead to."

Nell laughed. "The boy I got involved with too young was that Marcus you set me up with!"

Gillian frowned at her. "I didn't mean him and you know it. That chap who lived in the old house died, by the way, but only this last week. I was beginning to wonder if I'd get any wear out of the jacket and skirt I bought in Richmond with you that other Sunday; the weather's turning so warm!"

"Mum — you're all heart!" Nell laughed.

"At my age, funerals are quite frequent social events," Gillian told her. "You pretend you owe it to the deceased to look smart, but really you're along for the party after and you quite enjoy all the dressing up. Now — before we join Mimi with the coffee, tell me — who have you been going out with? Does he have . . . er . . . sterling qualities?"

"Do you mean money?" Patrick had been a rich boy. Gillian had approved of that aspect of him — but only that.

"Yes. Of course I do!" Gillian laughed. "If you have the choice of money or not-money, well, it can be a comfort in the difficult times."

"No it can't," Nell said bluntly. "Difficult times are just that — whatever the circumstances. I should know. And no — I don't think Steve is what you'd call loaded."

He's probably got a gun that is, though, she couldn't help thinking. "He teaches self-defence, personal safety. He's an ex-detective. I've been going to his classes — I told you about them."

"Ah, police. A solid citizen, then. He sounds a steady sort. That's also important." Nell seemed to remember that A Steady Sort had been Gillian's approving verdict on Alex, too.

"Yes. You'd think he was." Nell didn't much want to talk about Steve — she was saving dealing with him till she got home. Phone or email wasn't going to be enough — she wanted to see him; find out, if the letter business *was* him, what he thought he was playing at.

"Well, come on then." Gillian was impatient. "Do tell. Where does he live? Have you been there? What's it like?"

Nell smiled. What to say? That Steve's bed had a headboard with an extensive choice of convenient anchor points to which you could be chained or handcuffed; that he possessed a range of S&M gear that would be the envy of a brothel madam; and that if you got on the wrong side of him he had a cage you could be confined in while he debated the choice of weapon with which to beat your attitudes into shape?

"He's got a riverside flat in Putney. It's really quite nice but . . . don't rush out to buy the wedding hat just yet. I doubt if I'll be seeing him again, not as a date. Not that it really was. It was only lunch."

She wasn't going to mention Ed. Gillian might consider dating one man to be a minor and forgivable event. Dating two would look close to desperation.

"Oh!" Gillian looked so disappointed, Nell almost felt sorry she wasn't prepared to give Steve another chance. Maybe, in the interests of keeping her mother happy, she should try out a little light spanking. "Never mind," Gillian continued, "but do give any passing men a sporting chance. After all, at your age . . ."

This was new, Nell thought. Maybe she would — one day — mention Ed.

"Oh thanks!" Nell laughed. "At my age I'm supposed to be grateful for any attention going!"

"Well, I wasn't going to say that . . . and I wouldn't ever suggest a lowering of standards . . . but . . ."

"Good. Because I'm not looking for anyone, OK? I'm perfectly all right on my own."

"Quite. And you've got the children. Remember you wouldn't have those if you'd stayed with . . ."

Oh, here it came. What would Gillian say if she knew that Patrick was on hold in her computer, right now? She would probably be sharpening some kitchen knives and buying a nice new funeral outfit, something suitable for wearing to a murder victim's send-off. Though whether the victim would be Nell or Patrick was anyone's guess.

"Look, give it a rest, Mum. Patrick was over so many years ago, OK? Now — coffee? I can hear the kettle boiling away to itself in the kitchen. You really need a new one, you know."

"Oh, don't be silly!" Gillian said. "That one will see me out."

CHAPTER
SIXTEEN

Don't Look Back In Anger
(Oasis)

So that made two nights in a row without proper sleep. Nell, before six in the morning, went into the kitchen, switched on her computer and read again the flurry of emails between herself and Patrick from the evening before. No, he'd told her, there was no one else in his house who could have intercepted the mail. Yes, he did have someone he lived with, but she was in Brazil visiting her son. Not *his* son, Nell noted. And yes, he'd be delighted to see her again — how about lunch, Friday? She hadn't yet replied to this last one. It had rather taken her breath away and seemed so very, very soon. Somehow she'd imagined any kind of meeting would be in the safe middle distance. But then, wasn't this exactly what she'd hoped for? She thought about the numbers here. Five years of loving and fighting. Six weeks of pregnancy. Twenty years of silence and now five days till they met again. Well, sometimes you get what you wish for. That was the peculiar downside with wishes.

Patrick's emails left only one possibility — Steve was responsible for the intercepted letter. He was also, as a result, responsible for her sleepless night. Discovering that someone out there was manipulating your life was very frightening — what would they do next? He had, after all, been the one who'd changed her lock. In the middle of a long dark night, the possibility, however remote, that he might have held on to a key was a very chilling thought.

Nell felt about ninety years old, and a quick glance in the mirror told her she was possibly underestimating there. She lay on the sofa watching the day's early news on TV and eating stale croissants (just bearable if hot and smothered in blackcurrant jam) while looking up locksmiths in the phone book, wondering how soon she could get one to come over. There were plenty of twenty-four-hour ones for lockout emergencies, but this wasn't what she was after. What she needed was someone to change the new lock on the back door completely, and it wasn't a job she felt up to tackling by herself.

The previous night, in feverish paranoia, she had gone for maximum security in the ways that Steve had taught the class: she had taken to bed her trusty Maglite torch, stashed the front-door key in a white bag beside her, ready to throw down to the police if she had to summon them (oh, and they'd just love her, wouldn't they — calling them out two nights in succession). Both the landline phone and her mobile were on the pillow beside her, and every possible way into the house was locked. She even put on maximum-security nightwear: a pair of Mimi's coldest-weather flannelette pyjamas in candy pink and patterned with tiny, smiling ballerinas (more irony from Seb), fastened way up to her neck. She drew the line at locking, or even closing, her bedroom door, though, because there was Mimi to consider. If someone crept up the stairs in the night, it would be Mimi's room they came to before hers and she wanted to hear them coming. What kind of mother would lock herself in securely but leave her daughter vulnerable?

But in spite of all these precautions she had only managed the kind of sleep where the slightest rustle of a leaf at the far end of the garden had her eyes flashing wide open and her heart pounding; for what was the point of all this safety provision if the someone out there possessed a spare key to the back door? Now that she was up and about in reassuring daylight, Nell allowed herself to imagine the scene she'd been carefully avoiding: Steve at 3a.m. leaning casually on the bedroom door frame, pointing his high-beam police-issue torch at her, smiling and shaking his head and telling her, "Well you've only yourself to blame, Nell — did you count the keys I gave you after I fitted that lock? Didn't you wonder why there were only two of them?"

Of course this hadn't happened. It wouldn't. But in the middle of a very dark night all the worst things seemed possible, and no way now would she wander casually across the garden in the midnight hour just to collect something from the studio. Maybe even then he'd been around, lurking, watching. If he had been, she hoped he'd approved of the way she'd fought off Ed. It would almost have been funny (but OK, not very) if he'd emerged from behind the lilac tree to give her a round of applause — or more likely tell her what she was doing wrong.

Now, in the safe light of day, Nell had to wonder, realistically, why on earth she'd got herself into such a panic that she'd imagined Steve would even think of doing anything so sinister as creeping up on her in the night. If he'd wanted to see her, he'd have surely arranged it the simple way, by phoning and asking. And if he had any intentions towards her, they weren't likely to be about scaring her. It seemed to be more something to do with control, with power. What he had done with Patrick's letter . . . did that count as a form of stalking? She felt mildly guilty in this area, because how clear was her own conscience? Tracking down Patrick and checking up on where he lived, that wasn't exactly a hundred per cent above board either, surely. As she'd joked to Kate at the time, you could get an ASBO for that. It wasn't funny any more.

"It was all activity next door on Saturday night. Police, flashing blue lights, comings and goings, the lot," Charles told Ed in the kitchen that Monday morning. Unable to resist gloating, he emphasized the obvious with, "You missed it all."

"Why? What happened? Is Nell all right?" Ed looked out of the window to Nell's house. The car was still there on the driveway; the house windows seemed to be intact.

Charles smirked. "Aha! You're very quick to ask about *her*! Not the daughter, I notice!"

"Nell, Mimi, either, both. Come on, what happened? I know you're dying to tell me."

Charles started looking in cupboards, fussing with mugs, plates, inspecting the bread meticulously as if to check out every last crumb for uncomfortable roughage in the form of seeds, nuts or deadly mould. Ed waited, trying to stay patient, refusing to rise to the bait while Charles was deliberately doing his old-man act, bumbling around pretending he couldn't talk and be active at the same time. He'd give in before Ed did — he'd be unable to keep gossip bottled up for long.

"She went missing, that daughter you didn't ask about. Out all night, it seems. Poor Nell must have been frantic . . ." He looked round at Ed, expecting to see him agog for more information, but Ed wasn't there. Charles heard the front door close and smiled happily — there was only enough marmalade left for one lot of toast. It was all his.

Mimi drifted down the stairs half asleep and wondered why the door was wide open. For her, this was incredibly, almost unheard-of, early, but she was keen to get to school while she still had a bit of celebrity status. That was if she had — life's dramas had a fast turn-round among her group. Something might have happened on Saturday night that would eclipse all that she and Joel had done (or not done . . .). She closed the front door, quite pleased with herself for first having taken a look to make sure her mum wasn't out there chasing Isabelle-across-the-road's cat off the foxgloves. This was a sign she was becoming a grown-up, she realized: thinking of more than just the immediate problem, working out cause and effect. Shutting her mother out of the house at just past seven in the morning would be the *cause* of much fury. Being shouted at for Being That Stupid would be the *effect*. She yawned and rubbed her half-awake eyes, thinking Joel would be impressed at her logic: she would make a scientist yet. Still only half focused, Mimi stumbled into the kitchen, wailing, "Tea, I need tea." And there were her mum and Ed . . . oh God, not again!

"Mum? What are you *like*?" Mimi stood still in the kitchen doorway, her hand shielding her eyes from the scene but slowly taking in every detail she could see between splayed fingers. Nell was wearing her Ugg boots and Mimi's pyjamas. (*Why?* She'd got stuff of her own.) She supposed that had to be a slight improvement on what she'd been wearing the last time Mimi had found her with Ed. But this time she wasn't just sitting around laughing and drinking tea, she was all wrapped up with him, cuddled up close — like some *lerve* thing was going on. Ed was wearing the full complement of normal clothes (for him, anyway — why did men of his age think wine-coloured velvet was acceptable?) which was something, because, *euwww*, the alternative didn't bear thinking about, and he looked like he was about to go to work, which probably meant he hadn't actually been there all night. What he was doing in the kitchen this early, hugging Mimi's mother, was anyone's guess. And had she missed a big, full-on snog scene? It was too early in the day to think like this. In fact, and she felt slightly nauseous now, *any* time of day was too early for that.

"Er . . . Mum? Like . . . what, please, exactly is going on?" Mimi had gone through the imagining about what would happen if Nell started seeing someone; she'd even wondered about how it would be if another man moved in. What she was looking at felt strange . . . it was a long time since even her parents had been caught hugging each other. Grown-up displays of affection just weren't what she was used to seeing, not in this house. Tess's parents were always holding hands and tended to do that yucky thing of kissing each other as they passed in a room, which was something no adolescent of a sensitive nature should have to tolerate.

"Morning, Mimi," Nell said, moving only slightly away from Ed. He looked as if he didn't want to let go of her. She looked as if she didn't want him to. Mimi felt like some kind of gooseberry. What was she supposed to say? *"Don't mind me"?*

"Um . . . breakfast," Mimi muttered, heading for the fridge. She couldn't look at either of them properly. They weren't squashed up together any more, that was something, but Ed had hold of one of Nell's hands. *Let go*, Mimi wanted to squeal. *Not in front of me.*

"And work . . . I must get going," Ed said. "I'll call you later, Nell, OK? Will you be all right?"

"Yes, thanks. I will. Don't worry, and thanks so much for coming round. I'll give those lock people a call as soon as I've had a shower."

"Yes, do. Bye, Mimi!"

"Um . . . bye, Ed." She gave him a vague wave.

And he was gone. Mimi pounced on her mother as soon as the front door was closed.

"OK, Ma, what's going on here? Are you, like, dating the happy hippie from next door? Is he my new dad?"

Nell laughed. "Mimi, no, of course not! You've got a dad. You won't ever get a new one, don't be daft!"

Mimi felt as if she'd been slapped. "I'm not daft!" she shouted. "Don't patronize me! I just come down the stairs and find my *mum* and the *man next door* all loved-up and you call me *daft*! Well thanks *a whole lot*!"

"Mimi, just sit down, calm down. Look, there's tea here for you. I was going to bring a cup to your room, seeing as I was up so early. Ed was only here because he'd heard from Charles about you being missing all Friday night. There's no 'loved-up' about it, either. He was just concerned, that's all."

"Yeah, right. And I could see just *how concerned*. I suppose the *whole street* knows about me on Friday night. Are they all going to come round and give you some big love?" Mimi grouched. She slammed about, poured herself some muesli, broke off half a banana and pushed it into the middle of the bowl, chopping it viciously with her spoon so that milk splashed on to the table. Nell didn't comment, so Mimi chopped even harder, deliberately making maximum mess.

"Of course the whole street knows," Nell said. "But would you really prefer to live in a place where nobody cares?"

"They don't care, they're just fucking nosy," Mimi growled.

"OK, stop now. There's no need for that. Stop showing off, Mimi," Nell snapped. "Look, I'm going to have a shower and get dressed — I've got a lot to do today. Don't forget to come *straight* home after school, OK? And Mimi . . .?"

"What?"

"Don't . . . don't talk to strangers out there. No weird people, OK? Don't walk around texting; notice who's around you and what's going on." Nell kissed Mimi's tatty, bed-tangled hair and gave her a hug.

"Yeah, all right. S'pose," Mimi conceded. She heard Nell running up the stairs and thoughtfully chewed through the stodgy muesli. She wished she had the type of mum who'd buy really dodgy sugary cereals. You so needed something to zing you up in the mornings. Especially mornings like this one. She ate only half the muesli, tipped the rest down the waste disposal and put the bowl in the dishwasher. Then, recognizing with some regret that this was yet another sign of impending adulthood, she tore off some kitchen roll and carefully mopped up the spilled milk.

The lock was done. Nell handed over a vast amount of cash and the young man who had been sweet enough not to ask questions about the changing of a perfectly usable, obviously new, lock, handed over three keys. He'd probably had to deal with all sorts of domestic dramas — divorce, beatings, murders even. He must have heard stories of keys dropped down drains, keys hurled into the dark in a fit of anger, and could have written a book on the different reasons for lock-changing. She had also replied to Patrick, agreeing to meet him at the St Alban restaurant in Lower Regent Street on Friday, a prospect that now filled her with a mixture of pulse-banging excitement and deep, deep dread.

"Why didn't you just ask Steve for the other key back?" Kate asked her the next day when she and Nell met in the Ham House car park to walk the dachshund and Alvin along the riverbank again.

"Because I'd never know if he'd had more copies made," Nell told her. "I don't want even the slightest smidgen of doubt. I'm seeing him tonight. I told him I wouldn't be at the class but could meet him in the gym bar immediately after. And the minute I'm in the car leaving there, I'm going to call Ed to let him know I'm on my way home, just in case. I've told him the whole stupid, sorry story. If nothing else, those classes have sharpened up my personal-security skills no end. I suppose I've got Steve to thank for that at least."

"Yes, but you've also got Steve to thank for the fact that you *need* those security skills. You are sure it's him, aren't you? Are you a hundred per cent certain it couldn't be anyone else?"

Nell laughed. "I'm sure. Well, unless it's you . . . you're the only other one who knows I was even looking for Patrick!"

"God no, it's not me. I couldn't be arsed! And anyway, I want to know what happens next, not stop it happening. A woman like me, bogged down with a surprise infant and the daily domestic grind, has to get her thrills secondhand. Tragic, isn't it?"

"OK, so that's you out. Mimi has her own computer and doesn't even know my passwords so it isn't her — not that she knows anything about Patrick anyway. I think I know now why those letters were in the cupboard. Steve must have stuffed them in there, that time he was doing the lock. There'll be one missing — the one he nicked to copy the handwriting."

Kate shivered. "Spooky! But how are you going to make sure he doesn't keep up the pursuit? He might keep at it now he's getting a response."

"Oh, I don't think he will. I bet he has a target in every class. It's probably a challenge he sets himself each time a new course begins, see how far he gets with it. If he'd really fancied me that much he could have leapt on me that time I went back to his flat."

"And he didn't!" Kate sounded outraged. "How insulting. What a cop-out!"

"Well, I was a bit pissed; it would have come under Taking Advantage."

"Yeah? And? Why didn't he?"

"I wondered about that. Biding his time, I put it down to. And you know, if he'd made the right kind of effort I'd have been a pushover, that day," she giggled. "Literally! Maybe he prefers to work for it."

They stopped close to the Thames Young Mariners lagoon and walked down a path cut into the riverbank, right to the water's edge. The dog raced into the river and swam around, his long ears trailing and dragging and his tiny legs whirling beneath him. Alvin was released from his buggy and ran along the narrow strip of gritty shore, splashing in the river's shallows and throwing bread to squawking mallards that were pushing and shoving each other out of the way.

"Greedy buggers," Nell said, as some of the braver ones stepped out of the water and strolled right up to Alvin. They weren't much smaller than him, really. How did tiny children manage to grow, in what seemed like twenty short minutes, into great big adolescents with all their tricksiness and trouble?

"Man there!" Alvin shouted, pointing towards a clump of low trees behind him. Nell froze, almost scared to turn and look. There was no one else around, and this side of the Thames, with no buildings other than the securely locked Gun Club headquarters and with the woodsy fields of Ham Lands beyond, suddenly seemed a dangerously isolated place. Bloody Steve, she thought, blaming him for this edgy nervousness and wishing for a moment that they were all safely on the opposite bank, close to the residential main road through Strawberry Hill.

Alvin was staring, open-mouthed and fascinated, at a boy who was sitting on the ground, leaning against a tree, the warmth of the sun on his face. He was about Seb's age, reading the *Daily Mail* and calmly lighting a hand-rolled cigarette. He waved at Alvin and smiled, inhaling deeply. The sweet scent of cannabis smoke filled the air.

As Nell, Kate and Alvin strolled back towards the car park, Nell commented, "That's not something you see every day, is it?"

296

"What, someone smoking a spliff?" Kate laughed. "I think it is! Even the kids on the way to school light up in the bus shelter."

"No — I meant a spliff *and* the *Daily Mail*. It just doesn't match up, somehow."

"Ah — I see what you mean! Young people today, who can understand them?"

Nell was early. If she walked through the reception area and on towards the spa and the studios, she could look through the studio's glass doors and watch her own classmates having their final session. Steve had told her that she wasn't going to be missing a lot — most of it was simply a recap of what they'd already learned. "Just banging in the message," he'd said. It had made her laugh, thinking of Abi's lump-hammer. She waited for him in the bar, dawdling over a glass of iced white wine and adding more and more water till the taste of the Sauvignon was almost lost.

He'd sounded so cheerful on the phone, as if this was going to be a fun date, and she hadn't said anything to give him the impression that it wasn't. Perhaps he'd thought, when she'd told him she had something else to do that overlapped into the class, that she couldn't bear to finish the course without seeing him here one more time, or that she was coming to the gym to make sure he knew she wanted them to stay in touch. Tricky one, this. Maybe she should have dealt with it all by email — but then she wouldn't have been able to see how he reacted. She needed to be there, no question.

She looked at her watch. Only minutes to go. All around her, the thirty-something after-work gym bunnies were scuppering their health regimes by sinking bottles of wine and munching bar snacks. There was a gossipy, social buzz, and Nell felt disconnected from the comparatively youthful networking. She tried thinking it looked a bit Bridget Jones-like, all the girls in sexy post-workout ensembles that were not as carelessly casual as they pretended to be. Obviously, going to the gym you didn't do the full-scale glam-up straight after, but she supposed that if you were in the dating marketplace you also didn't fling on just any old thing, even if you were only hanging around before heading home for a solitary evening of microwaved food, a Johnny Depp DVD and an early night.

"Nell! You missed the class — how come you're out here but weren't in there?" Abi came bounding up to Nell's table and sat beside her. "I was going to get your phone number from Steve! We should stay in touch. Let's swop them now." She pulled out a notebook, tore off a page and handed it to Nell.

"Yes, definitely," Nell agreed, scribbling down her address and phone numbers. "We can go out on the town, safe in the knowledge that between us we could fight off all comers."

"I'll bring my hammer. You bring the scary torch."

Nell glanced past Abi to see the other class members drifting into the bar in groups. Mike grinned at her, approached the bar and signalled to her to see if she'd like a drink. She smiled back and shook her head, pointing to her own full glass. This was something she hadn't thought of, that there might be a kind of end-of-term drinks session and that it might not be easy to get Steve to herself. There'd be a moment though, somehow. She knew he'd make sure there was.

"Hey Nell, you missed a good one," Patsy came and told her. "Steve had Wilma pinned against the mirror and she threw him, like really *threw* him, against the wall! I don't think he was too delighted!"

And there he was, suddenly, doing that materializing-from-nowhere trick that he was so good at.

He said, mock-solemn, "I think you'll find, Patsy, that I *let* Wilma throw me. Just so she knows she can do it. I could have stopped her — but someone who doesn't know how to would land up on the floor, just like I did. Don't let on though, if you see her."

"Ooooh! Sir's got the hump!" Patsy giggled. "I'm getting a drink. Anyone want one?"

"Not for me, ta," Abi said. "I'm off home to see what the little sods are up to. They'd trashed the kitchen last week. Said they were cooking pasta. Now can anyone tell me how such a simple thing can leave a trail of cheese from the front door to the back one? No, I thought not." She got up to leave, nudging Nell hard in the ribs and whispering, "Whatever you're having with Steve — and don't deny y'are — have a real screamer for me, will you?"

"If I was . . ." Nell grinned at her and gave up. "OK, I'll do my best," she said; there was no point arguing the toss now.

Only a few of the class were left and they were at the bar, looking at the menu. Steve sat beside Nell, handing her another drink. She looked at it and at him, questioningly.

"According to what you've taught us, I shouldn't drink that. I didn't see you buy it, didn't see whether you put anything in it."

"Ah, but we're friends, aren't we?" he said, reaching across and putting his hand over hers. She slid hers out from under it.

"I don't know, Steve, are we? Aren't friends honest with each other? I'd have thought that was the absolute basic, wouldn't you?"

Steve put his glass of wine down. "What do you mean, Nell? What are you getting at?"

"Steve — you're the detective, I'll grant you the expertise. But you're not the only one who can work things out by deduction. Means, method and motive — aren't they the things you look for when you're solving a mystery? Or have I just read too many crime novels? And even if I have — what's good enough for Hercule Poirot is good enough for me. I know what you did."

Steve sighed and leaned back, folding his arms across his enviable abs and pecs. Abi would be salivating, Nell thought. He was quite something, if this was the something you were looking for. He was being checked out by several of the gym girls — he could have had his pick of them. Or perhaps he already had.

"How did you know?" Was he calculating that he'd get points for not denying?

Nell laughed. "When I had that horrible response from 'Patrick', did you really think I'd leave it at that?

After twenty years, do you think I'd let it rest with a slap in the face? I wrote to him again."

Steve frowned. "It was just delaying tactics. I . . . well, I wanted to have more time for us to get to know each other better."

"*Know* you better? Why would you think I'd want to 'know better' someone who deliberately stole my private mail, faked a reply and then *pounced* the moment they knew I'd be most vulnerable? You knew that time you invited me out to lunch that the postman would have delivered your fake letter! Were you watching him walk up my path? How could you do all that and not expect me to find out? How stupid do you think I am?"

In her head, Nell conceded that maybe she had been pretty stupid. No; *vulnerable*, possibly close to *needy*, were the right words. If she hadn't been so acutely single, so keen to blot up any drops of male appreciation, she wouldn't have been caught out. But he'd been persistent too, and clever and cunning. *Pounce* was exactly the word for what he'd done. She'd been a grazing antelope. Steve was a highly efficient lion.

"You can't say I really took advantage." He smirked. "I mean, I probably could have . . ."

"In your dreams, Steve," Nell said angrily. "In your fucking dreams. But you know, the silly, sad thing is that I liked you. I liked you a lot. If you'd behaved like a normal, non-controlling, non-crazy, non-stalking human being, you could easily — as the saying goes —

have been a contender. I don't think I need to ask you not to contact me again."

Out in the car park, Nell didn't dither around wondering where her car was, and once inside it, she quickly locked the doors, checking who was around her as she drove off. You never knew who might be following. Once she was clear of the gym area, she pulled over to the side of the road and called Ed.

"I can't go out, Joel. You know that. I'm grounded." Mimi lay on her bed thinking, oh, this is just like some American teen movie. She loved knowing that her life had some theatrical content to it. She even loved knowing she had something — in the form of not being allowed out — to complain about.

"It's not after school or at night though, not this time." Joel was becoming persuasive. "Your mum will never know. We'll be there and back by the end of school; well, just about — it's tight, timewise, but the trains should work out. I looked it all up. Oh *please*, Mimi. Seaside? Ice cream? Candyfloss?"

"Donkey rides?" she giggled.

"Er . . . I don't think they have those. Not where we're going."

"So are you going to tell me where that is this time? I'm not good with all these mysteries." Secretly she was thrilled that he still wanted to play these secretive games with her — or she would be, if this one didn't end up as cold and terrifying as the last one.

"I don't want to sleep another night with the ghosts and angels," she told him. "My mum will kill me if I do anything stupid again. Especially this soon. She'll say it's *becoming a habit*. And she'll tell Dad like she did last weekend and he'll say I've got to have *therapy* or something. That'll be his girlfriend's solution, I bet you anything, *so* New York."

"Wow — would they make you have therapy for taking one little trip on a train?" Joel sounded mystified. "I mean, people use them every day — they haven't all turned into crazies."

"They might have. Look, I'll think about it, OK? I can get out early in the mornings and . . ." She heard her mother's key in the front-door lock.

"Gotta go. She's back."

"Where's she been?"

"Out. She's always out. Bye." Mimi went down the stairs to greet Nell. It might be a good plan to soften her up a bit, maybe cook her something. She very much wanted to go on Thursday to wherever it was Joel wanted her to go. She felt close to him now, bonded by the overnight in the cemetery.

"You OK, Mum? Hungry?"

"Er . . . yes, a bit."

"Oh good. I'm going to cook spaghetti carbonara for you," Mimi told her. "You don't have to do anything. Just pour yourself a drink and go and sit on the sofa. I'll call you when it's ready."

"Good grief. What's all this about? Is there something disastrous you're about to tell me?"

Mimi smiled, knowing that even this would worry Nell. Parents — what strange things they were. You do things wrong and they're suspicious about you for evermore. You do things right, and it's the same old story. Having thought of this, she made her mind up instantly. On Thursday, she'd be at the bus stop at seven a.m. — whatever this trip was Joel had in mind for them to go on, she might as well just do it. What was to lose?

CHAPTER
SEVENTEEN

Castles Made Of Sand
(Jimi Hendrix)

No one in their right mind would choose six thirty in the morning to have any kind of conversation with a fifteen-year-old, let alone one in which you were more than fifty per cent sure they were being shifty about something. Nell sat on the stairs, tightly wrapped in her blue silky robe against the gale from the open front door, and wondered why Mimi had thought she could get out of the house this early without being spotted, *and* wearing jeans and a varied layering of tops, not her school clothes. Seven thirty (and in uniform) would have been fine. Even seven — at a push — if, the night before, she'd preambled with a claim that there was some vital homework book she'd left at school that she *really needed* and if she didn't find it and do the work *immediately* then there'd be detention, for sure. But six thirty, not a chance. That was just not on. School wouldn't even be open.

"We've got a trip to . . . to . . . um . . . somewhere near Brighton. I forgot to tell you. It's to look at rock formations. White cliffs — and that."

"That's pretty lame, Mimi. Can't you do better than that? And why tell me now and not last night?"

Mimi looked panic-stricken. "Because I forgot! OK? I forget things. I've got stuff on my mind, all the coursework and exams and like *soo* much to remember! You don't know what it's like! Tess texted me — look, if you don't believe me!" She held out her phone. Nell didn't doubt it would tell her there was a trip to Brighton. It was the alibi network all over again. Unless . . . it wasn't.

"OK — I'll give you a lift." She called Mimi's bluff, heading back up the stairs. "Just give me a minute to get some clothes on."

"No! No, honestly Mum, there's no need. I'm meeting Tess at the bus stop. It's all right. I'm out the door now — it's fine, everything's cool. See you later!" And she was gone, leaving Nell marooned halfway up the stairs with the distinct feeling that she'd been had. She could do several things about this. She could go after Mimi in the car and pick her up at the bus stop — if that was where she'd gone. Or she could phone the school later and check that there was a trip. Or she could do nothing and see how it played out. If she did either of the first two, was it a sign that, deep down, she no longer trusted her daughter *at all*? She didn't want to feel like that — it would lead to a horrible checking up on everything she did. She'd end up — and she couldn't help thinking along these lines — almost stalking her own daughter. You couldn't live like that.

She went into the kitchen to make some tea and think about what to do. No one told you how exhausting it would be, being the only parent and having to make all the decisions. Sure, Alex had been absent a lot, but essentially there had been two of them running this show. She could, she thought with sly glee, phone him right now (close to 2a.m. in New York?) and ask what he'd advise . . . but then that had a downside, too — she didn't want to look as if she couldn't cope. She could, really. On the kitchen table was the note that Mimi had hoped would be her only contact with her mother till the day's end. "*School trip to Brighton — sorry, forgot! Lotsa love, Me. xxxx*" Oh, maybe it was true. Surely it was better to trust than not? What she *did* believe with Mimi, was that she wouldn't knowingly do something dangerous or frightening. Definitely not frightening, anyway. She'd had enough of that in the cemetery.

Still indecisive, she shoved her feet into her trusty Uggs, opened the front door and went to the gate. It was just too late, she realized as she gazed along the deserted road, to check which direction Mimi had taken. And besides, if she was being truly devious she'd have gone in the usual school direction and then cut through a side road if there was somewhere else she wanted to be. Nell hated herself for her suspicions and turned to go back in. Ed was in the adjoining drive, putting a bag in his car.

"Hey — we can't keep meeting like this," he said. "The neighbours will talk. Are you all right?"

"I don't know," she admitted. "Mimi says she's got a school trip — one she conveniently forgot to tell me about till she was sliding out of the house just now. I don't like myself for not believing her."

Ed leaned against his car door and thought for a moment. "Well, if I remember teen years well enough, I think if I was planning something that *wasn't* a genuine school trip, I'd have given it a bit of a lead-up. Wouldn't she have got a story worked out further back to tell you? I mean, what would you have done?"

Nell laughed. "I did once tell my mother that the school was finishing a day later than it said on the calendar they'd sent. I said it was a mistake. I gave them two weeks' notice of that and prayed they wouldn't phone and check, and then I went to a very glamorous party in London at the home of a massively sophisticated girl in my year."

"How old were you?"

"Fifteen . . . yes, I see what you mean. You know, the odd thing is, if I'd asked my folks, I'd have been allowed to go, no problem. My mum would probably have given me the money for a new dress in the hope that I'd meet a Nice Suitable Boy. I just enjoyed the sneaky drama of it all." She looked at the bag on the back seat of the car. "Are you going away for the weekend already? No college tomorrow?"

"They've got an inset day, so I'm off a day early. You should come down, Nell. You'd love it."

Nell smiled. "You know, Ed, I can't think of anything I'd like more, right now. A peaceful country weekend would be wonderful. The trouble is, teenagers can run away from us but we can't run away from them. Ask me again sometime though, won't you?"

"I will. And here's the phone number, and my mobile one. If it all goes pear-shaped with Mimi at the end of today, give me a call. I'll come back."

"Oh . . . Ed, thanks so much." She felt incredibly touched. Would he really do that? How sweet, how generous.

"I'm sure it'll be fine. I'm just overreacting after last weekend. I'll hang on to your number and I'll give you a call, let you know either way." He gently pulled her towards him and kissed her, just briefly, on the exact point on her mouth that was most electric. As he drove away and she went back into the house, she could still taste him, still feel the warm pressure of his hand on her arm through the blue silk.

"Oh shit! Now what?" Mimi looked at the train that was leaving the platform and at the smirking face of the train manager, who had been so delighted to evict them from his domain. They were at Exeter.

Joel kicked the bag that lay at his feet. "Dunno." He shrugged. "Hitch a lift home? I wonder which way is the nearest motorway?" He looked up and down the railway track as if he expected a convenient road to run alongside it, complete with drivers who couldn't wait to pick up a pair of stranded teenagers and share enclosed space with them all the way back to London. Mimi gave him a look. "Joel — are you mad? If I hitch my mum will go ape. And don't say she won't find out. I think something's telling me that I'm no good at lying. She's going to know about this for sure — I bet she knows already. Parents have radar."

Joel sat on the platform bench, looking puzzled. "Do they? I don't think mine do. But then . . . well, I told them exactly what I was doing today. They were doing the *Guardian* crossword together and they just said 'fine'. I don't think they heard, actually. You see, Mimi, you've just got to pick your moments."

Mimi paced up and down the platform, trying to think. What was she doing here in the middle of . . . oh yes, Devon, that was the county. She should have known it was all going to end in trouble when they got to Plymouth on the way down. "Going back tonight?" the train manager had asked, as he gathered his belongings and left the train at the same time as her and Joel.

"Oh yes, this afternoon," Joel had said, like it was what he did every day. They'd caught a local train to Saltash, paying for a ticket this time, just so they could cross the Tamar on Brunel's fantastic bridge. And it *was* fantastic, Mimi hadn't had to fake her delight here. Then, after they'd bought a sandwich at the Spar in Saltash, admired the bridge's arches from the Cornwall side, they'd taken a train back to Plymouth, got on the next train for London and been caught by the same manager who had so cheerfully waved them off a few hours earlier.

"I hoped I'd see you again," he'd told them as he gleefully copped that they had no tickets. "You've made my day." On balance, Joel probably shouldn't have told him he'd been watching too many American cop movies. He might have let them stay on the train, might have let them call home and get some kind parent to

310

fork out a creditcard payment for tickets over the phone. But no. And so here they were, horribly stranded.

"I'm going to call my mum," Mimi decided. She looked at Joel. He was looking sad, as if he'd let her down. Well, he had. But . . . she went and sat beside him on the bench. "It'll be all right." She giggled. "At least it's daylight. And there aren't any ghosts."

Nell had decided what to wear for the lunch date with Patrick the next day. It hadn't been easy and she'd wasted too much energy and time thinking about it. After twenty years she wasn't going to be able to pretend she hadn't aged in the slightest, but all the same, any woman would want to look as tasty as possible. It wasn't a matter of showing Patrick what he'd been missing, merely a matter of simple personal vanity; not something she was particularly proud of. She had tried various permutations early that morning, spreading heaps of clothes across her bed and discarding them in turn till she was wishing she'd bought something new. The Joseph caramel suede skirt went (she decided she looked like a biscuit in it), along with the black and white Whistles dress with the frill across the front (too girly), the net Only Hearts dress (it wasn't a party), and the classic DVF wrapover (too safe and dull), and she finally came down in favour of a quirky little dark blue crepe and cashmere Empire-line number teamed with a grey-blue jacket that had trailing bits of artfully tattered fabric and looked like something

311

a first-year design student would come up with for a project.

Now, emerging from Toni and Guy with her hair newly cut, she realized she was putting far too much effort in for this date. She had work backing up in the studio that she should be getting on with and yet, until she'd seen Patrick, she knew her hand would be too trembly to hold the paintbrushes steady. Part of her wished the next day's lunch was all over, so she could get back to real life, a prospect that seemed incredibly desirable and restful. She'd fantasized about this moment on and off for several years — the reality would either be a huge disappointment or would set off too many pointless regrets. This was ridiculous. She had half a mind to cancel. And then her phone rang.

"Isn't it brilliant how a beach brings out the small child in even the most image-burdened teenagers?" Ed was saying as he and Nell sat together on the promenade above Exmouth beach, eating gooey Magnum ice creams and watching Joel and Mimi building a massive and elaborate fort out of sand. The effort they were putting into it, the concentration, was impressive. If Mimi put half this much thought into her coursework, she would be on track for straight A stars. The late-afternoon sun was surprisingly strong — Nell could feel its warmth through every bit of her body. What a delight. It made her feel sleek, powerful, content.

"This was so kind of you," she said for about the fourth time to Ed. "It's a long way from your place."

"It's not really that far. And it's a pleasure. You know it is. Someone had to come and rescue them. I was just that much nearer to here than you were at the time."

"I suppose I should have taken them straight back home," Nell said. "After what they did, they don't deserve this. It's too much of a treat. But then . . . it's so lovely today. Call it serendipity or something."

She'd booked rooms at a hotel in the town. Alex had agreed to foot the bill — guilt money, she supposed, though at the cost of admitting that once more, Mimi was causing trouble.

"It's all my fault anyway, so I suppose there's no reason why they should suffer."

"How can it be your fault?" Ed asked. "You're a brilliant parent. I mean, look at Mimi — she's great. There's nothing wrong with being adventurous. Would you want a spiritless child?"

"No — it *is* my fault. I took my eye right off the ball. Off the entire pitch, lately. Tomorrow I was supposed to be having lunch with the only old boyfriend who's ever mattered. I left him all those years ago because . . ." Nell wondered why she was telling Ed this. How could he want to know? Or did she just need to say it?

"Go on . . ." He took hold of her hand. "Just tell me, it's fine." His hand was warm, calming.

"Because if I'd stayed with him, we'd never have had children."

"Oh — because he couldn't? That's a shame, but then lots of people don't . . ."

"No — it was a choice thing. There'd have been no children and no going to beaches, either. When he was ten . . . he was on a beach in Wales and his parents told him to take care of his little sister while they went to the pub. Patrick took her for a ride on a pedalo. She fell off and . . . she drowned." Such a simple, tragic tale.

"God, that's horrendous! Poor kids, both of them. But . . . I mean, at ten? Who has to be responsible for another child at ten?"

"I know, I know. But you can imagine how it would affect someone, a brother. And the family never spoke about her, he told me, not ever again. It was almost as if she hadn't existed, as if the whole horrible thing hadn't happened. And after the one drunk night in Oxford when he told me about it, Patrick never mentioned it to me again either. I can understand that, I suppose. Once told, no point going over it."

"So you chose the possibility of a family," Ed said, turning her hand over and stroking her palm, soothing now.

"I did. The big decision was when I got pregnant and he went completely hysterical. When I refused to go back to him, he came to my parents' house and smashed all my mother's car windows."

And today she'd chosen children over Patrick again, in a way: choosing to come down to Devon to get Mimi and Joel rather than pay her way out of the situation, throw credit-card money at it. She'd phoned Patrick, told him about Mimi being stranded in Devon, that she was going to Exeter for the night and wouldn't be back in time for lunch, swanky hard-to-get-into St Alban restaurant or not. She hadn't for a moment thought, oh, I'm talking to Patrick for the first time in twenty years; she hadn't fluttered and palpitated and wondered how she was coming across, or thought about whether his voice sounded the same or older, or anything silly and trivial. She'd simply told him what had happened and that another time would be better.

"What did he say when you bailed out of the lunch date? Wasn't he horribly disappointed?"

Nell could feel her mouth twitching with laughter. "Um . . . he said something that, in a million years, I'd never have expected arty, bad-boy, rebel Patrick to say." The laughter bubbled up. "He said, 'That's a total pain: I'd cancelled my golf just to see you.' Golf! Ye gods!"

Ed laughed, then became serious again. "But the real reasons you two didn't stay together back then . . ."

"Hmm. You're quick. It's taken me twenty whole years to get to this one! He didn't love me enough to reconsider the children option. I didn't love him enough to stay and try to change his mind. Simple as that. And nothing's going to be any different there now, is it?"

"Yes, well — that's what you get when you go digging around — sometimes the thing you unearth is the simple truth."

"Exactly." Nell watched Mimi and Joel excavating a channel from their fort to the rapidly approaching sea. The two of them shouted and yelled abuse at it for crumbling their carefully constructed foundations, then gave up the fight, laughing madly as they danced on what they'd created and then leapt into the waves, hand in hand, splashing like little children. Those Philippe Starck Ghost chairs, Nell thought suddenly as she and Ed snuggled closer together: she must order them for the kitchen.

This Is Dedicated To The One I Love (The Shirelles)

Also available in ISIS Large Print:

This Age We're Living In

David Wilson

George Worth is a grumpy lifestyle columnist who works in a woman's world. He hates fashion, mobile phones, computers and Young People. At night he goes home to a borrowed Labrador and feelings of guilt about his dead wife.

Justin Smith is a Young Person. A bright newcomer, he's always on his mobile to his girlfriend, surfing the Net and keeping abreast of the latest trends.

Then comes the day when Justin's girlfriend throws him out and he finds himself having to share a flat with George. As the women around them watch and wonder, both men start to work out what really matters among the obsessions and distractions of modern life.

ISBN 978-0-7531-7936-9 (hb)
ISBN 978-0-7531-7937-6 (pb)

The Truth About Ruby Valentine

Alison Bond

When Hollywood legend Ruby Valentine shocks the world with her mysterious suicide, Kelly's father reveals something even more shocking — she's Ruby's daughter.

So Kelly sets off for Tinseltown to find some answers, diving head first into Hollywood society with her new family of jet-setters and fashionistas. But she soon discovers that Ruby's real life was laced with more drama, tragedy and intrigue than any screenwriter could imagine.

When Ruby's fortune turns out to be non-existent, and Kelly learns of the intense relationship her mother had with her slick, powerful agent, she begins to get suspicious about what's really going on. And the more she digs, the closer she gets to uncovering the most unbelievable secret of them all.

ISBN 978-0-7531-7866-9 (hb)
ISBN 978-0-7531-7867-6 (pb)

Lucky Girl

Fiona Gibson

Everyone always told Stella Moon how lucky she was to have a famous dad.

She just wished he was more like everyone else's. And when her mum died, and he withdrew to his allotment leaving Stella and her brother alone to play in rusty cars and exist for a whole week on Black Forest gateaux, she didn't feel lucky at all.

Now in her thirties, Stella has made sure her life couldn't be further from her chaotic upbringing, with a strict routine as a music teacher and a peaceful, tidy home. Until two noisy little girls move in next door.

At first, she feels besieged. The girls hound her, bearing sticky gifts of edible jewellery and firing personal questions about her mum, her dad and her love life. But it's their friendship that helps her to confront the truth about her own childhood and start living life to the full.

ISBN 978-0-7531-7778-5 (hb)
ISBN 978-0-7531-7779-2 (pb)

The Betrayal of Grace Mulcahy

Colette Caddle

The life and marriage of Grace and Michael Mulcahy has all the signs of being a successful and fulfilled one: a daughter, rewarding jobs and plenty of friends. But when Grace discovers that her partner in her interior design business, 52-year-old Miriam, is embezzling her, the seeds are sown for Grace's bind.

When confronted with her betrayal, Miriam begs Grace not to tell anyone in order to preserve Miriam's marriage, which will fall apart if the truth outs. Grace agrees to keep quiet but finds it leads to all sorts of complications and misunderstandings that put a strain on all of her relationships, both professional and personal. By the time she notices how close things are to crumbling, it could be too late to piece together the ties that bind her to those she loves.

ISBN 978-0-7531-7728-0 (hb)
ISBN 978-0-7531-7729-7 (pb)

6P.

VV

ST

WP.

BRH.

Whi

BM

ET